CHRISTMAS FOR ONE

As a child, Meg always dreamed of the perfect Christmas... This year, she can make it come true for her own little boy. There will be a turkey and all the trimmings, a glittering tree, and a stocking hung over a roaring fire. Who cares if there's no devoted husband in the picture? She and Lucas will be just fine on their own. But then a chance meeting with a stranger in New York unravels everything she's planned. Will Meg finally get everything she wished for? Or will she be alone this Christmas after all?

CHRISTMAS FOR ONE

CHRISTMAS FOR ONE

by

Amanda Prowse

Magna Large Print Books
Long Preston, North Yorkshire,
BD23 4ND, England.

British Library Cataloguing in Publication Data.

Prowse, Amanda
Christmas for one.

A catalogue record of this book is
available from the British Library

ISBN 978-0-7505-4042-1

First published in Great Britain in 2014 by Head of Zeus, Ltd.

Published in Large Print 2015 by arrangement with
Head of Zeus

Magna Large Print is an imprint of Library Magna Books Ltd.

Printed and bound in Great Britain by
T.J. (International) Ltd., Cornwall, PL28 8RW

The publishers hope that this book has given you enjoyable reading. Large Print Books are especially designed to be as easy to see and hold as possible. If you wish a complete list of our books please ask at your local library or write directly to:

Magna Large Print Books
Magna House, Long Preston,
Skipton, North Yorkshire.
BD23 4ND

This book is for Jo Ward. She has always been there for me, a brilliant mum to Luke and Alice, a great sister, fabulous aunt and a lovely friend.

Prologue

Megan woke to the sound of squealing coming from the landing. It was Kirsty, the daughter of the foster family she was staying with.

Today was a special day: Christmas.

'I got a Sylvanian Families tree-house! I love it! I love it! Thank you, Mummy and Daddy!' Kirsty screamed, her excitement pushing her voice up an octave higher than usual.

Megan pulled the duvet up over her shoulders and swallowed, unsure if she should get up or stay put. It was the same way she felt every morning in Tall Trees Avenue. Sometimes she got up early, put her school uniform on and slid back under the duvet, waiting for Pam, Kirsty's mum, to knock on the door and invite her down to the kitchen for her Frosties.

What was the right thing to do today? Should she stay silently in the bedroom trying to be as little bother as possible or should she go and join in? Megan knew that Christmas morning was a big deal and, despite being only seven, she was smart enough to realise that if the Bartram family were opening gifts without her, they probably wanted some time to themselves.

She laid her cheek on the pillow and tried to imagine what her mum was doing right that moment. Then she thought about each of her brothers and sisters: Janey, Mel, Jason and Robbie. She blinked. Her heart was beating very fast between her ribs. Like a little bird trapped inside a cage, that was how she always pictured it. Patting her chest, she whispered, 'Ssssshhh....,' as though it were a living thing that she could calm.

There was a tap on the bedroom door and Megan sat up. Pam came in, wearing her sweatshirt with huskies on the front. Megan thought Pam might have dressed up today, maybe in a red sequined dress like the one she had seen a lady on the telly wearing. The sight of the huskies with their real googly eyes that moved when Pam jumped was a bit disappointing.

'Morning, Megan. Looks like Santa's been! There's a little pile of presents under the tree with your name on them.'

Megan felt her tummy flutter with excitement. Pam walked briskly to the window and drew the curtains, lifting the catch to let the breeze whip around the room. Megan wondered, as she did every time Pam performed this little ritual, if she smelt. She had been living with the Bartrams for three months, but she still didn't really know if they liked having her there.

Suddenly the door burst open and Kirsty rushed in. 'Come on, Megan! It's Christmas!' She smiled, reaching for Megan's hand, pulling her from the warmth of the bed.

Megan understood that today there was to be a truce. No hair-pulling or pinching, no stealing her chips when the adults were out of the room.

She sat on the floral-patterned carpet in her nightie and slowly removed the paper from her gifts: some new white socks, a small pink stuffed unicorn with a furry mane and big eyes, and a Blockbusters board game. She beamed. Nice presents!

Two hours later, Megan sat on the sofa in Kirsty's old bridesmaid's dress, running her hands over the layers of lilac tulle that reached her ankles. She felt like a princess. Delicious smells wafted from the kitchen – roast potatoes, Christmas pudding and brandy butter. Her mouth watered, even though she knew that she wouldn't get to eat any of it.

When Kirsty's dad, Len, reached for the car keys, she started quivering with nerves. Out of sight of the others, she placed her small hand against her chest and whispered, 'Ssssshhh.'

'Come on then, flower.' Len waved the keys in her direction.

She liked Len. She liked being called 'flower'.

Megan zipped her navy school coat over her fancy frock and waved goodbye to the family, who were all sitting round the Christmas tree. Megan blushed with guilt. She knew she should be excited about going to see *her* family, but part of her wanted to stay there, among strangers, and eat proper turkey and gravy, followed by Christmas pudding, brandy butter and charades.

'Take these with you!' Kirsty removed the seal from the tin of Quality Street that had sat so temptingly under the tree for the last week and shoved four sweets into Megan's palm. Two were flat gold circles, one was a green triangle and the other an orange bon-bon shape.

'Thank you,' Megan whispered as she placed the sweets in her coat pocket.

Len was a man of few words. Rather than make Megan feel even more awkward, the thirty-minute drive in comfortable silence helped her relax a little.

As Megan stepped through the front door of her mum's flat, she was met by laughter. 'What the bloody hell have you got on?' her mum asked, leaning on the kitchen door frame, her cigarette held up to her mouth between two long red nails. She was in vest and jeans, despite the season.

'Kirsty said I could wear it.' Megan

bunched the skirt in her fists and let it fall. She felt sick, like she had done something wrong.

Her mum shook her head and narrowed her eyes against the yellow wisps of smoke. 'Everyone's in the front room.' She nodded her head towards the sound of the telly and went into the kitchen.

Megan unzipped her coat and followed her in. Her mum was standing in front of the sink. A man she had never seen before stood by her side. He wasn't wearing a top and had a tattoo of a big ugly dog on his bicep. Megan stared at it until he flexed his arm and barked, making it look like the dog was jumping in her direction. Megan gasped and swallowed. She noticed that neither of them was wearing shoes or socks and that their hair was messy, like they had just got up.

'I got you a present,' she whispered as she stepped forward.

Her mum turned around and gathered the pink unicorn into her hands. 'Oh.' She looked at the man with the messy hair and gave a crooked smile. 'That's just what I always wanted. Thanks, Meggy.' She bent down and kissed her daughter's head.

Megan inhaled the scent of cigarettes and something else that she couldn't identify, but it made her tummy flip nonetheless.

'And I got you these.' She unclenched her fingers and placed the four sweets on the sticky work surface where they shone like brightly wrapped jewels.

'Ooh, my favourite!' The man dived forward and took one of the gold circles into his big hands. Megan instantly wished that she had saved them for herself. They weren't meant for him.

She wandered along the hallway to the lounge. Hovering in the doorway, she gazed at the room, which looked just like it did on any other day. No Christmas tree, no decorations, no presents. Her brothers, sisters and cousins sat flopped and sagged against the stained sofa cushions and greasy chair arms. They were eating crisps and watching the big telly, which was showing a gravy advert. A smiling mum in an apron ferried steaming plates of home-cooked goodies to a table spread with a clean white tablecloth. A dad, wearing a tie, sat at the head, beaming at his handsome offspring. Megan stared at their own lounge with its curtains that didn't quite fit the windows and were held shut by clothes pegs, and the rusty Calor gas heater pumping out warmth. It was a world away from Tall Trees Avenue.

'Fuck me, it's Cinderella!' Jason wheezed as he winked at his little sister.

'It's not mine,' she whispered, embarrassed, no longer feeling like a princess.

She sat on the floor next to Mel and watched the last hour of *Who Framed Roger*

Rabbit, wondering how long it would be until Len came to fetch her.

'Did your mum get you a present?' Len asked casually as she clicked her seat belt.

'She got me lots of presents, too many for me to carry and so I left them all there.' Megan felt her cheeks flame as the lie slipped from her lips.

'Probably best.' Len winked at her.

Back at Tall Trees Avenue, Megan hung up her coat and walked into the dining room. The table still gleamed with tinsel and candles, and Christmas carols were playing on the stereo. Megan closed her eyes and made a promise that when she was grown up she would be just like the gravy advert lady. She would serve a lovely Christmas dinner to her family, carrying the plates to the table and putting them on a clean white cloth. She would buy everyone the presents they had always wanted and after lunch they would play charades and laugh as they passed around the tin of Quality Street.

She sat down by the tree in the lounge and fanned her princess dress out on the floor around her, feeling both happy and sad. Happy to be able to run her hands over the shiny baubles and to sit watching the twinkling lights, but sad for her mum, Janey, Mel, Jason and Robbie, that their home didn't have any magic in it. None at all.

One

Meg stood in the middle of the pavement and stared at the display in the tall glass window. She had been with Plum Patisserie, working for cousins Pru and Milly Plum, for four years, yet continued to be wonderstruck by the incredible confections that creative director Guy Baudin and his team produced.

She beamed and held her scarf against her throat. It was December the first and the window conjured thoughts of snow and sparkle. The single-tier cake sat on a silver and glass podium within a vast glass snow globe. Long shards of crystal hung from invisible wires and caught the light, sending dazzling miniature rainbows out into the grey December day. Thc cakc itsclf was a foot wide and two feet deep, its sides and edges shaped into a brilliant white snowscape of jagged icing and fondant peaks. In the crevices and dips there was the faintest tinge of grey. On top of the cake, glistening inside this snowy crater, was a frozen pond of the palest blue, made from the smoothest, most blemish-free icing that Meg had ever seen. It was glass-like in its perfection, complete with tiny ice fissures at the edges where a slightly darker blue icing shone through from below. Atop this perfect pond skated a male and female figure. Dressed in silver lamé and white fur, they swirled and glided in intricate animatronic loops around each other, their arms outstretched, missing each other by a hair's breadth. Where their skates had touched the ice there were left the tiniest scratches, fine flecks of icing sitting like dust to either side of the needle-like tracks, as if kicked up by a flashing blade. Delicate snowflakes danced and fluttered around the two, hitting the roof of the snow globe then falling to the floor before being lifted once again by a gentle wave of air.

Guy's 'Winter Fiesta' was nothing short of magical and Meg found herself instantly transported into Christmas. She pictured roaring fires and warm mulled wine held between chilly palms; thick socks and brisk walks; hot buttery toast; the smell of pine and cinnamon; and beautifully wrapped presents nestling under a fat Norway spruce. She saw herself in her beautiful Mayfair flat, serving a lovely Christmas dinner to her family, carrying the plates to the table and putting them on a clean white cloth.

A little girl shouted, 'Look! Mummy, look!' as she dragged her mother by the hand to stand next to Meg. 'Wow!' she mouthed as she placed her mittened palms on the glass and stared, transfixed. Meg smiled at her;

this was exactly the reaction it deserved. It was a full minute before her mother, promising to bring her back another day, yanked her arm and they continued on their way.

Meg looked at the two miniature skaters and felt a familiar pang of loneliness. She bent low, peered into the faces of the little figures and began whispering to them. 'I envy you two. Nothing to worry about and nothing to do all day apart from smile at each other and skate around in your little boots. Must be nice. I shall call you Dimitri and Anna. I think you are madly in love, but your families disapprove and so you meet on the ice every day to conduct your romance.'

She shook her head. *What's got into you, Meg? You've been reading too many stories.* She leant closer to the window. 'Careful you don't fall, Dimitri and Anna,' she murmured. 'It looks bloody freezing in there – I hope you've both got your thermals on, my loves.'

Even though Meg had seen at least a dozen of Guy's showstopping display cakes, the feeling of wonder as she peered through the glass never diminished. She thought back to the first time she had seen one of his famous Plum Patisserie windows. She could still picture the cake perfectly: eight tiers of white icing, with one side covered in tiny red sugar-paste rosebuds and petals. The flowers had looked so real she could almost smell them. Pregnant with Lucas at the time, and raw with grief over the infidelity and death of her fiancé Bill, Meg had been in a terrible state. She had nowhere else to go. She had stood gazing at the dozens of candle bulbs that flickered around the display, wondering how much a cake like that might cost and how long it had taken to make. It had seemed like something from a different universe. With only a couple of quid in her pocket and no idea where she was going to lay her head that night, she had questioned the point of such a fanciful creation. What sort of life could possibly fit that sort of cake?

Four years on, Meg still pinched herself at the direction things had taken. Exquisite cakes had become the stuff of her daily life. All thanks to Pru and Milly Plum, who had taken her in and made her feel like family. They had been grieving too – it was their niece, Bobby Plum, who'd been Bill's other woman, and she'd died alongside Bill in the car crash. But instead of chucking Meg out, the Plum cousins had all but adopted her, giving her a home and a job in their fancy bakery. At the time, the extent of Meg's cake knowledge was limited to rustling up a flat Victoria sponge and on occasion treating herself to a fondant fancy. But with hard work, a keen eye and patient guidance from Pru, Milly and Guy, she had learnt fast, becoming very skilled at sugarwork and decoration. Since then, though, she had moved into a managerial role at Plum's, which left her little time to practise and improve. More often than not her fingers danced across pages of figures and spreadsheets rather than dough and sugar paste.

She smiled ruefully at the memory of that first day as she let herself in at the front door next to the café. Guy waved briefly at her from the window. It looked busy in there, which was good.

Meg climbed the stairs and opened the door to her flat. 'Only me!' she called as she kicked off her boots and shrugged her arms from her coat.

'Mummy!' Lucas came hurtling down the hallway on his red truck, powering it with his bare feet, Flintstones style, thumping against the marble floor. He steered with his right hand and in his left gripped a large plastic dagger.

'Hello, mate! How are you? Have you had fun?'

Lucas gave an exaggerated nod. Meg bent down and kissed her son on the face, smoothing his long, dark hair from his forehead. He gave her his signature smile, through eyes half closed and with his lips pursed, looking exactly like his dad. It fascinated Meg that even though Bill had died before Lucas was born, their little boy shared many of his habits and mannerisms. It was both comforting and heartbreaking to see this little reminder of the man she had loved. When she saw him asleep, sprawled face down with his arms above his head, in the favourite pose of his father, it made her ache with longing for the man that had left them too soon.

'Milly's stuck in the pirate ship!' He excitedly executed a three-point turn and scooted back the way he'd come. Meg followed him and poked her head into the beautiful Georgian sitting room. It looked like a burglary had taken place. The two wingback armchairs that usually sat either side of the fireplace had been tipped onto their sides and were covered with a large white sheet. A broom handle had been stuck through the middle of the sheet, and from it hung a rather limp skull and crossbones. A pile of 'treasure' consisting of mismatched buttons and beads was spilling from an old cardboard box and several blue towels had been placed around the 'ship' with plastic fish scattered on top of them.

'Mills? Are you in there?' Meg crouched down and peeked beneath the sheet.

Milly was lying on the floor between the two chairs. Her head was crooked at a rather unnatural angle and she was wearing a pirate bandana and a patch over her left eye. She tilted her neck back and peered at Meg. 'It's Cap'n Mills to you and I can't come out, I am surrounded by shark-infested waters.'

Meg looked down at her feet, which were on a blue towel. 'Oh dear, I think I must be shark bait.'

Milly scrabbled her way out from under the sheet. In the light, Meg could see she had drawn a natty cavalier-style beard on her chin and a matching moustache.

'Nice tash!' Meg said.

'Urgh, thanks! We have a slight problem with my facial hair.'

'Oh?' Meg watched as Milly rubbed at her face with her cutlass-free hand.

'I picked up the wrong pen and accidentally used this.' Milly pulled from her pocket a black marker with the words 'INDELIBLE INK' stamped on the side.

Meg laughed loudly. 'You nutter!'

'I'm supposed to be playing bridge tonight,' Milly huffed. 'How can I turn up looking like the love child of Charles the bloody First?'

Meg snorted her laughter.

'Lucas, I've been rescued, I'm going to have a tea break with Mum and then we can go back to pirating, okay?'

'Aye aye, Captain!' Lucas shouted from his truck. Milly had him well trained in pirate-speak.

'You're early!' Milly moaned. 'We've still got a damsel in distress to rescue and a dragon to slay.'

Meg grinned. 'Aren't you confusing

knights' tales with pirate adventures?'

'Blimey, who are you, the fairy-tale police?' Milly tutted. 'I think you'll find we can be whoever we want to be, isn't that right, Spiderman-Pirate?' she called into the hallway.

'Aye aye, Captain!' Lucas replied.

'We weren't expecting you until after tea. Not that I'm complaining – you can be the dragon.'

'Can't I be the princess?' Meg asked.

Milly shook her head as she filled the kettle. 'Definitely not. You don't just turn up at the eleventh hour and get the best role of the day. I need commitment! We've been playing for four hours and Lucas started off as cabin boy and has only recently been appointed first mate.'

Meg's eyes began to well up with tears. Milly set the kettle on the side and put her arm across her back. 'All right, all right, no need to go all wobbly on me. I didn't realise it meant that much to you. You can be the princess if you like!'

Meg shook her head. 'It's not that. I've had a shitty day. Piers and I have finished.' She looked up in time to see Milly placing her palms together in a silent prayer of thanks, her eyes skyward.

'I know you didn't like him, Mills, but I did.'

'No you didn't, not really,' Milly said

matter-of-factly. 'And it's not that I didn't like him; I liked him very much actually. I just didn't like how you became when you were with him. I hated seeing you having to try so hard; it shouldn't be like that. You weren't yourself and that's no good, love.'

'Oh God, I know!' Meg covered her eyes with her palms and sighed. 'I know. You're right.'

'Come and sit down.' Milly removed her bandana and led Meg by the hand until the two slumped down on the soft sofa. 'Here you go.' She handed her a tissue.

'Thank you.' Meg sniffed and blew her nose.

'Darling, you can't beat yourself up. You were still properly grieving for Bill when you met him. I reckon you weren't firing on all cylinders and if he in some small way helped you move forward, then it wasn't all bad, was it?' Milly tried to be serious, but her beard and moustache were quite distracting.

'I guess not.' Meg considered. 'I just hate the idea that I've upset him. Piers didn't deserve that. He was busy making plans for Christmas and wondering how to make it perfect for Lucas–'

Milly tutted. 'What were you supposed to do, marry him because you didn't want to hurt his feelings? Now that would be bonkers!'

Meg bit her lip and didn't confess that she

had actually considered this. 'I know you're right and at the end of the day it boils down to one thing. I didn't love him, Mills, and I don't think he really loved me, not the real me.'

Meg closed her eyes briefly and replayed the previous evening in her head. They had been about to walk into the restaurant to meet Piers' school friend and his new fiancée when Piers had turned to her and casually remarked, 'By the way, I told them you're an orphan – thought that would be easier than mentioning the whole being in care thing.' He'd then grimaced. Meg had stood in front of him and it was as if a veil had been lifted. 'Easier for who, Piers?' she'd asked.

'Oh, Mills, I feel so stupid for letting it go on so long.'

Milly sighed. 'Well, you've found the courage now and I bet Piers will be hooked up with some suitable young filly before the New Year's invites go out.'

Meg ignored the churn to her stomach, unable to explain that even though she didn't want him, she didn't want him hooking up with someone else quite so soon either, especially not someone from the right background, with the right contacts. Someone his mother would adore and fawn over, someone that wasn't like her.

'I guess.' She fiddled with the fringe of the scarf that lay in her lap. 'And what about

Christmas?' she groaned. 'We were supposed to be staying in town together and going up to his parents' house on Boxing Day.'

'Well at least you don't have to endure that now!' Milly grinned.

Meg smiled. Piers' parents hardly approved of her single-parent status or the fact that their son was smitten with someone who had gone to a comprehensive school.

'Why don't I look at flights for you both to come out to Barbados? The villa sounds plenty big enough; Pru and Christopher would love it! Just think,' Milly chirped, 'Christmas by the pool, a fancy lunch – lobster, the works – and a large cocktail. It'll be fab.'

'Barbarbados!' Lucas shouted as he scooted by the open door.

Meg shook her head. 'Thanks, Mills, but I'd like to stay here. I love him waking up in his own bed on Christmas morning...' Meg let this trail, unable to explain that it was the aspect of her childhood that irked her the most: no warm memories of Christmas morning with presents and a glowing fire. No afternoons on the sofa with full tummies and charades. She was determined to give Lucas a bucketful of traditional festive memories to last him a lifetime. She also wanted to take him to see Bill's mother, Isabel, in Oxford. It was important that he retained links to his dad's family.

'The offer's there if you change your mind.' Milly smacked the arm of the sofa.

Meg looked at Milly. 'Truth is, Mills, I'm scared of being lonely.'

'Lonely? Don't be ridiculous. How can you be lonely when you've got Lucas? And besides, you're at the threshold of life, about to jump in. Take it from one who knows about loneliness, you're just starting out.' Milly folded her arms across her chest as if to emphasise her sixty-nine years on the planet as a single woman. 'There would be nothing more 'orrible than being saddled with someone you didn't love or who didn't love you exactly the way you were.'

Milly let this point linger. Meg cringed a little. Had it been that obvious that Piers had tried to mould Meg into his ideal woman?

Milly continued. 'It wouldn't have been fair on either of you. If you had stayed with Piers it would have been a half life and that is no life at all, not for you or the boy.'

Lucas, having abandoned his scooter, ran into the room on cue. Meg smiled at her son.

'I know you're right. I keep telling myself to man up and get on with things, but I quite liked being someone's girlfriend. It wasn't like it was with Bill, not cosy or special, but it made me feel good nonetheless.'

'And you will feel like that again.' Milly patted her leg. 'But next time, don't settle for someone just because he makes all the right noises and is perfect on paper. Go for someone who knocks your socks off and gets your knickers in a spin.'

'A bit like Dimitri and Anna,' Meg muttered to herself.

'Knocks your socks off!' Lucas shouted loudly as he charged around the room with his dagger held high.

Meg looked at Milly and laughed, relieved that Lucas had chosen that part of the phrase to repeat.

Two

Meg walked briskly along Piccadilly, blowing out foggy breath into the crisp, cold day. Nearly home. She now felt entirely comfortable in this postcode, where, years ago, she had felt like an interloper, looking over her shoulder in case she got turfed out and sent back to her cousin's grim flat in Marylebone. Home was still the apartment above Milly's, and Meg wondered, as she did on occasion, whether she should spread her wings and move from the safety of Curzon Street. But with Milly on the floor below and her friend Guy in the bakery, always ready to natter over a cup of coffee or amuse Lucas at a moment's notice, there was nowhere she'd rather be.

A small part of her felt she *should* fly the nest that had kept her safe during the worst of her grief over Bill. But as Pru had once told her, the road to recovery was more like a dance, with steps left, right and backwards; as long as you arrived at happiness, Pru had advised, no one would give a fig how you'd got there. It was now December the second, about forty-eight hours since she and Piers had broken up, and bar a couple of drunken texts sent in the wee small hours, in which he'd declared his undying love and suggested they meet, there had been no contact between them. Her hectic schedule as Plum Patisserie enjoyed its pre-Christmas surge meant Meg hardly had time to think. But Lucas was happy and seemed quite oblivious to his mum's working hours.

In the last two years, Plum Patisserie had opened new bakeries and cafés in towns and cities all over Britain, as well as branches in Barcelona and Auckland. It was Meg's responsibility to oversee them. She had been at the Windsor store that day, one of several she'd visited in the last couple of weeks. Since Pru had stepped down from day-to-day operations, spending more and more time with her new husband in Salcombe, Meg and Milly had worked side by side, taking the business to new heights. Pru and Milly both agreed that Meg's energy and ideas had given Plum Patisserie the shot in the arm that was needed to expand. And expand it had, all the while remaining faithful to the spirit and style of the Curzon Street flagship. Meg loved the way that in each of their outlets, whether in Bath with its beautiful Georgian façade or Edinburgh where the café nestled within walls of dark grey stone, the interior always echoed that of the Mayfair original. The brass and glass display cabinets, dark wood, bistro panelling and vintage lighting were all replicated perfectly. She felt at home in every one of them.

The recipes for the cakes, tortes, buns and breads sold in each store and café were also executed to Plum's exacting standards. Finding the right calibre of staff had been easy. Plum's reputation went before it and bakers and pâtissiers of note sent their applications by the sackload, keen to be part of the growing success story that was Plum Patisserie.

Guy and his managers personally trained every team of bakers and whether they were in Solihull or Lymington, everyone used the same ingredients and followed the prescribed methods. Pru and Milly had insisted on this. 'Quality and presentation are everything!' Meg had had this drummed into her and could now at a glance tell if the sirop de citron was made with fresh lemons, just by the colour of the glaze on a bun. And if a cherry, no matter how hidden in its almond-infused crème pâtissière, was not the dark, dark colour required, it would be rejected. Canned or frozen substitutes just wouldn't do.

This year, every one of the outlets was carrying the Plum Patisserie Christmas range that Meg and Guy had spent hours perfecting. The results were stunning: spiced apple and mincemeat tarts with flaky pastry tops dusted in powdered sugar; brandy-infused mini Christmas puddings with tiny crystallised pomegranate berries garnishing their shiny domes; chunky individual cranberry and walnut loaves that came wrapped in Plum Patisserie waxed paper and were best eaten warm, when the moist crumbs melted on your tongue; soft-baked cinnamon and oat-crusted Christmas cookies threaded with chunks of dark chocolate and crushed macadamia nuts. There was a whole range of festive drinks to accompany them, including pumpkin-spiced cinnamon latte and cranberry and orange tea. Meg's favourite, though, was the luxuriously rich chocolat chaud just perfect on a cold day. Made from the finest bittersweet organic French chocolate, it was served in a large white bowl that required both hands for sipping. It arrived in front of grateful customers with dark curls of mint-infused chocolat noir scattered across the surface. These stuck to the roof of the mouth and sent one's tastebuds crazy. Each drink came with a generous paper twist of candied peel and nuts, just one of the little touches that set Plum Patisserie apart from its rivals.

Meg yawned. It had been a long day; her train from Windsor had arrived in Waterloo an hour ago. She had battled through the windswept city, trying to hide her face from the light rain that fell. En route she had been tempted by yet another gift for Lucas. This time it was a brightly coloured jack-in-the-box that caught her eye. She knew that when the lid flipped and the garish clown popped his head from the tin her little boy would shriek and make her do it again and again. She couldn't wait to give him all his gifts on Christmas morning. She loved the fact that he now properly understood Christmas and was as interested in his presents as he was in the wrapping paper and boxes they arrived in. It gave her so much joy to see Lucas having the type of Christmas that she had only ever dreamt of. Her thoughts flew to the three-bedroomed semi-detached house in Tall Trees Avenue and a stuffed pink unicorn that had been hers for the briefest time.

Nipping into Babbo's in Mayfair, Meg picked up two hearty portions of chicken parmigiana; that would be plenty for the three of them. Lucas would love the spaghetti and she and Milly would scoop the garlicky tomato sauce, thick slices of milky mozzarella and crunchy breaded chicken on to warm, fresh-baked crusty bread. She considered buying a bottle of red but decided against it, knowing her capacity for alcohol was limited and she had another busy day tomorrow.

The last time she had drunk had been at a pub lunch with Piers, at the Old Red Cow in Smithfield. They had shared a cheese board, with pear chutney and oat cakes, as they sipped at cold pints of strong dark ale. Piers had tutted at her choice of drink, asking if she wouldn't prefer something a little more ladylike. She had snorted her laughter and asked what he would suggest – Babycham? She felt the familiar cringe and wave of sadness wash through her. She had tried too hard to be the girlfriend she thought he wanted and in doing so had lost part of herself. Never again. She would heed Milly's advice and the next time would only jump for someone who got her knickers in a spin and knocked her socks off, someone who loved her exactly how she was. She smiled at the idea of taking advice from a woman who drew moustaches on her face with indelible ink and spent hours of each day dressed as a pirate. No wonder she was single.

Meg's knee-high boots clicked on the icy

pavement. Gathering her warm, camel-coloured coat about her neck, she lowered her head against the cold wind that whipped up the leaves and sent the litter in the gutters swirling. She slowed as she approached the display window at Plum's. 'Evening, Dimitri, Anna. Still smiling? Good, good. And if you don't mind me saying, I think that triple salchow is really coming on.'

Meg looked up at the foggy window of the café. It was twenty minutes until closing time and Guy looked dead on his feet. She knew he had had quite a day; the team from *Good Housekeeping* magazine had been in to photograph the Plum Patisserie range for Valentine's Day – as always, they were thinking and planning ahead, crucial if they were to meet the long lead time of the glossies. The shop and café were packed and a queue of customers, both tourists and locals, snaked down Curzon Street. Everyone was eager for some warm freshly baked boules de campagne and a few slices of the ever-popular, deliciously crumbly winter-spiced tarte aux pommes.

Guy caught sight of Meg and knocked on the window. She let herself in, to the accompaniment of the little brass bell that tinkled overhead on the doorframe. She inhaled the smell of freshly ground coffee, hoping it might give her a lift.

'Hey, chérie! How was Windsor? Has the

Queen been in to the new store yet?' Guy smiled.

'Not yet!' Meg laughed. 'Busy day?'

'Phew! You are not kidding.' Guy mopped at his noticeably un-fevered, powdered brow. 'It's been crazy! I'm looking forward to a hot bath, a foot rub and a large glass of gin – not necessarily in that order.' He giggled. 'Want to see the photos we got today? The Valentine's Day range is simply magnifique!'

'Ooh yes!' Meg called on the last of her energy reserves and followed him down the back stairs to the floor below. Guy raced ahead so that when she entered the office he was already standing there with his arms spread wide and two large prints dangling from his hands. They showed a beautiful selection of romantic fancies: cupcakes crowned with fondant red hearts, white chocolate tortes with pink mallow hearts falling in a decadent flutter from tier to tier, and brioches baked in heart-shaped moulds and dusted with sliced strawberries and icing sugar.

'Oh, they look wonderful!' Meg enthused.

'They do, don't they? I had to sample them all.' He patted his flat stomach.

'You get all the good jobs, Guy. Mind you, if I ate what you did every day, I'd be the size of a bloody bus!'

Swooping forward, he kissed her forehead.

'You would be the prettiest bus in Mayfair.'
'Thanks. I think.' Meg laughed. 'Better be getting back. I've got supper here and Lucas will be getting hungry.' She lifted the bag of chicken parmigiana.
'That poor child will think all food comes in brown paper bags. Do you ever cook for him?' Guy tutted.
'When I have the time!' Meg replied without hesitation.
'Touché. Ooh, give him this from me!' Guy reached behind her and plucked one of the Valentine's cupcakes from the shelf. 'Tell him his Uncle Guy made it from scratch. Or should I put it into a paper bag so he knows it's food?' He winked.
'You are so not funny.' Meg inhaled the rich vanilla-scented sponge and lightly prodded the thick pool of fondant icing. 'And I can't lie. I haven't eaten all day and this will probably not survive the walk up the stairs.'
'I'll be checking – Lucas tells me *everything!*' Guy turned on his heel and swept out of the office. Meg laughed. He was right, he and Lucas certainly shared a lovely bond.

She walked into the flat to find Milly on the phone and pacing the hallway as she tutted and shook her head in response to the caller. Meg waved and pointed at the bag of supper. Milly rolled her eyes and pointed to the sitting room, indicating that that was where she would find her little boy.

Over the four years Meg had lived in the flat, she had stamped her own personality on the interior; gone were some of the fusty oil paintings, replaced by big, bold prints that added a splash of colour to the neutral decor. An enormous leather beanbag sat in pride of place in the sitting room and Lucas's toys were dotted around, bringing just the right amount of hominess to the grand Georgian design.

Meg leant against the wall and pulled off her boots, flexing her newly freed toes against the marble floor, enjoying the coolness of the tiles beneath her tired feet.

'Lucas!' she called, holding the cupcake out like bait.

'Mummy!' He ran from the sitting room.

'Hey, baby.' She bent down and smothered his face with kisses. 'Guy sent you a cake. You can have it after your tea, okay?'

Lucas nodded and went back to the telly. Having grown up with fine patisserie and fresh baking all around him, such a gift was nothing special.

She switched the oven on and removed the lids of the foil containers, releasing the glorious smell of garlicky chicken parmigiana into the room before placing the food on the top shelf to heat through.

Milly walked in and stood with her hands

on her hips and her eyes closed. 'Blimey, Meg, that was a long one. I've got a hot ear.' She placed her fingers against her reddened lobe.

'What's the matter?' Meg had heard enough of the conversation to know there was a problem somewhere. She licked her fingers clean of stray tomato sauce, laid three plates on top of the stove to take the chill from the white china, then rummaged in the cutlery drawer for knives, forks and spoons.

Milly rubbed her top lip, which was thankfully on the mend and no longer so tender, after having been scoured with a rough sponge to remove her indelible-pen moustache. 'Bloody New York, that's what's the matter.' She let out a large sigh.

'Is that the whole city you're fed up with or just a particular part of it?' Meg smiled as she washed a handful of lettuce in the colander.

'One particular part of it, sadly, that sits on Bleecker Street and West 11th.'

'The new store? Why, what's up?' Meg tore the lettuce and arranged it in piles on the plates before adding some thinly sliced rings of red pepper and some leftover sweetcorn that she had stored in a little glass bowl for just such an occasion. She couldn't abide waste.

'They're really behind schedule. The café

isn't even close to ready for opening – there's a problem with the lighting or something, I couldn't really figure it out. But what I do know is that all the electrics are behind. Three of the staff are having a bit of a wobble, worrying this great new venture might not even get off the ground. Juno hinted they're threatening to walk and I can tell she's trying to give me the good news all the time, and not being that honest. She's stressed.' Milly rested her bum against the counter top and folded her arms. 'They need a visit. It needs a bit of steering.'

Meg paused from her dinner preparations and looked over at Milly. She knew what was coming next.

'Would you mind, Meg? I know you hate leaving Lucas, but he'll be fine, I promise, and it will only be in and out, four days tops.'

Milly was right, she did hate leaving her little boy. And although she'd handled the complex problems that some of the new British stores had thrown up, this felt like a big deal. New York? She'd only ever seen it on the TV. She'd barely even been out of the UK, just on a couple of breaks to France with Milly and Pru. She'd never been abroad for work, had never even dreamt of travelling that far away by herself. As ever, she was only one memory away from being the little girl with her clothes in a carrier bag, feeling awkward in a stranger's house and wanting to go back to her mum. All she really wanted was to be at home, preparing for Lucas's fourth Christmas, wrapping presents, stocking up on chocolates and watching a bit of telly.

Milly drew breath. 'You could go at the beginning of next week and be back in no time. There's no one else I trust to sort it out, Meg. I'd go myself, but I've got all the Christmas press interviews to give and I want to be on hand for the holiday stock deliveries for the new shops. Guy is brilliant here, but he's not really one of life's problem-solvers.'

Meg snorted her laughter at the memory of Guy's behaviour the previous week. After a particularly stressful couple of days, he'd run out of live yeast before baking had finished for the day and had broken down in tears, weeping and waving his hanky. Meg had sat him down and given him a cup of strong, sugary tea before calling their suppliers and arranging for more to be delivered by courier, pronto.

'I wouldn't ask, love, if it wasn't important, but I think things are going a bit tits-up over there and we can't have one of our sites crashing before they've even opened.'

'I know.' Meg put her hands on her hips, thinking about the logistics of such a trip.

'I could ask Pru if she and Chris would nip over...' Milly let this hang in the air. Pru and

Chris, at seventy and seventy-two, were still living like newlyweds, enjoying the South Devon coast and settling into semi-retirement, he from public life as a politician and she from running Plum Patisserie.

Since Milly had taken the reins and Meg's role and responsibilities had increased, it was an unspoken agreement that they would not bother Pru, who was loath to leave her cottage in Salcombe. She was entirely content to potter in the garden or sit on the terrace watching the comings and goings on the estuary. They didn't want to disturb her new-found domestic bliss, and they also wanted to prove that they could cope without having to call on her to bail them out, tempting though that was.

'No, I'll go. It's not fair on Juno to expect her to deal with it alone.' Meg gave Milly her brightest false smile. 'Anyway, it'll only be for couple of days, as you said.'

'That's my girl.' Milly clapped her hands together. 'I'll give the airline a call.'

'Are you sure I can manage it?' Meg chewed on her thumbnail.

'What have I told you?' Milly scolded. 'You can do anything you set your mind to. Of course you can handle it!'

Lucas ran into the kitchen. 'I'm hungee!'

'I know, little one. I'm just heating supper up now.' Meg bent down and gathered her son into her chest. 'I love you, Lucas.'

She stood with him in her arms and squeezed him tight, inhaling the scent of him and already dreading their separation. She remembered what it had been like saying goodbye to her own mum. The thought of leaving him made her miss him already.

Three

The plane touched down at John F. Kennedy Airport, where winter had arrived in force. Meg had been unsure what to pack, torn between the weather forecast, which had predicted minus temperatures, and fantasies about living the high life in Manhattan, which according to *Sex and the City* meant a large selection of heels and floaty tops. She wished her planning had been a little more considered as she hauled her large suitcase along on its wheels with her hand luggage bumping against her hip. *Oh God, I wish I could just jump on a plane and go straight home. I can't do this! Why did you think you could, Meg?*

Meg dug deep and straightened her back as she took her place in the taxi queue. Milly's assurance that all Meg needed was the address of her hotel and a credit card challenged the nerves that bubbled in her stomach. Milly was a smart woman and if she had faith in her abilities then maybe Meg should too.

'Where to?' the taxi-queue man asked. Meg noted his padded navy bomber jacket, stiff peaked hat and the truncheon-like stick dangling by his side. Having read all about how dangerous New York could be, she gulped at the thought that even the taxi-rank man had to carry a deterrent.

'It's Greenwich Village.' She hoped she had pronounced it right and that it wasn't 'Green-Witch', as she had once heard an American refer to 'Dull-Witch' in south London. Her titter in the train station all those years ago now felt horribly misplaced.

'Sure thing. Just hop into the next cab that pulls up. Have a great day.' He smiled. Meg felt a pulse of excitement; he sounded exactly like every character in every movie she had ever seen. *I'm in New York! I am actually in New York!* Despite the eight-hour flight, her fatigue evaporated.

Meg felt her limbs jump and her skin prickle as the bitter wind and driving snow slashed at every patch of exposed skin. She dipped her chin into her coat, trying to muster some warmth.

A taxi pulled into the pick-up lane and the driver popped the boot. 'Too cold!' He rubbed his hands together.

She nodded, slightly disappointed by his

Eastern European accent. She had been hoping for someone who sounded like Robert De Niro in *Taxi Driver.*

Climbing into the back of the yellow cab was a moment she wouldn't forget. Despite the plastic screen separating her from the driver, the slightly funky smell of dirty carpet and the fact that she could only make out every other word of the driver's heavily accented commentary over the clatter of the engine, it was a huge thrill to be travelling for the first time in such an iconic vehicle. As the car cruised the expressway from JFK, Meg craned her neck to follow the spires of the skyscrapers in the distance and made a plan to photograph the signs that read 'Brooklyn Bridge' and 'Walk. Don't Walk'. She couldn't wait to show them to Lucas. She also planned to eat a hot dog from a street cart and to visit the coffee shop that featured in *Friends.*

A feeling of loneliness washed over her as she contemplated exploring the city alone. This was one of the places Bill had spoken about very fondly, promising to bring her here. Like so many of his promises, it lay unfulfilled. *Oh, Bill.*

Meg realised that she thought of him less and less now. The all-consuming grief in the immediate aftermath of his death had eventually given way to flares of distress before fading to a constant hum of yearning.

It now felt closer to anger, something she would never dream of confessing to his mother, Isabel. She was angry that he had left her without the future that they had planned and angry that he'd left Lucas without a dad; she was angry that she had been forced to spend time with Piers who she hadn't really loved, but primarily she was mad that he had cheated on her, lied to her, been about to marry another woman.

Meg shook her head. 'I can really pick 'em.' She spoke to the view of the New York skyline with the Statue of Liberty looking diminutive in the distance, far smaller than she had envisaged and further away from the city than she had imagined.

The taxi trundled along the potholed roads into Manhattan, the driver muttering as his chassis jarred against the uneven tarmac. Meg felt a swell of childlike excitement as she stared at the shop windows full of elaborate Christmas displays, the curls of twinkling lights and the be-ribboned doors. It was December the eighth and retailers were on the big festive countdown. The pavements were heaving with New Yorkers and tourists, all muffled up in coats and scarves and weighed down with large fancy carrier bags. Those who were in a hurry stepped into the road, keeping close to the kerb and tutting as wheels bounced into rain- and sleet-filled holes, sending showers over their shiny shoes and greatcoats. Horns honked in chorus as cars jerked forward, unconcerned if they blocked others in the process. Bike couriers in balaclavas and layers of lycra weaved in and out of the stationary traffic at alarming speeds, bumping over gratings that hissed steam from the depths.

Meg tilted her head to take in the looming skyscrapers which all but blocked the last of the day's light from the streets. New York, she decided, made her feel very small. A street-cart vendor with an apron over his padded coat and an 'NYPD' beanie pulled over his ears stood on the corner of Church and Canal selling fat, soft pretzels with a choice of sweet mustard or sourcream dip. Meg's taste-buds prickled and her stomach groaned; she wanted one. She smiled. New York looked and sounded like nowhere else she'd ever been and she wanted to experience it all.

Oblivious to the beeps and shouts from the cars behind him, the taxi driver suddenly swung the cab into West 11th, Greenwich Village and pulled up outside a tall, slim brownstone building with black window frames, one of several identical terraces. This was the Inn on 11th, where she was to stay. As Milly had pointed out, it would be far more congenial than a faceless chain hotel and hopefully the 'suite-style' bedroom would be spacious enough to make her feel at home. Plus it was a couple of blocks from the new Plum Patisserie.

Meg paid the driver from her stash of dollars, counting the unfamiliar currency slowly from her palm before watching as he roared away, leaving a plume of smoke in his wake. She took a deep breath and walked backwards up the steps that led to the front door, bumping her suitcase up with her arms stretched out in front of her. At the top she gripped the freezing scrolled-iron railing for support and pushed the tarnished brass bell on the black front door. She was nose to nose with a vast and tawdry wreath, its red plastic berries and spiky green fronds covered in fake frosting, its tartan ribbon distinctly faded. She hoped this wasn't a clue as to what lay within.

The front door opened eventually to reveal an elderly, miserable-looking man, whose gold name-badge read 'Salvatore'. He gave a long sigh and appeared to be in no hurry. 'My wife and I are happy to welcome you to the Inn on 11th.' He looked past her to the middle distance and held out his upturned palm before letting it fall to his thigh. He sounded anything but happy.

'Thank you! It's good to be here, finally. Bit of a long journey, exciting though.' Meg stamped her boots on the thick coconut mat inlaid on the hallway floor, trying to restore some feeling to her toes. 'It's so cold!'

Salvatore ignored her pleasantries, clearly

in no mood for making small talk. Meg pictured how Milly would have reacted to his welcome; he was what she might describe as a right old smiler! She spoke to the man's back as he shuffled forward in his shiny black shoes. He was dressed smartly, in navy slacks and a crisp white shirt under a royal-blue V-neck sweater, and still held the echoes of his handsome youth, with his trim figure, good skin and bright, clear eyes. His thick shock of grey hair was cut and combed into a side parting that brought to mind the Rat Pack. It was only his stoop and slightly unstable gait that betrayed his eight decades on the planet.

Meg let her eyes rove over the large, square, open-plan hallway cum sitting room with its flock wallpaper, dark wood floors and oversized green marble fireplace. There was an eclectic mix of antiques and retro pieces: comfy-looking leather chairs with cracks of age on thc broad arms, trunks covered in vintage labels, which doubled as tables, and a cast-iron hat-stand from which hung fairy lights. A six-foot fake Christmas tree in a red plastic pot leant against the wall behind the reception desk. Its branches were crammed full of angels, baubles, wooden Santas, snowmen and reindeer, all in a riot of colours. She winced at the lack of uniformity, having learnt a thing or two about display and design during her time at

Plum's. The tree seemed to have been decorated haphazardly, possibly by an impatient or grumpy Salvatore, in the way Lucas might do it, leaving Meg, unable to resist, to put things right after he'd gone to bed. The fairy lights blinked and stuttered. Meg wasn't sure if this was an effect or the result of an electrical fault; she hoped they didn't leave them on overnight.

The place looked like a treasure trove and wasn't what she had expected. It was like entering a portal to the 1950s or 60s. As Salvatore rummaged on the shelf of the bureau that served as the reception desk, she studied the large stag's head above the door and the kidney-shaped bar with optics hanging on the wall behind it. The clutter of randomly hung pictures above the fireplace looked as if they were fighting for space.

'I like your pictures.' Meg pointed at the cluster of crude oils depicting everything from a nude woman reclining on a chaise longue to the obligatory bowl of fruit.

'My wife's an artist, apparently. What she lacks in talent she makes up for in productivity. Go figure.' Salvatore spoke from a stern mouth. Meg couldn't decide if he was intentionally dry or was simply the most unintentionally hilarious man she had ever met. She smiled at him, either way.

'What's your name?' Salvatore mumbled, turning his attention to the task in hand.

‘It’s Hope, Meg Hope. I’m here for three nights.’

‘You are in the garden room. There is no lift.’ Salvatore eyed her large suitcase before popping on his half-moon specs and slowly opening the red leather guest-book. His licked his fingers and fumbled with the fine gilt-edged pages that seemed to be stuck together. Meg liked his New York–Italian accent; he sounded like a gangster.

‘Yes, thank you. I booked the garden room because it sounded so nice when I checked it out online. I live in a flat in London and so don’t have a garden.’ She tried again to engage him with a smile, which he ignored.

‘Breakfast is served in the library between seven and ten.’ He waved his hand in the general direction of the back of the property. From where Meg stood, it seemed a rather grand term for the single-storey lean-to with its floor-to-ceiling bookshelf, plethora of tropical plants and mismatched wicker furniture. Nonetheless, it looked like a wonderful room in which to sit drinking coffee and browsing the papers.

‘That’s great, thank you. Although I’m off to work at the bakery we are opening not too far from here – so I might have breakfast there.’

Salvatore reached under the counter and produced a folded map, which he slid across the top of the bureau with two fingers. ‘This shows the closest subway and places of interest.'

'Thanks.' Meg twitched her nose. He clearly didn't want to chat.

'Hey, you must be Meg!' came a voice from the stairs. 'Hello, hello! I am Elene, co-owner of the Inn on 11th.' Salvatore's wife, the prolific artist, swept into the room, resplendent in a leopard-skin-patterned scarf, which was tied at her neck in an elaborate bow. The diminutive innkeeper was immaculate in gold pumps, tailored camel trousers and matching jacket, with a heavy gold ring on her little finger. She wore a generous smudge of kohl around her eyes and a shock of red lipstick that almost sat on her lips. Elene's make-up was heavy and seemed to have been dabbed on in generally the right areas, suggesting that failing eyesight or an unsteady hand might be to blame. But Meg loved her look.

'I saw your booking a few days ago. It's our pleasure to welcome you here, Meg. I was in London in 1963, stayed in Earls Court. Had the time of my life! My first time away from my parents and I saw the Beatles at the Palladium. Couldn't hear a thing apart from the girls screaming – they were going crazy. But I was as close to them as I am to you. Paul looked right at me, I swear. It was amazing! I hooked up with a guy called Joe, an East London Jew. He was adorable.' She let both hands flop over at the wrist. 'I was in love, of course, but his parents soon put a stop to that!'

Meg smiled, wondering if Salvatore's quiet reticence was a reaction to his wife's over-sharing.

'It was before I met Sali.' She waved dismissively in his general direction. 'Joe was ten years older than me, swept me off my feet. It was a whirlwind thing, the kind that's good for your soul but has no future. He was the most beautiful dancer I have ever seen – we waltzed in Trafalgar Square, one of the best nights of my entire life!' she shouted.

'Ah, how lovely!' Meg said tentatively. She wasn't sure of the correct response and felt a little awkward discussing Elene's illicit love in front of her husband.

'And I hear you are involved in the new store that's opening? Plum's, isn't it?' Meg smiled at Elene's pronunciation – *stawwerr.* 'I peep in when I walk past, looks real fancy. If a little dark.' She nodded.

'Yes, that's the one. This'll be the first time I've seen it. It's very exciting.' Meg didn't want any negativity around the project leaking out into the community and was under no illusion that if anyone were good at leaking information, it would be Elene.

'Well, make sure I'm invited to the grand opening. I'll bring my friends, especially Stella. If anyone knows patisserie, it's her.'

She raised her index finger as if giving a lesson. 'She's ninety but I swear doesn't look a day over seventy-five. She lived in Montmartre after the war.' She winked at Meg, as though this information were code for something far more risqué. 'I might even bring Sali if he promises to behave!' This she bellowed at Salvatore. Who ignored her, muttering under his breath.

'Will do. It'd be lovely to see you there.' Meg collected her case, not sure if Plum's was even considering a grand opening.

'Do you have supper plans, honey?' Elene was equal parts motherly and nosy.

'No. Think I might just nip out, grab something and eat in my room. It's been a very long day.' Meg sighed and felt the familiar ache at the memory of kissing Lucas goodbye twelve hours earlier. She glanced at her watch. He'd be tucked up now, sound asleep, if Milly hadn't let him stay up and play superhero pirates, which was entirely possible.

'Try the Greenwich Avenue Deli. It's the best in the Village! Say Elene sent you.' She winked again. 'Go out the door, turn right, walk forward a block and a half and you can't miss it.'

Meg nodded her thanks.

She let herself into her room with its view of the garden. The outside space was no more than a ten-foot square crammed full of ornate statues and with a rather elaborate fountain in the middle that she suspected was switched on very rarely. It sat on a small patch of faux grass that reminded her of Astro Turf. Various plant pots in once bright colours sat in faded piles, their contents long since shrivelled to dust. She had expected an Italianate courtyard as per the description; this was more back yard of the local pub, out of season.

Meg liked the spacious room, which was old-fashioned, fussy and a little dusty. The faded gold velvet curtains and pelmet were both fringed with maroon tassels. The bathroom was large, tiled in white, with greying grout and an orangey imprint on the white floor where countless feet had alighted from the tub. Vintage brass taps graced the tub and wide china sink. Burgundy towels with appliqué flowers were folded over the heated towel rail.

Meg heaved her suitcase up on to the luggage stand and flipped it open. She unpacked her clothes into the tall walnut wardrobe but hung her shirts and trousers on the back of the bathroom door. The steam from her shower would help the creases drop – a neat trick she had learnt from Pru. The wide, soft bed with its quilted jade-coloured counterpane and matching headboard was calling to her, but Meg knew that if she crawled between the starched white sheets and succumbed to sleep at 5 p.m. she would then be up in the early hours, pacing the floor, only to be thoroughly exhausted by 3 p.m. the next day. She had to adapt to the local time zone the moment she arrived. The rule was to go to bed when everyone else did – Pru's husband Christopher had taught her *that.*

Securing her striped scarf around her neck and pulling the matching hat with its large bobble over her ears, she tiptoed back through the reception area. There was no sign of Elene or Salvatore. The hat sat snugly on her thick hair and, according to Milly, made her look like a pixie. She smiled at her reflection; at least she'd be a warm pixie. Reluctantly, she set out into the cold New York evening from which she had only just escaped.

She stood on the pavement and let the chilly evening air filter into her lungs. She stared at the yellow cabs and wide cars that sped by and stood back to allow the smart ladies in belted macs, fashionable spectacles and trainers pass by. *I'm in New York!* Again she felt a rush of excitement. Remembering Elene's instructions, she made her way to the best deli in the Village. It shone like a glittering beacon in the winter gloom. Her mouth watered and her stomach rumbled as she caught sight of the salamis and sausages hanging from hooks in the brightly lit windows. She was clearly more hungry than she'd realised. Boxes of panettone, traditional Italian Christmas bread, were lined up just inside the glass. The packaging was cleverly both vintage and festive and made her think of her childhood. A memory came to her, sharp and bittersweet.

It was Christmastime; she couldn't have been more than seven and was staying with her foster family in Tall Trees Avenue. It had been a long day, traipsing around the shops buying last-minute Christmas 'bits and bobs', as Pam had called them. They had gone into town by bus, to avoid having to look for a parking space. Megan liked sitting on the top deck, drawing pictures with her finger on the steamed-up windows. As they waited in the cold shelter for their bus home, neon lights shone on the dark, wet pavements. She watched the bright headlights prowling the streets and illuminating the raindrops. It was quite hypnotic.

When they eventually arrived home, she and Kirsty were sent into the lounge, where a real fire blazed and a fat aunt sat on the sofa. Megan had felt a smile twitch on her lips when she saw that the woman's husband was very, very thin. The two of them reminded her of Jack Spratt and his wife, from the nursery rhyme they'd learnt in school. She watched as the woman shrugged her wobbly arms from her coat to reveal her Sunday best.

The woman tilted her head to one side and spoke to Pam through a half-closed mouth. 'Who is she again?' Then, 'How long have you got her for?' Everyone took up their places on the sofa or the floor. Conversation flew over Megan's head and she listened while they all laughed at memories she couldn't relate to and talked about people she had never heard of. When no one was looking, she placed her small hand against her chest and whispered, 'Ssssshhh.'

Pam brought in a chocolate-covered Yule log, already cut into slices, and placed it on the table. Even now, standing in front of the deli, Meg could almost smell the thick chocolate from all those years ago, which had melted slightly in the heat of the room.

'Help yourselves!' Pam urged.

Kirsty, the fat aunt, her skinny husband and Len all shoved out their hands and grasped fat slices of the sponge, quickly cramming it into their mouths and licking any residue from their fingers. It was only when Megan crept towards the table that she realised there was nothing but crumbs left. She hadn't meant to cry, but hot tears stung her eyes and clogged her nose nonetheless.

'We forgot Megan!' Kirsty mumbled through her last half-chewed mouthful.

'Oh, Megan!' they chorused. Their pity was genuine and that somehow made the situation much worse. She wished they weren't being nice to her, it made her feel even sadder. How could she admit to hating them all just then, when they were being sympathetic?

'I've got something that'll last much longer than Yule log.' Pam winked at Megan and left the room, returning with the box the cake had come in. 'Look, Megan! It's got a lovely picture on it of holly and berries and it still smells of chocolate.' Pam smiled as she handed it to her.

Megan had gathered the box to her chest and sniffed its interior. It was torture, only reminding her of what she'd missed out on. Funny she should think of that now.

Meg walked inside the warm, busy deli and inhaled the heady mixture of food, spices and coffee. It was noisy: people shouted greetings and laughed, the till chimed, and Dean Martin crooned 'White Christmas' through the speakers on the wall. In front of the counter sat straw panniers full of large red apples and bags of designer vegetable crisps. To the side was a wooden cart loaded with every type of cheese imaginable, from wedges of creamy blue Roquefort to vast wheels of Grana Padano, displayed amid full clusters of red and green grapes. Six dark-haired men stood behind the counters in white tunics with 'The Greenwich Avenue Deli' embroidered above the breast pocket. Masters of the sandwich, they swiped at rounds of warm ciabatta, loaves of organic San Francisco sourdough and Cuban batons, depending on the customer's preference, slitting them with long, sharp knives before loading them up with savouries from the cold counter. They slid and slipped around each other in the small space like dancers with well-choreographed moves, never missing a beat.

Meg stood in the queue, watching with fascination as succulent slices of milky mozzarella were laid on top of sundried tomatoes, smoked peppers and salad, before being finished with a rip of fresh basil and a twist of coarsely ground black pepper. The ciabatta was then quickly sealed, wrapped inside waxed paper and handed to a young guy in a grubby baseball cap and black square-framed glasses who was nodding to whatever his earphones were pumping into his head. She decided to have the same. It looked delicious.

The woman in front of her ordered sourdough piled high with peppery rocket, crispy bacon, slices of white chicken meat and a generous dollop of homemade spicy slaw. Meg decided to have that instead.

Suddenly it was her turn. Her indecisiveness made her nervous.

'What'll it be, lady?' The man stood with knife in hand. Every second of hesitation caused his mouth to twitch. His leg jumped as the knife banged against his thigh. He was like every other New Yorker, in a desperate hurry.

'Oooh... I'm not sure. It all looks so good!'

He didn't react to her compliment; keen to keep the line moving, conversation would only slow proceedings.

She was about to settle on sourdough cut into thick doorsteps 'I think I'll go for...' – when a roll of dark German rye caught her eye. She hesitated. 'Actually, no. I think ... erm...' She tapped her finger against her mouth, unable to decide. The bread was the foundation on which her sandwich would be built; get it wrong and the whole thing could be a disaster. And if there was one thing Meg knew about, it was bread. She let her eyes wander over the crusty batons and seeded loaves. Fatigue was getting the better of her.

A large arm in a blue denim shirt, rolled above the elbow, reached over her shoulder and a voice boomed in her ear. 'I'll take a hoagie with pastrami, pickle and sauerkraut, coupla slices of Swiss and tomato, lots of black pepper, hold the mayo.'

Meg turned to face the overbearing New Yorker who had queue-jumped her. 'Excuse me! I was just about to order!'

The tall auburn-haired man grinned. 'Ah well, that's where you went wrong. "Just about to" will never get you anywhere here. You need to pounce, not dally.'

'You want mustard with that, pal?'

Meg stared at the sandwich guy, complicit in bumping her place in the queue.

'Sure.'

'"Dally"?' Meg was aware that her voice had a squeaky tone to it. 'I'm not dallying, I'm just very tired!'

The man laughed. 'Well, hey, Mary Poppins, top tip for ya: try being tired at the back of the queue not the front.'

'Mary Poppins?' Meg wasn't sure whether to laugh or cry.

'Yeah, you've got that whole spoonful of sugar thing going on there!' He circled his forefinger in front of his mouth and laughed again.

'You seem to know a lot about Mary Poppins for a grown man.' She closed her eyes and turned away.

'I wasn't always a grown man. I was born real small and it's taken thirty years to get to this.' He ran his open palms down his body, which she couldn't help but notice was well built and toned. His skin was darker than the type she usually associated with red hair and the freckles that peppered his forearms were darker still. *Angel's kisses...* That's what she'd heard her foster mum say to Kirsty, as she'd kissed her little nose and waved her off into the winter's morning for school. Megan had rather liked the term.

Meg shook her head and turned back to the counter.

'What'll it be?' The next server nodded in her direction, with an expression that was just as impatient as his colleague's.

'Erm... I'd like...' Meg felt flustered all over again.

'Do you need help there?' Denim-shirt guy bent low and spoke into her ear.

'What I *need* is for you to leave me alone,' she snapped, staring at the array of produce in front of her. 'I'd like a cheese sandwich please.'

'On what?' the server fired back.

'Brown bread?' She hated her uncertainty.

Thankfully he grabbed two slices of multigrain from an open bag on the shelf behind him and slapped them down on the counter. 'Which cheese?' He ground his teeth together, his lower jaw jutting with impatience. He eyed the queue building up behind this indecisive broad.

'I'm not sure...' Meg felt her face colour and considered giving up on the whole thing.

'We got cream cheese, goat's cheese, American cheese, Italian cheese, French, Swiss – could you at least narrow it down to a country?' The man spoke quickly.

Red hair laughed and again leant towards her. 'Try the Swiss with a pickle, and mustard and mayo. You can't go wrong.' He winked at her as he grabbed his sandwich and went off to pay.

Meg turned to him with her mouth

opening and closing like a fish. It wasn't often she was rendered speechless.

Clutching her waxed paper parcel, she decided to eat her sandwich at the counter, to give her some energy for the walk back to the Inn on 11th. Climbing with effort up on to the high stool, she removed her scarf and bobble hat and placed them on her lap before unwrapping the paper. Meg held her first New York deli sandwich at eye level and she had to admit, it looked delicious.

Police sirens wailed and flashed in the gathering darkness beyond the window. Couples linked arm in arm strode the pavement purposefully, whether tired at the end of a busy day or in anticipation of a fun night ahead, she couldn't tell. Meg looked at the shops opposite, all of them with apartments above, and decided that New York was a bit like an anthill, with only a fraction of life visible on the street and the rest going on way above your head. She tried to immerse herself in the comings and goings on Greenwich Avenue, doing her best to ignore the obnoxious queue jumper, who was now seated two stools away from her.

She heard the scrape of the stool's metal legs against the tiled floor as he took the place next to her. Meg kept her gaze fixed on the window, not wanting to engage with him any further. *Please just go away.*

'I bet you are single.' He was direct, his

voice calm and she could tell from his delivery that he was smiling.

Meg shook her head and bit into her sandwich, which was just as good as it looked.

'I'm right, aren't I?' he pushed. 'You aren't married or even involved.' He folded his arms across his chest as if to state that he wasn't leaving any time soon.

Meg looked at her lonely supper and her single serving of milk as she flexed her ring-free fingers. 'I don't see that whether I am single or not is anything to do with you.' She turned back to her sandwich.

'You sound adorable. I could listen to you all night.' He smiled.

Meg rolled her eyes. As if that was going to happen.

'I'm right, aren't I? Come on! Throw me a bone here. You're single, I can tell.'

'Why do you think I'm single?' she asked, partly to hurry the exchange along and get it over with and also, she had to admit, she was curious.

He leant forward and she noticed for the first time his very, very blue eyes, a similar colour to his shirt. 'It's just a guess, but mainly I've come to that conclusion because you are really, really ugly.'

Meg coughed, nearly choking on her pickle. She wasn't sure whether to laugh or cry.

'I'm kidding! I'm kidding! Don't asphyxiate, my Heimlich skills leave a lot to be desired.' He wiped his mouth with the back of his palm and chuckled. 'And why are you so tired, if you don't mind me asking?'

'I do mind, actually.' Meg folded her food back into its wrapper and decided to take it back to her room as originally planned; she was not in the mood for his approaches.

'Hey, come on, haven't you heard of friendly New York banter?' He feigned distress, putting his hand on his heart.

'Haven't you heard of piss off and leave me alone?' Her tone sharper than she had intended.

'Aw, come on, I'm only messing with you, Mary. We've got a thing going on here, this is good!' He grinned.

'We definitely do not have a thing going on and my name isn't Mary!'

'Well, that's easily fixed. If you tell me your real name then I won't have to call you Mary any more, will I, Mary?'

Meg jumped down from her stool and walked quickly from the deli without looking back at denim-shirt guy, the idiot. She was tired, hungry and dreaming of her bed at home. It would take more than a pair of sparkly blue eyes to get around her tonight.

Four

It took a full second for Meg to remember where she was as she slid reluctantly from between the crisp, warm sheets, reaching for her phone alarm as it pipped her awake. She had texted her safe arrival to Milly the previous night and now she desperately wanted to speak to Lucas, wanted to hear his breathy gabble down the line reassuring her that he was far too busy to talk. She checked her watch, which was still on UK time; he'd be at pre-school. Their chat would have to wait until later. It was going to be the most frustrating thing about being here, trying to schedule their contact around bedtime, work time and a five-hour time difference.

She groped, bleary-eyed, around the bedroom until she located the bathroom door. The hot shower was just the kick-start she needed. Meg stood with the outdated showerhead angled just so and let the water pummel her back. She dug her nails into her scalp, rubbing vigorously to rid her skin of the greasy film that built up after travelling. Then she wrapped herself in the white fluffy towel and combed her hair. After slipping into her fitted black wool trousers and her favourite grey polo neck, she twisted her hair up into a messy topknot and was ready to face the day.

Passing through reception, Meg spied Salvatore sitting in one of the leather chairs, immaculate as ever. He was scouring *The Villager* with his glasses in his hand hovering over the print, using them like a magnifying glass.

'Good morning!' she said cheerily, still trying to win him over, as she buttoned up her coat and wrapped her scarf around her neck.

'Don't know what's good about it!' He tapped the open page with the arm of his spectacles. 'Are they going to pull down every goddam historical building and replace them all with flashy glass condos? The mayor's a schmuck. They're destroying the city, piece by piece. What's good about that?' Salvatore shook his head.

Meg paused as she got to the front door, unsure whether he wanted a response or was just venting his spleen. 'I don't know what's good about it, you are right. But I hope something happens today to make you smile.' She flashed a grin at the top of Salvatore's head, but he continued reading and mumbling as though he were alone.

'Well, I'll be off then.' She nodded and reached for the brass handle. It was time to get on with her day.

'Don't let the heat out!' He waved his glasses in her direction and shouted at her disappearing form.

Meg laughed. How was she supposed to step outside into the frosty winter morning without opening the front door? Standing on the top step, she took a deep breath and ventured out on to the streets of Greenwich Village.

She liked this time of day in any city. It was a little too early for other tourists to have hit the streets and was the preserve of natives making their way to work and runners pounding the pavements in mismatched T-shirts and joggers. Here, the sun was yet to rise over the skyscrapers and the early haze of morning threw a bluey-grey veil over the cityscape. She let her eyes wander, watching as New York stretched and yawned, coming alive, full of all the wonderful possibilities that the day might hold.

Passing the Greenwich Avenue Deli, she resisted the temptation to go in and grab a coffee and one of the plump banana and nut muffins that sat so enticingly in the window, their crunchy crusts of dark brown sugar all but impossible to ignore. She didn't want to arrive with breakfast in her hand, especially not a baked breakfast, feeling that would be disloyal to the Plum brand. She'd simply have to wait. She hoped that they had at least managed to get the coffee machine working and had run off a batch of chocolate brioche. Meg inhaled their imaginary scent, which was enough to make her mouth water. She glanced at the stools and counter inside the window and shook her head, remembering the rude man in the denim shirt the night before. Mary Poppins? What a dickhead.

She fell into step with the other commuters and felt a rush of happiness as she considered her situation. Meg from London, Megan who had been in and out of care, quiet Megan who would never amount to much, here she was, strolling around New York, off to work as though it were second nature. If she could, what would she say to her seven-year-old self, who felt like the world was so complicated, when it took all of her strength just to figure out her place in it? She would say, 'Hang on in there, Meggy. You might have a few bumps ahead of you, but I promise, it all gets a lot, lot easier.' And she'd probably buy her a pair of pink fluffy earmuffs like Izzy Fox's because she'd know how much she coveted them. She smiled at the idea.

Meg walked the few blocks quickly to try and prevent the chill of the frosty morning from creeping into her bones. She took a circuitous route, wanting to see some of this incredible city. Having passed through Washington Square and skirted the New York University building, she now stood watching Juno, the young manager of Plum's New York branch, from across the street as she waited for a gap in the traffic.

Juno was nervous. She paced the pavement in front of the shop, smoothing her dark hair back into its immaculate ballerina bun and craning her neck left and right before returning inside and peeking regularly from the open door. Meg recognised her instantly from their many conversations on Skype. She sensed her anxiety and felt for her. She knew that until Juno had worked for the company for a while, she would be jumpy, uneasy about how she might be viewed when things were running less than smoothly. But everyone in London had confidence in Juno's abilities. She had been awarded the ribbon for excellence on her course in pastry arts, cake- and bread-making at the New York Institute of Culinary Arts, and she had impressed at her interview. Her artisan loaf had wowed Guy, which was no mean feat, and her passion for the project was infectious, just what they needed for a new team in a competitive environment. Milly was right, it was important not to let her enthusiasm flag before Plum's had even opened its doors for business, especially if there was a whiff of dissent in the ranks.

Juno came out on to Bleecker Street again just as the cloud seemed to lift and rays of sunshine pierced the sky. Shielding her eyes, she glanced up and down the busy street, wiping her palms down the side of her long black skirt, over which she wore her starched black atelier's apron that buttoned on to her white shirt. The Plum Patisserie double 'P' logo stood out in gold embroidery. Meg had expected her to be in jeans, as they weren't yet open. She waved from the other side of Bleecker Street, catching Juno's eye immediately before a large truck with a shiny chrome fender blocked her from view. A gap finally appeared in the traffic and Meg took her chance and darted across the road.

'Morning, Juno!' She stepped forward, smiling. 'It's really great to meet you properly in person.'

'Hey, Meg. You too. I'm really sorry about this.' Juno looked close to tears as she gestured at the shopfront behind her. The gold 'Plum Patisserie' lettering shone handsomely against the bottle-green frontage.

'What are you sorry for?'

'For the whole mess and that you had to come out so near to Christmas to check up on things. I know how busy you must be. I told Milly things were getting sorted and they are, it's just that we have hit a couple of roadblocks...' She twisted her fingers inside her cupped palms and blinked rapidly.

Meg took a deep breath. 'Listen to me, Juno, we are a team, a family and we will do whatever it takes to get things sorted, okay?'

She placed her hand on the girl's shoulder and felt the tension leave her muscles.

'Okay.' Juno nodded, giving her first smile of the day, even if it was a little forced.

'That's better. And I'm here to support you, not check up on you. What kind of team would we be if we left you to sort out all the crap alone?' Meg remembered Pru's hand on her back when she had needed it most; the extraordinarily feeling that she wasn't alone was one that she would never forget.

Juno nodded again. 'Okay.' She exhaled, relieved and determined.

'Now, why don't we grab a cup of coffee and we can go through where we are at. The shopfront looks marvellous, by the way. They've done a great job.'

'They have.' Juno beamed. This time her smile was genuine.

Meg stepped over the brass tread with its plastic wrap still in place and looked around at the spacious shop. The bakery occupied the back wall, with the café and counter at the front. The front door was wedged open by an improvised rough wooden block, allowing as much natural light as possible to fill the space.

The solid wood floor was a beautiful burnished oak, the honey tones of which made the whole room seem bright; it too was being kept under wraps beneath a layer of plastic that was taped down at the edges and corners. The counter stretched across the right-hand wall, along with glass display cabinets and blackboards. The walls had been beautifully panelled in dark wood and the ornamental brass rails and window seats were awaiting the standard button-backed cushions. Wooden bistro chairs were stacked in corners; on the tables, which had been pushed to the side, sat shallow packing cases full of crockery, glassware, cake stands and glass cloches, all nestling in white polystyrene squiggles. Everything from head height down looked to be near completion. The problem became evident when Meg looked up.

Long electrical flexes hung in loops from jagged fist-sized holes that had been roughly cut in the new ceiling. There were no light fittings; instead, bright bulbs sat inside round wire cages that had been pegged up on wooden splints, providing temporary lighting. They were plugged into cables that dragged along the floor and were crisscrossed into place with yellow-and-black tape printed with the words 'Trip Hazard'. *No kidding,* Meg thought as she sidestepped one particular snaking cable that threatened to ensnare her ankle.

Dust fell at regular intervals, sending a fine mist of debris into the room whenever something was disturbed. It clung to Meg's clothes and filled her nose and mouth with a grey, gritty soot that turned to paste on her tongue.

'Oh dear.' Meg shielded her eyes as she peered up at the ceiling.

Juno sighed. 'Yes, oh dear. We have the mop out every hour trying to keep on top of the dust, but it's not easy with all the cables and stuff in the way.'

'I bet.' Meg sympathised, liking Juno's attempts at keeping order.

'We've tried every way we can think of to get around it, but the problem is Mr Redlitch, who lives in the apartment above. He won't answer his door or respond to calls or letters. Mrs Pakeffelar two doors down is his friend from the bridge club and thinks he may have gone to stay with his daughter, Nancy, in Boca Raton. Apparently he goes for long periods, otherwise he can't cope with the journey and why wouldn't you go for a long time, weather's gotta be better than here, right?' Juno held her upturned palms in thc air.

'Right.' Meg nodded although she wasn't entirely sure what she was agreeing to. Juno spoke very quickly and her hand gestures were a little distracting. 'But what's our ceiling got to do with Mr...?' Meg had lost the thread and was busy wondering where Boca Raton was.

'Redlitch,' Juno prompted.

'Yes, Mr Redlitch.'

Juno sighed again. It clearly wasn't the first

time she had recounted the story. 'He owns the apartment above and we need access to finish the electrical work. The architect thought it could all be done from this side...' She pointed upwards. 'But apparently it was a false ceiling with a botched electrical job done decades ago, so the wiring's old and messy. We need to pull up Mr Redlitch's floor and come from the top down to sort it all out. That's if we can get his permission, which we still haven't–'

'Because he's gone to stay with Nancy,' Meg concluded.

'Right.' Juno nodded.

The two stared silently at the ceiling as if, if they stared long enough, a solution might present itself.

'I'm probably stating the obvious, but does anyone have a number for Nancy?' Meg was in full solution mode.

Juno shook her head. 'No. We thought of that, of course. I even tried buttering up the building superintendent to let me in. I figured we could get in, pull up the floor and have everything back in place before Mr Redlitch came home – he'd never suspect a thing!'

Meg pulled a face at Juno's cunning, concerned and impressed in equal parts.

'But he cited some clause at me about violating people's property and breaking and entering, yadda yadda...'

'So we can't get the lighting done until Mr Redlitch appears or we get hold of Nancy's number?' Meg placed her hands on her hips.

'That's about the sum of it.'

'And we have no lighting until that time?'

'It's not just that: no ceiling lighting and no lit displays, but also no electrical safety certificate. And without that, no general liability insurance, meaning we can't let the public set foot over the door.' Juno inhaled strongly.

'Shit,' Meg muttered under her breath.

'Yes, shit. A couple of the kitchen team are getting jumpy, worried that we aren't going to open and that their jobs are in jeopardy. No one wants to be out of work three weeks before Christmas. I keep telling them everything is fine, but I guess they're worried that if we can't get up and running, it might never get off the ground.'

'Arc you worricd too, Juno?' Meg looked her in the eye.

The girl tilted her oval face towards her narrow shoulder. 'A little, I guess.'

'Well don't be. I promise you we *are* going to open, no matter how long it takes. I'll have a word with everyone else individually.' Meg started to mentally rehearse the reassurances. This was far more than a hand-holding project. 'And where is the architect? I can't believe we are in this mess at this point so close to opening.' The firm of architects responsible for the design and fit of the building was also overseeing the project and sending regular reports back to Milly and Pru in the UK.

'I asked him to meet us here.' Juno looked at her watch. 'I know he's crazy busy though. Seems at this time of the year everyone wants things finished.'

Meg lifted down a couple of the chairs from the stack by the wall and ran her fingertips over the dusty seat before sitting down. 'I don't care about everyone else's projects. I only care about ours.'

She once again looked up at the ceiling and the electrical vines hanging down. They made the room look part cable factory, part jungle. Meg breathed deeply, trying to calm her pulse. Her palms were clammy despite the cold. She hoped she would know what to do, hoped she'd be able to find the answers and get the place up and running. It was a familiar feeling of not wanting to let Milly and Pru down and wondering if she was good enough to get the job done. Pru's words drifted into her head: *'You can do anything you put your mind to, Meg. You are smart and if you don't know what to do straight off you'll figure it out.'* Meg lifted her chin and opened her case. It was important to convey confidence and leadership to Juno and the team. *Yes. I will figure this out.*

The two spent the next couple of hours running through the training programme for the serving staff, who were all on standby, waiting for a start date.

Juno fidgeted with strands of hair that had worked loose from her bun. 'The problem we have is that even though the staff are super keen, some might begin looking for other jobs and there are more available at this time of year than any other, even if they're only temporary. My worry is they might take temp work rather than hang around waiting for us and then we will have lost them for the opening and will have to start the hiring process all over again.' She put her head in her hand, depressed at the prospect.

Meg knew how time-consuming and tedious that whole process could be. 'Well, we shall have to let them start right away. Let's get them involved in the setting-up of the premises and begin table training and, more crucially, let's start paying them – it's only a few weeks early. It might cost us in wages, but it will save us money in the long-term. At least they'll be fully on board, reassured and invested in the project if they've been here since the very beginning and watched it open.'

Juno bobbed her head, relieved. 'That's great, Meg.'

'You see?' Meg smiled. 'There is nothing we can't sort with a bit of team work!'

'Oh good – finally!' Juno directed her gaze over Meg's shoulder. 'Here's Mr Architect!'

Meg glanced at her watch. It was nearly 11 a.m. She watched Juno's cheeks flush ever so slightly at the sight of the architect. Meg turned and came face to face with the man in whom she would have to trust as he guided her through the process of sorting the electrics and getting the whole venture up and running, in time and on budget. She looked on as he dumped his brown leather satchel and yellow hardhat on the floor.

The man took a step forward and held out his hand. 'Edward Kelly – Edd.' He beamed, eyes shining, a beacon of confidence.

Meg placed her palm against his and looked him up and down. *You have got to be kidding me.* Her face fell and her shoulders sagged. 'Poppins, Mary Poppins.'

'Ah! Yes, that...' He looked at the floor and sucked his breath in through his clenched teeth.

'Yes, that. And for your information, I'd literally just landed.' She enjoyed watching him squirm.

'Well, that explains why you were so tired.' He tried to break the ice, putting his hands on his hips and nodding slightly.

'That's right. Tired, not dallying,' Meg whispered. She noted his sturdy tan Timberland work boots, jeans, white T-shirt and favoured denim shirt, over which he wore a navy pea coat, buttoned up against the cold weather.

Edd dropped her hand and removed his coat, which he placed over the back of Meg's chair. The sleeves of his shirt were again rolled above his dark, freckled forearms, despite the season. He indicated the door over his shoulder with his thumb. 'Can we rewind and start over?'

'What, all the way back to last night?' she asked, conscious that Juno was all ears.

'Well, no, I was thinking just the last few minutes, give myself a chance to do over.'

'"Do over"?' Meg looked confused.

'A "do-over" is where you get to start again from the beginning, usually because you did it badly the first time,' Juno explained.

'Oh.' Meg looked up. 'A do-over...'

'What do you call it?' Edd asked.

'We just say, get it right the first time, you muppet.' She allowed the smallest smile to form on her lips.

'"Muppet" as in...?' Edd rolled his hand, hoping for clarification.

'As in Miss Piggy, Kermit, Gonzo and gang.'

The two stared at each other and then the floor. Juno coughed. 'Shall I go get us all some coffee?' she offered with a wistful air. Clearly the newly arrived Brit had made far more progress with Mr Architect in the last twenty-four hours than she had in over a month.

'Please.' They both nodded at her in unison.

'What about something to eat?' Juno ventured.

Meg felt a ripple of hunger in her stomach. 'Oh, yes please, a good firm golden croissant that hasn't been anywhere near shrink-wrap. Yes!' She clicked her fingers imagining the breakfast she craved. 'Organic honey to dip it in would be perfect. Or some warm brioche, the ones that pull apart with ease, chocolate preferably, but only if they're warm. Or a muffin, any flavour, but definitely one of the big greasy ones with something drizzled on top. You know the ones?' She turned to Edd. 'They are mass-produced with too much corn oil, keeps them softer and fresher for longer, but it leaves that small slick of grease on your lips – my guilty pleasure! They need to be washed down with strong black coffee to balance the sweetness.' She looked back to Juno. 'In fact, get me all three, would you? I'm absolutely starving!' She rubbed her stomach, having no difficulty in voicing exactly what she wanted to eat. She smiled, vindicated.

Juno beamed, knowing that Meg was a kindred spirit. It was rare to find someone whose whole demeanour was elevated simply through describing baked goods!

'And for you, Edd?' Juno asked as she headed for the door.

'Just the coffee.' He smiled, a little sheepishly.

'Sure. Is that flat white? Latte? Tall black?'

Edd looked at Juno and then Meg. He could swear this was a conspiracy. 'Just a regular white coffee, thanks.'

Juno crept from the room and out onto the street.

Edd sighed and ruffled his hair. 'I'm sorry if I offended you last night. It had been one helluva day. I'd been here for nearly twelve hours and hadn't eaten a thing. I was just letting off steam. You're Megan Hope, right?'

Meg nodded. 'Right.'

'My client and effectively my boss.' He ran his palm over his chin and open mouth, shaking his head. His eyes crinkled as he smiled.

Five

The muffins and coffee restored Meg's wellbeing and the trio now sat at one of the bistro tables with the blueprints for the building spread out in front of them. Edd had pulled his tortoiseshell square-framed glasses from his top pocket and, with the end of his propelling pencil against the paper, was talking Meg through the issues.

'So you see how it's gone from being an easy job into this nightmare? It's often the way: the complex aspects of a build glide along, only for the small unforeseen snags to escalate into a drama. I'm aware that this is costing us all time and money.'

Meg knitted her fingers together in front of her, business-like. 'How long do you think it will take to get everything fixed once we get access?'

Edd tapped his pencil on the drawing. 'I've got the contractors on standby. A day. Two days, max.'

Meg sipped her coffee, then slammed the Styrofoam cup on the tabletop and gasped, 'Oh my God!'

'What? What's wrong?' Edd and Juno asked in unison.

Meg slapped her forehead lightly. 'I have just had an idea that is either complete genius or extreme madness. I'm not sure which.' *You can do anything you put your mind to, Meg.*

'Are you going to share it with us?' Edd removed his glasses and sat back in the chair, intrigued.

Meg turned to Juno. 'Do you have the superintendent's number?'

Juno nodded. 'It's in my cell.' She jumped up to retrieve the phone from her bag.

Edd stared at the crazy English woman who was talking in riddles. Juno flipped open the cover of her phone and let her fingers slide down the list of numbers.

'Can you get him on the phone for me?' Meg cocked her head and smiled before popping the last bite of muffin into her mouth.

A couple of hours later, Meg stood on the pavement and patted her hair behind her ears. She licked her lips, which were dry with nerves, and sucked spit from her cheeks to unstick her tongue from the roof of her mouth. Her hands were shaking. Was she really going to do this?

The man approached slowly. When she was able to tear her eyes away from the thin combover of hair on his balding head, she focused on the vast bunch of keys swinging from the belt loop on his khaki-brown trousers. *Come to Mumma!* She smiled. From a similar loop on the opposite side to his keys hung a torch. The paunch of his belly sat over the top of his waistband and was barely contained within the shirt buttons that strained under the tension. Where the material gaped, pouches of white flesh that sprouted dark hairs could be seen. His shirt and trousers were of the same material and from a distance she wondered if he was wearing an ill-fitting jumpsuit. A large white cotton patch was sewn above his breast pocket, edged in red and with his name embroidered in a red scroll font: 'Victor'.

'Victor?' Meg smiled sweetly as she stepped forward.

'Yup.'

Meg noted how Victor's bottom lip rose up over his top lip as he stood with his legs splayed and his fingers twitching down by his thighs. He looked like a petulant gunslinger.

'Thank you for coming down here to meet me. I really appreciate it. Juno, the girl in the café, had your number, thank goodness, or I don't know what I would have done!' She simpered, figuring that if Edd had seen fit to flirt with her the night before, it couldn't be that hard to woo Victor. She just hoped he didn't see the sweat that peppered her top lip or notice the tremor to her voice.

'You not from round here?' Victor tilted his head to one side.

'No. England, as I said on the phone, I've come to visit my grandpa and I can't believe he's not here. Must have gone to my mum's.'

'In Boca?' Victor prompted.

'Yes, in Poker. There's been a mix-up with dates and I don't have my key.' She patted her pockets as though that was where her key might lurk. She caught Edd's eye as he shook his head and covered his face with his palm.

'I'm not sure I can let you in, ma'am. It's 'gainst the rules to allow anyone access without the permission of the owner.'

'I should think so too,' Meg countered. 'But I figured if you're with me and I can prove my ID...' She smiled. She had no idea how she was going to stay inside once she got there, but was hoping that somehow, with enough smoke and bluster, she might just pull it off. She knew that if she thought too far ahead she would actually throw up.

'You like soccer?' Victor hovered as he asked the random question. It looked like it might be the deal breaker.

'Yes, very much. Do you?'

Victor nodded. 'I support Chelsea, big fan of Mourinho.'

Meg crossed her fingers behind her back. 'Me too! Go the Blues!' She heard the creak of her actual granddad as he spun in the cemetery in Dalston. He, like his ancestors as well as his descendants, was a lifelong Hammers supporter.

'You ever met any of Motörhead?' Victor asked, his eyes bright.

Meg exhaled through bloated cheeks, wondering where the line of questioning would go next. She decided to come clean on this one. 'No, sadly not. But I did once mosh to "Ace of Spades" at a school disco. If I remember correctly, I'd been swigging neat Malibu behind the bike sheds with some of the bigger girls.'

'Malibu?' Victor's lip curled in revulsion.

‘Yes, it was all that could be stolen from some unsuspecting mum’s booze cupboard apparently.’

Victor smiled. ‘I got everything Motorhead ever wrote, including a rare EP with a picture sleeve.’

Meg stared at Victor, not sure of where to go next.

‘Your granddad expecting you, you say?’

‘Hmm?’ Meg looked confused; she hadn’t actually ever met her granddad. Edd coughed. It was enough of an alert to bring her back to earth.

‘My granddad! Yes! Yes, he is. That’s right.’

‘Well, I guess I can let you in and you tell Mr Redlitch to come see me when he gets back. I got a stack of mail for him and it’ll be good to know he’s back on the block.’

‘I sure will.’ Meg accompanied this with a salute, she wasn’t sure why.

Victor trod the stairs with Meg trailing behind. She felt a tremor of unease; was she actually about to break into an elderly man’s apartment? Might it be better to wait until he got back from ... wherever that place was?

Victor took a left turn at the top of the dark wood staircase, his rubber-soled shoes squeaking on the tiled hall floor that bore the dull veneer of a hundred years of grime. The ceramic squares, once bright blue, green and yellow, had paled with age. He pulled sharply at the keys on his belt loop, loosening the bunch. Meg smiled as she saw that they remained fastened to his body by means of a spring-loaded key fob on a length of cord. You never could be too careful.

Victor raised the key towards the lock, then hesitated. His eyes blinked rapidly and he breathed out.

'Are you okay, Victor?' He looked a little unsteady on his feet.

'All good, ma'am.' He turned to her and smiled. 'Say, would you mind fetching the young man from the store up here?'

'Edd? Yes, sure.' Meg trotted down to the bakery and returned minutes later with Edd in tow, as requested.

As soon as they turned the corner at the top of the stairs, the stench from the opened front door hit their nostrils.

'Oh shit!' Edd gasped as he inhaled. The smell was sickly sweet, offensive, sour. 'Stay here, Megan.' He gripped the top of her arm, his face stern, his voice steady and commanding.

Meg cupped her palm over her mouth and spoke through her fingers. 'God in heaven! What is that smell?' She felt her gut twist as her breakfast muffin readied itself for expulsion. She leant heavily on the wooden banister and was strangely rooted to the spot, even though her instinct told her to run. It was as if time slowed a little and Meg had the distinct feeling that she knew what was happening in advance, a kind of hazy déjà vu. She remembered feeling similar when her mum had walked into the lounge one day and told her to put on her school uniform and wait on her bed. Megan knew something was afoot because it was Saturday and there was no school, but her sixth sense told her not to make a fuss. She remembered sitting on the duvet with her pyjamas in a carrier bag by her side, waiting for the knock on the door and the woman who would whisk her off to Tall Trees Avenue. The lady had been kind, her voice soothing as she gripped Megan's hand and led her to the car outside. She had looked over her shoulder at her mum, who was watching from the kitchen window. Megan had mouthed, 'I'm sorry,' and hoped that one day she would be given the chance to make amends for whatever it was she had done that meant she had to be sent away.

This felt similar, as though she were spiralling downwards, a sick feeling in the pit of her stomach.

Victor appeared in the hallway, shaken and pale. Edd followed closely behind. 'I'm so sorry, ma'am. I'm afraid it ain't good news.' He paused. 'Your grandpa has ... passed on.' Victor lowered his gaze.

Meg was shocked by the news, no matter that she had never met Mr Redlitch. Her legs wobbled and she sank down on to the step. She placed her hand on her chest and whispered, 'Sssshhh.'

Edd helped her up and as they made their way down the landing, Meg couldn't help but glance back through the open door through the banister railings. She saw what looked like a dark cloud hovering just below the ceiling. It was only when it started to disperse and hum that she realised it was a swarm of flies.

As darkness fell on the city, the cab carrying Edd and Meg drew to a halt. Edd offered Meg his hand as she clambered out.

'You okay?' His tone was one of concern.

She nodded, but felt far from okay. She felt sick, scared and tearful but was trying to keep it all bottled up as she arrived at the park with this strange man in this strange city.

Edd shook his head. 'I thought a walk in the park might help clear our heads. That was quite a shock back there.'

'Yes it was.' Her voice was small.

They entered Central Park and walked side by side along the wide, meandering path with the New York skyline twinkling in the twilight behind them.

'Take deep breaths,' he instructed, so she did.

Their shoulders bumped from time to time as they strolled in silence, matching each other's pace. Meg yanked her pixie hat down over her cold ears and pulled her scarf over her chin, letting her warm breath gather in droplets on the wool. Edd shoved his hands inside his coat pockets and lifted his shoulders, as if adopting a hunched posture might make him warmer.

'I hope his daughter is okay.'

Meg liked the fact Edd was concerned. She nodded her agreement. 'They are going to get the friend he played bridge with to call her. At least the news won't be coming from an unfamiliar voice. Oh God, I feel so terrible about lying!' Meg placed her hand over her eyes. That was what she was to Mr Redlitch: an unfamiliar person who had lied to get into his apartment. And all the time he was lying there…

'It's not your fault, Megan.'

'I still feel horrible. I shouldn't have done it.' She shook her head as they slowed down a little.

Edd seemed deep in thought. 'It was a stranger, a policeman, that confirmed my dad had died–'

'Oh. I didn't know your dad had died,' Meg replied, interrupting him as the two halted on the path.

He gave a dry smile. 'Yep, little while ago.'

'Do you remember him?' She thought of Lucas, who would only ever know Bill by a photograph and the familiar tales told by his grandma.

'Yes, it wasn't *that* long ago. Thirteen years to be precise.'

'I know there's nothing I can say that probably hasn't been said a million times to you before, so I'm not going to tell you how sorry I am,' she thought of the countless times this had tripped from strangers' tongues, 'but I would like to tell you that I know what it feels like to have that sadness inside of you. I know how horrible it feels. Don't know if that helps?' she smiled.

'More than you know.' Edd nodded.

'Did he just die or was it in an accident?' She was curious.

Edward took a deep breath. 'Oh, there was nothing accidental about it. He was killed while he was working.'

'Oh, Edd!' Megan placed her hand over her mouth, the horror of his statement only magnified by the events of the day.

He started to walk and Megan kept pace.

'I have every second of that day imprinted in my brain, what we wore, where we sat, everything. I can picture every detail of that cop's face as he looked my mom in the eye and told her. And I just watched as she fell apart. It was as if time stood still. Even now, it's like it's not real. Then something will happen that makes me realise it is true and it shocks me all over again. Sometimes, regularly in fact, I think, oh, I haven't spoken to Pop in a few days, and I reach for my cell to call him.' He kicked his toe against the path. 'It sounds stupid.'

'Actually it doesn't.' She looked at him. 'My fiancé died too. He had a car accident. It didn't feel real for years. The police gave me the news over the phone. I often think it would have been easier coming from someone that knew me, that knew us...' She let this hang, trying to think of who that person might have been.

'Jesus. I don't know what to say to you, Megan.' Edd sighed and it was a little while before he spoke, as if he were feeling the weight of their combined story. 'My dad was missing for some time, and that was possibly the worst part for me.' Edd drew a sharp breath as a jogger ran past at speed. Meg got the impression that this admission was rare. 'I just wanted to know either way, so I could either get on with grieving and looking after my mom, or I could set about welcoming him home and organising a big celebration. The biggest celebration ever.' His voice wavered with emotion. He coughed to clear his throat. 'When they confirmed he was dead, I felt very guilty because I had prayed for the news. I figured living with the uncertainty was worse, but it wasn't. As soon as I knew he had passed on, I prayed that there might have been a mistake and that there was still a possibility he might be found alive and well. That hope was like an energy and I missed it. I had the best safety net in the world: two parents that loved me so much and made home a place I couldn't wait to get back to. My dad used to say, "The real world is what is behind our front door, everything on the other side ain't important."'

Meg felt a familiar stab of raw pain. 'I envy people that haven't been through it. It's the worst thing,' she whispered.

'Do you? I don't envy them.' Edd stopped on the path and paused. 'I think that because the worst thing has happened to me, I'm equipped to deal with whatever comes my way. If anything, losing someone you love puts everything into perspective. Makes you understand what's important, reminds you not to sweat the small stuff.'

Meg looked up at him. 'I hadn't thought of it like that.'

'It's true though, right? You hear someone going nutso because a train is late or their phone has no signal and I think, half your luck, pal, if that's all you've got to worry about.'

Meg gave a small laugh; this was very, very true. 'I guess I'm used to dealing with crap. I didn't have a mum that gave me a safety net or a dad that I looked up to. I grew up without a dad or stability or a bed that was all mine.' She looked into his face, trying to gauge his expression.

'That doesn't sound like much fun.'

'It wasn't.'

'Are things better between you now?' he asked.

Meg shook her head. 'I haven't seen her for nearly a decade.'

Edd gave a small whistle. 'Wow! I can't imagine that.' He looked sad.

'It's just how it is for me. When I was little, what I wanted more than anything in the world was someone to look after me. And I found them! The day I met Pru is one I will never forget, she rescued me from a really shitty time. That was the start of a change in my life, a change in me. Bill had just died and I was in a really bad place. It hit me like a rock.' Meg placed her hand on her chest as words rang inside her head that she wasn't willing to share just yet. *And he was cheating on me and I was pregnant with Lucas.* She smiled as she pictured her crumpled newborn.

'You've had a really hard time and I admire you for coming out the other side.' His hands jerked, as if he had been about to reach for her but had decided against it.

Her heart leapt with both relief and disappointment. 'Sometimes I'm not sure that I am on the other side, not yet.'

'I know how that feels.' He nodded into the distance, looking out across the clusters of trees and the winding path.

'You'd think I'd be used to disappointment, but I'm not.' She hesitated. 'I always believe things are going to get better, but then something comes along and pulls the rug from under me. Admittedly it's different worries now. When I was little, I used to worry about becoming homeless. I used to wonder what would happen if agencies and charities stopped gathering up my clean pyjamas and Neville, my ratty teddy bear, and giving us both shelter.' She glanced at him, it was rare for *her* to make admissions like this. 'It was only ever me that left, being that much younger than the others. I was the one that was whisked away when things started to crack, always being told that being taken away from my family was only temporary, just until my mum got her act together and I could go home again. It was temporary for a week and then it was temporary for a month and, once, it was temporary for four years...' Meg sniffed, imagining Lucas being bundled out in the middle of the night. 'Oh God, look at me!' She swiped her tears, embarrassed. 'I think it's the shock of finding Mr Redlitch like that. It's made me sad.'

'Of course. It was horrible.' Edd shook his head. 'Look, it's getting colder.' He shivered. 'We could go and get something to drink if you like?'

Meg nodded; she liked the idea very much. 'I know, we could go to the coffee shop that they use in *Friends*. That's near Central Park, isn't it?' She smiled.

'I hate to be the bearer of bad news, but there is no such coffee shop. It's a studio set.'

'Oh.' Meg looked at the floor, feeling a little stupid.

'And I was thinking of a *drink* drink – something a little stronger than coffee?' He narrowed his eyes.

'Drink up.' Edd filled her glass with red wine. Her second or third, she had lost count.

Meg looked around the dark interior of the dimly lit wine bar a couple of blocks from the Grand Army Plaza entrance to Central Park. It was half past five and the place was practically empty apart from her and Edd, two men in suits on another table, their ties slackened and faces flushed, and the three waitresses that hovered by the bar, enjoying the lull between the late lunchers and the dinner crowds.

'I feel terrible.' Meg propped her head on her palm. 'Poor Mr Redlitch.' She sipped at the warm vino, which was making things better and worse at the same time. 'I was making out that I knew him and all the time he was dead. Poor man.'

Edd lifted the bottle and let the remains of the house red glug into his glass. 'You weren't to know.'

Meg shrugged. It made little difference, she still felt bad. 'And the way Victor looked at me when I had to confess I didn't know him at all – that was just as bad. He looked so disappointed. I'm sorry, Victor.' Meg leant on the table with her arms folded inwards, cradling her glass of plonk against her chest.

'Look at it this way, if you hadn't lied to Victor, Mr Redlitch would have lain there a lot longer and that would have been worse for everyone.'

'How long do you think he'd been dead?' she asked, biting her nails.

'They said about a fortnight, which coincides with when we first tried to contact him.'

'Did they say how he died?'

Edd sighed. 'It looks like he had a heart attack and just keeled over. It would have been very quick and painless.'

Meg looked at him, suspecting he offered the last detail by way of comfort and based on no particular knowledge. 'I wish I knew what his first name was.' She felt her tears pool.

'It began with G, I know that, but that's all. It doesn't really matter now.'

'It matters to me. I want to say a little prayer for him, and "Mr Redlitch" sounds so formal.'

'Do you believe in God?'

'Sometimes,' Meg confessed, 'and

sometimes not. You?'

'Same, I guess. I think it's hard to believe, when you've been tested...' He let this trail and waved his hand in the air for the waitress – they required another bottle.

Meg once again rested her head against her upturned palm. 'I saw him.'

'You saw who?'

'Mr G. Redlitch. Well, I saw part of him.'

'Oh.'

Meg nodded. 'I saw his hand and arm as I looked back into his flat. It was dark and seemed a bit deflated.'

Edd exhaled. 'You need to put that out of your head. It wasn't him. Just the shell of him.'

'That doesn't sound like the words of someone who doesn't believe in God.'

Edd flicked the edge of the cardboard drinks coaster with his thumb. 'Well, as I said, sometimes I do.'

The middle-aged waitress popped the cork and leant forward, placing the bottle on the table. 'To young lovers!' She smiled as she sauntered back to the bar.

Edd gave her the smile that had been absent for the last hour or two. Meg blushed, awkward and yet excited as she thought about the previous evening and their inauspicious, flirtatious meeting in the deli. She felt comfortable in his company, despite only having known him for such a short time, but couldn't say if the glow she felt was down to the wine or something else entirely.

'I think we should finish this and go and get some fresh air.' Edd reached for the bottle and refilled both their glasses.

'That's a good idea. Where shall we go?' Meg sat forward, enjoying the wine-soaked euphoria that flooded through her body.

'Central Park again?'

'No! Let's go to the top of the Empire State Building!' She clapped.

'Okay!' He laughed. 'If that's what you want to do.'

'It is! Have you done it before?'

Edd considered this. 'Yes, years ago. I went on a trip with my school.'

Meg laughed loudly, then instantly felt guilty as she remembered someone had died. 'You went on a school trip to the Empire State Building? I went on a school trip to Ealing Bus Station to learn about transport and you went to the top of the Empire State Building!'

'Only because Ealing Bus Station was already booked.' He smiled, wondering where Ealing Bus Station was.

Meg nipped to the loo and met Edd outside, where he had managed to hail a cab. She wobbled on the pavement before sliding into the back and sitting close to him, happy to feel his form next to hers.

She leant across him as they drove southwards, peering into the windows of Macy's. Santa Claus sat in a huge red leather chair with a giant Christmas tree lit up behind him. Presents were stacked high all around and he waved to children as they stopped to stare at the festive scene. Meg's head was fuzzy with wine and excitement. 'Look, it's Santa and it's nearly Christmas!' She cheered, bouncing up and down on the seat.

'Don't remind me, I have a deadline to make, remember?' he quipped.

'It'll all be okay, Edd. And you know what? Seeing Mr G. Redlitch like that earlier has made me think. You're right, it does put things into perspective. We can't worry too much about opening dates, we just need to live a little and count our blessings!' She flung her arms wide.

'That's a good motto. And I shall remind you of it tomorrow.' Edd laughed; she was clearly more inebriated than him.

The cab pulled up at 350 Fifth Avenue and the two rushed inside. They joined the throng of tourists waiting for the elevator to the top, then squashed into it like beans in a can. Meg lost sight of Edd as she was squeezed into the corner, surrounded by people taller than her.

They made their way to the glass double doors and on to the balcony of the 86th Floor. It was a lot narrower than Meg had imagined, quite different from what she'd come to expect from countless movie shots. The chill wind whipped her face, but it was a minor discomfort and worth it for the view, which was breathtaking.

'Wow!' Her eyes scanned the New York landmarks lit up against the crisp dark sky. It was the perfect time of day to appreciate the sights.

Edd stood close behind her and pointed over her shoulder into the distance. 'There's the Brooklyn Bridge and you can just make out Central Park.' They walked around a bit further. 'And the Chrysler Building!'

Meg smiled and held her scarf close around her neck. 'This has a much, much better view than Ealing Bus Station.' She stood back, teetering slightly as she peered at the spire. 'Poor old King Kong.' She frowned.

'I know, right?' Edd shook his head. 'I don't tell many people this, but I cried when they shot him at the end. I cried like a baby.'

'Oh, Edd! How old were you?'

'Twenty-three,' Edd replied.

Meg couldn't tell if he was joking. She stared at him, her expression solemn. 'Well, as we are confessing, I'm embarrassed to admit that until very recently I didn't know that seahorses were real. I always believed them to be mythical creatures like unicorns and yetis. I had of course seen pictures and I remember the famous scene in *Bedknobs and Broomsticks* when they dance around on the bottom of the sea, but I never for a moment imagined they existed, not in real life. I mean c'mon! A little horse-faced creature with a curly tail that lives in water, with the males carrying all the babies – who were they trying to kid?'

'What, you thought they were invented? Like Donald Duck or the Little Mermaid?' Edd smirked.

'Yes! Exactly like that! Can you imagine my shock when I saw one, in fact not one but a whole bunch of them in a tank at the London Aquarium? I screamed and pointed. People laughed at me, three tourists took my picture! I just stood there, shaking my head in confusion. I tried to explain that for me it was the equivalent of coming face to face with a centaur clip-clopping down the high street while a griffin circled overhead. I still get shuddery if I think about it, a real live sea-horse! I thought they were beautiful as imaginary beings, but in real life they were even more stunning. They fascinate me.'

'Are you for real?'

Meg nodded.

'That is possibly the cutest thing I have ever heard.' He laughed.

For some reason Meg felt very close to tears. How could she explain to someone like Edd that she had never gone anywhere and hadn't seen enough to challenge her imagination? She gazed up at him, happier to look at him than the view of New York State that stretched for miles behind her.

Edd took a step towards her. 'And just for the record, I don't really think you are ugly, Mary Poppins.'

Meg smiled. 'But you were right. I am single.'

'Well, that makes me very happy to hear.' He grinned and reached for her hands, which he held inside his own. Then he bent down, hesitated and kissed her very gently on the mouth. As he did so, the gentlest flutter of snowflakes landed on her upturned face.

Meg closed her eyes and spoke quietly. 'It's snowing and you just kissed me on top of the Empire State Building.'

'Yes I did.'

'I think you knocked my socks off...' She decided not to mention her spinning knickers.

'Is that a good thing?' he asked, a little self-consciously.

Meg opened her eyes. 'It's a very good thing.'

'What should we do now?' Edd whispered into her hair.

'I'd quite like another one of those kisses,' she whispered back as she threw her arms around his neck.

Six

Meg woke with a start. Her mouth was dry and her eyes heavy. She sat up in the bed and gasped, clutching at the unfamiliar white sheets in the unfamiliar room. Some walls were exposed brick, the others were painted white; all were picture-free. The contemporary chandelier that hung low over the bed was fashioned from green glass bottles with the bottoms cut out to reveal retro-looking light bulbs with quirky-shaped filaments. Wherever she was, it definitely wasn't her chintzy room at the Inn on 11th. She opened and closed her mouth. Her tongue felt thick and she clearly hadn't cleaned her teeth before falling asleep – a big no-no.

'Morning.'

She turned her head. Edd's broad, naked back was stretched out in the space next to her.

'Oh my God!' She tucked her hair behind her ears and ran the pad of her index finger over her eyelashes, confirming she still had yesterday's make-up on – a double no-no. She could only guess at how bad she looked.

'Headache?' he asked.

'Yes, but that's not what's bothering me!'

She placed her hand over her mouth.

'What's wrong?'

'I'm a tart!' she wailed.

'What?' He turned his head towards her and opened his eyes.

'I'm such a tart! I've only known you five minutes and I'm waking up in your bed!' She shook her head. 'Oh my God! I can't believe it. I *never* do anything like this. I mean never, ever!'

Edd laughed. 'Don't worry, you didn't "do anything like this"! We got back here late and you kind of collapsed. I didn't know where you were staying and so it just seemed logical.' He let his palms fall against the mattress.

'Oh.' She exhaled. 'So nothing happened?' She looked away from him – easier to hear the details without looking at his face.

'Well, not nothing ... just a little making out. But no more than second base, I swear!' He raised his hands as if taking an oath.

'What's second base?' She turned back to face him.

Edd chuckled. 'It's a baseball metaphor. Nothing you wouldn't do as a tenth grader, particularly if you were Jennifer Molowski.'

'What's tenth grade? Is that a baseball term too?'

'No, jheesh! It's a school grade, aged about sixteen, seventeen.'

Meg peeled back the sheets and looked

down at her body. Thankfully she wasn't naked; she had her pants on and an oversized sports top of some description. 'What *am* I wearing?' She plucked at the white fabric run through with a navy pinstripe.

'You have the honour of wearing my third most treasured possession in the world.' He grinned. 'And I had the honour of helping you into it.'

'Well thank you.' She blushed. 'What is it?' She ran her hand over the appliquéd logo on the front.

Edd turned over and sat up against the padded black headboard, seemingly less awkward in his near-naked state than Meg. 'It's my Yankees shirt.'

'Are they a football team?' she asked, glancing surreptitiously at his hard chest and muscular arms, all dappled with dark freckles that matched the ones on his nose. She was delighted to see that he was wearing red and yellow plaid pyjama bottoms.

'Football?' He tutted. 'You see, if they didn't spend all their time in British schools teaching you witchcraft and wizardry, you might know that there are very important sports in the world other than football and Quidditch.'

'You got me! I'm a Hogwarts graduate!' She smiled, thinking of her own inner-city school, where the cosmopolitan mix meant that much of the lesson time was taken up with trying to make instructions understood in five different languages and where if you made it to the fifth form without leaving to have a baby or being sent to a youth detention centre, you were considered a high achiever.

'The Yankees are the greatest team on earth and they play baseball.' He looked serious.

'Are you baseball obsessed? You've mentioned it a lot.'

'In a word, yes.'

'Don't think we have much baseball in England.' Meg pondered this.

'Then it's nowhere I could ever live,' he said, quite matter-of-factly.

'What are your other two?'

'My other two what?'

'Treasured possessions?'

'The second is this.' He reached for the black leather-bound notebook on the bedside table and flipped it open in the middle, pulling from it a fabric badge shaped like a shield. It had the words 'New York's Bravest' on it. Blocks of blue and red sat behind the city skyline and the whole thing was edged with a thick gold embroidered border. 'It's my dad's old one.'

Meg ran her fingers over it. 'It's nice. Was your dad a policeman?' She handed the badge back to him and watched as he ran his fingers over it before placing it back between the pages of his notebook.

'No, a firefighter. You know it's the only way I can picture him, in his uniform, either coming in from or heading out to work.'

'That's a nice memory to have.' She considered what she knew about his death. 'Was he caught in a fire?'

Edd stared at her, letting his eyes travel over her face and form. 'He was killed in 9/11.' He paused, letting this sink in. 'After the first plane hit, they got the call and had just arrived when the second plane hit the South Tower. We know he was making his way into the South Tower when it collapsed.'

'Oh my God.' Meg stared at the book with the badge lying between its pages. 'Edd...' She shook her head, searching for the right words.

'I don't talk about it to most people.'

She smiled, acknowledging the compliment as he continued,

'It's strange for me. That's the day that the whole of New York mourns and so my grief isn't special.'

'Does that make it harder or easier?' she wondered.

'Easier at first, I didn't feel alone because there was so much support, I could feel the love and thoughts of everyone in the city, the country all pulling together. We got messages from all over the world. It was incredible.'

'But now?' she asked.

'Now, I sometimes feel like shouting that I know it's everyone's tragedy, but he was my dad! *My* dad and I lost him and only I know what that feels like. Does that make sense?'

She nodded.

'Like I said, it's not something we talk about often, but every New Yorker carries it around in a little pocket just below their heart and once in a while we let it out, release the pain and sadness and then we tuck it away again, so we can get on with everyday life.' He looked up at her. 'I think that's why I can talk to you about it because you weren't here, you don't have your own version of the day. It makes it easier somehow.'

'I'm glad.' She beamed. 'What's your first treasured thing?' she asked buoyantly, changing the pace and tone of their conversation.

'Agh, I never tell that on a first date.' He lifted the sheet over the bottom of his face and batted his eyelashes, feigning coy.

Meg swung her legs from the side of the bed, taking in the spacious room. It was dominated by the grey metal window frame and its metal blinds, which had been raised to reveal the sprawl of New York below. The bed was a large wooden frame on the floor. There was very little furniture, bar a tall, slightly battered red metal locker unit standing against an exposed brick wall, with cubbyholes and numbered cupboard doors.

It looked like it would be more at home in a stinky changing room. And there was a clear Perspex console table on which someone had neatly lined up bottles of aftershave and hair oil. Above the unit on the wall hung a huge flatscreen TV.

She wandered to the window in a bit of a daze. Closing her eyes, she exhaled, hating this morning-after feeling. She wasn't used to it. Her bare feet stuck to the wooden floor. She gave a long, loud, open-mouthed yawn and jabbed with her index finger as she mined the corner of her eye to remove the sleepy dust, coloured black with eyeliner. She was fastidious about removing her make-up before falling asleep and wasn't used to the sticky feeling of her lashes. She was certain she looked like Chi Chi the panda.

Leaning against the wall, she peered through the window as she ran her fingers through her thick, wavy hair, twisting it into a bun, from which it instantly unwound to hang down her back in a shiny blonde curtain. The view was semi-industrial. Immediately opposite sat a square red-brick warehouse with worn writing on the side in a three-dimensional font: 'Mortimer Inc., Import and Export'. Meg was drawn to the bottle-green fire escapes that criss-crossed the building like laces. To the left was a more modern block, obviously converted from the original warehouse into apartments as many of the windows boasted window boxes and all manner of curtains, blinds and shades. Meg turned her head left and right: in every direction she could see nothing but rooftops and reflections, with a small bend of blue water in the distance between two buildings, and the city skyline stretching all the way to the horizon. 'Where are we?' she asked.

'We're on East 12th, Greenwich Village.'

'Oh, sounds interesting!' She smiled.

'It's very upscale.' He raised his eyebrows.

'Blimey. Better be on my best behaviour then.' She stood upright and gripped the window frame. Any position other than horizontal when your blood was still one-third alcohol was not a good idea. The last thing she wanted was to be sick in this gorgeous man's apartment.

'Can I get you some coffee?' The proximity of his voice made her jump. Edd leant on the doorframe in his tartan PJ bottoms and slipped his arms into a top with a black and white image of a smiling young man on the front. Meg stared at his T-shirt. Edd looked down and smiled, pointing at the toothy grinning face. 'This is Yogi Berra.'

'Let me guess, he played baseball?' She folded her arms.

Edd shook his head. 'No. He *is* baseball.'

Meg smiled. 'I see. Coffee would be great, thank you.'

She watched as he padded out of the room.

Even at this early hour and after a night of drinking and little sleep, he still looked wonderful. His thick hair flopped and curled effortlessly in a way that imitators would take hours to perfect. His skin was tawny and blemish-free and his twenty-four-hour stubble only highlighted his white teeth and full, pouty lips. She felt her muscles tense as she looked at her own flat chest, bony feet and mottled legs, which today had taken on a rather bluish tinge. Without the benefit of her wine goggles, she realised that she had been punching above her weight the day before. Sucking in her slightly pouchy mummy tummy and trying to curb her embarrassment, she ventured from the bedroom.

The rest of the apartment was surprisingly small, tiny in fact. The bedroom was by far the biggest space. Edd's taste and style were also apparent in the open-plan sitting cum dining room: more exposed brick walls, wacky industrial lighting and a slick grey glossy kitchen area in the corner. Meg glanced at the oversized chrome clock. It was 7 a.m.

'Is this going to be weird today, working together after...?' She ran out of words, as she wasn't sure quite what 'this' was. What she did know was that she was heading back to London tomorrow and this was just a little fling, a diversion.

Edd was at the sink, inserting a stainless

steel tube of water into a complicated, industrial-looking coffee machine, the only appliance on the work surface in the immaculate kitchen.

He turned towards her and shook his head. 'No, not at all. It's only as weird as we make it. We are just friends, right? New friends, admittedly, who simply had a couple of drinks and fell asleep.'

'Do you do second base with all your friends?' she asked from behind lowered lids.

Edd laughed loudly. 'You don't "do" second base, you "go to" second base.'

'Sorry. Do you go *to* second base with all your friends?' She twisted her legs together and leant on the counter top.

'No! No, I don't. Most of them are too stubbly and have beer bellies.' He laughed as he collected two plain white china mugs from a cupboard and placed them in front of the coffee machine.

'Just checking.' She smiled.

'God, we drank a lot yesterday, but I think it was probably justified. Things like that don't happen every day, thank God. It was a shock, right?'

'Poor Mr Redlitch.' Meg felt a flush of guilt that she hadn't thought about him until that point.

'I know. Poor guy.' He sighed. 'I never ever drink during the week, it's my rule.' Edd grinned at her over his shoulder.

'I hardly drink at all, weekday or not. I'm practically teetotal,' Meg countered as she toyed with her hair. *But I like drinking with you... And I did it because I wanted you to like me, wanted to be like every other girl who might have caught your eye. I wanted you to think I was cosmopolitan and outgoing and not scared. Lonely and scared.*

'Teetotal?' Edd threw his head back and guffawed. 'That's funny. For a teetotaller you did pretty good. You must be like those vegetarians who give up meat at sixteen but continue to eat bacon, then eventually progress to chicken so that by the time they hit twenty they are ripping the leg off every cow that passes and slapping it in a bun. They think they've been embracing a vegetarian lifestyle when really they've simply been denying themselves what they crave.' His eyes twinkled at her. 'I think you are like that.'

She laughed. 'I am so not like that!'

'You were *so* like that last night. At one point I held up my hands – no more! And while I was in the bathroom you ordered Flaming Russians, two each!'

'I don't even know what a Flaming Russian is!' Meg covered her eyes with her hands, cringing. 'You must think I'm terrible.'

'I do. I really do.' He nodded vigorously. 'I think you are one of the most terrible human beings I have ever met.' He stared at her, his expression suggesting the exact opposite.

The delicious smell of freshly brewed coffee wafted from the machine and filled the apartment. Edd poured generous amounts into the waiting mugs and walked over to the firm, pale silver sofa in the middle of the room. Meg followed him.

'Nice cushions!' She pulled one of the mauve pillows from the sofa and admired the floral sequin design. 'Very fancy-pants!'

'I hate them. Unnecessary sofa ornaments. They spend more time on the floor when I'm home–' Edd checked himself and shook his head as he plumped down on the sofa. They sat sideways, facing each other, without any of the awkwardness that might have followed, being that they were new friends who were only half dressed.

'How long have you worked for Plum's?' he asked, cupping his coffee mug under his chin in a way that she found very attractive.

'Four years.' Meg sipped the restorative brew. 'I lived with Milly and her cousin Pru first. I was going through a particularly rough patch and they really helped me out. And now I work for them.'

Meg wasn't sure how much to share. It was hard to explain that as well as being her employers they were the closest thing to family that Meg had – well, reliable family. The only exception being her cousin Liam, who ran a car dealership in Lewisham that only just operated on the right side of the law. Milly had been there for Lucas's birth and had earned a special place in her son's heart as well as in her own. Having left school at sixteen without qualifications or a clue as to where her future lay, Meg never, ever took her very good fortune for granted.

She took a deep breath and mentally rehearsed how to tell Edd that her non-working hours were filled with Lucas, her heart, her anchor and her greatest joy.

'I have a son,' she blurted, a little louder and more bluntly than she intended, but there it was, out in the open.

'You do?' His eyes widened.

Meg nodded, unable to tell from his tone if he was shocked, disapproving or not that fussed.

'How old?' He tilted his head as though interested.

'He's four. He's called Lucas.'

'Lucas,' Edd repeated. He sipped his coffee, keeping his eyes on Meg's face. 'Where is Lucas's dad?'

'His dad was Bill, my fiancé who died.' Meg wriggled further into the sofa.

Edd lowered his cup. 'Oh right! Sorry, Megan. That's unimaginable. You must be a very strong woman to have coped.'

'I don't think I'm strong. Life has always just kind of happened to me without too much planning. My childhood wasn't always easy and I learnt not to think much beyond the next day. And then I met Bill. And everything changed.' She sighed. 'Like seahorses, I didn't know that someone like him could exist. He was Captain William Fellsley, an army officer who didn't speak or act like anyone I'd ever known. He was smart and ambitious, but the most remarkable thing about Bill was that he loved me. Me! Of all the posh girls he could have picked, he chose me. I figured that if someone like that had picked me, then I must be valuable and special and once I realised that, I began living in the real world and not just existing with my nose pressed up against it.'

'He sounds like a good guy. Losing him must have been awful.' Edd raised his hand and let it fall at the understatement.

Meg nodded. 'It was awful, but not for the reasons you might think. I found out some stuff after he'd gone that changed things.' Meg toyed with the hem of the Yankees shirt. 'He was seeing someone else, stringing us both along and, well, who knows what would have happened had he lived.'

Edd reached out and placed his hand on her thigh. 'I'm sorry you had to go through that, Megan. All of it.'

'No one calls me Megan any more. It's Meg. If someone calls me Megan, I always think I'm in trouble or am being asked to fill out a form.'

'Meg,' he repeated.

'Bill, that's Lucas's dad, had a friend called Piers. I saw him for a while. Couple of years actually.' She pictured his kindly face. 'He was lovely in some ways, but not for me. A bit too proper, always worried about what other people might think and a bit too connected to Bill for me to ever feel comfortable. He's old before his time–' She bit her lip. 'That sounds mean and I don't want it to.'

'Old how?' Edd chuckled. 'Did he talk about the old days and smoke a pipe?'

'No!' She laughed. 'But he did wear an old Barbour that might have belonged to his grandpa.'

'Ah. Not a young man of fashion like my good self.' He grinned.

Meg shook her head and thought about Piers' frequent mentions of Bill and their mutual friends, their shared experiences. How he would continually ask, 'How are you doing?' assuming a doleful expression as he did so.

'He made it hard for me to move on. So I moved on from him instead. I think I used him as a bit of a safety blanket, if I'm being honest. It was more like a habit, without any real emotion.' She paused. 'I'm not proud of that.' This was the first time she had said this out loud to anyone other than Milly. 'And I only admitted to myself quite recently that he wanted me to be someone that I wasn't.'

'Well, hey, we all know that story.' Edd ran his fingers through his hair and stretched his long legs out in front of him, crossing his feet at the ankles. He rested his mug on his chest. 'It's the same for me, with Flavia. We met through a mutual friend and on paper she was brilliant. She's a great girl, but there was no spark that makes you...' Edd hesitated. 'I don't know how you describe it.'

'She didn't knock your socks off?' Meg offered.

Edd turned to face her, remembering her words at the top of the Empire State Building. 'No.' He shook his head. 'She never did.'

Meg looked at the fine straight line of his nose and mouth and placed her palm over the back of his hand, which still rested on her thigh. She wondered what he saw as he stared at her, feeling the wave of warmth rise within her from their point of contact. Shc wanted him to see her as a sexy, available partner and not how she often felt on the inside, a knackered working single mum who was trying very hard to have it all.

She pulled the sequined cushion from the side of the sofa and held it into her chest.

'I'm not very confident, Edd. I'm a bit bruised,' she whispered.

'I think we all are in one way or another.' He looked at the floor. Easier to have this conversation with his eyes averted.

'Do you think I'm sexy?' she whispered. 'I just wondered.' Instantly she regretted the question; her nerves caused her to ramble. 'You don't have to answer. I only ask because sometimes I'm so focused on being a mum and getting things done for Plum's that I don't know what I've become. I don't know if anyone will ever find me attractive. I have the chest of a fourteen-year-old boy. I wish I had boobs...' Meg felt her cheeks flush at the admission.

Edd spluttered on his coffee, laughing and choking simultaneously. 'That's funny! And for your information, I was once a fourteen-year-old boy and my chest wasn't anything like that. If it had been, I'd never have left the house.' Edd looked at her shyly. The bolshie, flirty man from the Greenwich Avenue Deli had disappeared behind his coffee cup. 'And in answer to your question – of course.'

'Of course what?'

'You are very sexy. I love the way you look, and your little cockney voice. Any man that cheated on you would want his head examined.'

They both laughed. She stared at him as her eyes misted slightly. 'I've never thought being a cockney was a sexy thing.'

'Well it is, trust me.' Edd placed his coffee cup on the floor and removed hers from her grasp. He threw the cushions to the ground and took her hand in his, pulling her into an upright position.

'Where are we going?' she asked, with one eye on the clock.

'We are going back to bed and we are going to make things a whole lot weirder.'

He kissed her hard on the mouth. Meg knotted her hands behind his neck as they moved towards the bedroom, trying desperately to ignore the nerves that fizzed in her stomach. She hoped she was going to be all Edd wanted and more.

Seven

Meg looped by the Inn on 11th on her way to work. Having showered, retouched her make-up and changed into her black wool minidress, over-the-knee black boots and thick woolly tights, she felt ready to face the day. She had a spring in her step and a grin on her face.

She'd ignored Elene's subtle line of questioning – 'Is that you coming in or going out, Meg?' – her eyes bright with interest. And she'd resisted the temptation to respond with, *'Oh, coming in, actually. I got so sloshed last night that I slept in a strange man's bed and then slept with him this morning. We had a lovely time, went to fifth base, which was great and apparently further than Jennifer Molowski let anyone go, even on Prom night.'* Instead, she managed to deflect the question with a burst of unnatural laughter and by babbling about the cold weather and plans for Christmas before smiling sweetly and returning her key to the disinterested Salvatore. He hung it on the rack where it had spent the night.

Meg was pleased to see that Plum Patisserie on Bleecker Street was a hive of activity. Nancy, Mr Redlitch's daughter, had left a message asking Meg to come up and see her. As she trod the stairs to the apartments above, she felt even more like an intruder than she had the day before. She slowly approached Mr Redlitch's front door, which she found ajar, knocked on it and entered. Trying not to stare at the spot where his body had lain only twenty-four hours earlier, she stepped around the space, taking in the detail of his apartment.

A pair of ruby-red velvet slippers with the backs trodden down sat neatly aligned by the wall. In the sitting room, thick-lensed spectacles perched on top of a haphazard pile of newspapers and magazines. The papers rested on a stool by the side of an olive green couch, which had a couple of lace antimacassars. A wood-veneer side table was crammed with medicine bottles, blister packs of pills in various colours and pots of ointment. The sight of these personal items that were now ownerless caused a lump to rise in Meg's throat. She thought how sad it was that, following a death, things of use and value were quickly relegated to thrift-shop fodder.

The heavy, dusty curtains had been pulled back and the windows opened to let in the daylight and the cold December air. A framed black and white photograph sat on a dresser. It was of a young couple beaming into the shutter from a sunny dockside, she was wearing net petticoats, he was in a shoestring tie and Brylcreem. She studied the picture, focusing on the young man's hand clamped around the tiny belted waist of his girl. She tried not to think about the hand it had become, lying limply on the sticky linoleum in the cold dark room, unnoticed for a fortnight.

Nancy was a heavy-set woman in a neon floral blouse; Meg counted seven rings on her tanned fingers. She had settled herself in the corner of her father's sitting room and was sniffing into a soggy square of kitchen roll while her big-haired friend made tea, noisily, in the cramped kitchen. She seemed glad to have someone to talk to, even if that someone was a stranger like Meg. Despite her obvious grief, she was gracious and kind, saying immediately that of course the contractors could have access to her dad's apartment later in the day.

'I'm so grateful you raised the alarm with the superintendent, dear. Thank you.'

Meg blushed, still embarrassed at having been so underhand about it.

'And I wanted to ask you something.' Nancy paused.

'You can ask me anything.' Meg was sincere.

'When you saw him, did ... did he look peaceful?' Nancy asked hopefully between fractured breaths.

Meg pictured the swarm of flies and the horrific, sickly-sweet smell, which, despite the bleach and industrial clean-up, still lingered in the fabric of the apartment. She smiled at Nancy, sensing she would not be able to cope with any of the detail. Her mind flew to that silent white room in St Thomas' hospital, London four years before, when she'd held the hand of her fiancé, trying to understand that he had gone from her. Grazing his knuckles with her lips, she had squeezed Bill's hand, hoping beyond hope for a response as her fingers lay against his cooled skin. It would have helped such a lot to have known that his last minutes had been calm and pain-free. But his cuts, bruises and bloody wounds told a very different story.

Meg smiled at Nancy. 'Yes he did. I thought he looked very peaceful.' She watched as Nancy's shoulders sagged and her sob formed.

'Thank you,' she mouthed, patting Meg's arm. 'Thank you so much.'

There was a silent interval. 'Can I ask you something?' Meg eventually whispered.

'Of course, sweetie.' Nancy leant forward.

'I was wondering, what was your dad's name?'

'It was Gabriel.' Nancy heaved, finding it distressing to use the past tense. 'He was a Christmas baby; it would have been his birthday next week.' She drew a deep breath. 'My grandma used to tell me that she thought she'd been blessed with an angel. An angel at Christmas, what else were they gonna call him?' She smiled.

'Gabriel,' Meg repeated.

Downstairs, Meg sat at one of the tables in the café, poring over the stock order for the Christmas period. She glanced up to see the man she had been waiting for on the pavement outside. Quickly, she set aside the paperwork and raced out into the street.

'Hey, Victor.'

'Hey.' He nodded, barely acknowledging her, fiddling with the keys on his belt loop.

Meg knotted her fingers behind her back. 'How are you feeling today? It must have been horrible for you yesterday, finding Mr Redlitch like that. I thought you were amazing. I just wanted to say that.'

Victor shrugged. 'I always just try to do the right thing.'

Meg nodded in acknowledgement. *Yes, and I duped you and I am sorry, really sorry.* 'I was chatting to Nancy earlier, Mr Redlitch's daughter. She's busy getting things sorted upstairs, but she seems okay. Her friend is with her.' It felt odd discussing this intimate situation with a man she didn't know, about a woman who was a stranger.

'Is that Nancy who *isn't* your mother?' he asked, looking past her towards the upstairs apartment.

Meg felt her blush spread up her neck. 'I'm sorry I lied to you. I really am. It seemed like a good idea at the time. I guess none of us could have imagined how it would end up.'

Victor shrugged. 'No matter.' He tapped his torch against his palm and switched it on and off.

Always good to test your battery, Meg thought wryly.

'Turned out right in the end.'

'Yes, poor Mr Redlitch.' She vowed to come up with a better way of referring to him. *Gabriel…*

'I suppose you don't even support Chelsea?' Victor asked, his eyes downcast.

Meg sighed and shook her head. 'No, West Ham. But I did mosh to "Ace of Spades" at a school disco – that was the truth and it was good fun!'

Victor twisted his mouth into a small smile.

Meg looked up the street, searching for a way to bring the conversation to a close, just as Edd rounded the corner and came into view. Her heart flipped and her stomach turned over at the sight of him. No words left her lips; she simply turned away from Victor with her eyes fixed on the man walking towards her.

Oh my God...

Meg had been thankful that Edd had had to be somewhere else first thing, knowing she could not have concentrated or hidden her grin earlier on. It would have been horribly insensitive, talking to the tearful Nancy with a coquettish giggle. She beamed at him, noting he had swapped his denim shirt for a white cotton one but was still in his regulation jeans and Timberland boots. She couldn't help but picture the body underneath, the memory of which made her smile even more broadly. As he got closer, she noted his stern expression and her stomach turned again for an entirely different reason. Was he regretting the last twenty-four hours or having second thoughts about getting involved with a knackered single mum with the chest of a fourteen-year-old boy? She swallowed as he sped up, coming to a stop inches from her on the pavement.

'When do you leave for England?' he asked without preamble. His face earnest, voice steady.

Meg swallowed. 'Thursday. Tomorrow!'

Victor ambled into the apartment block, feeling even more invisible than usual.

Edd was breathing quickly as he shook his head. 'I don't know what's happening, but ... I can't stop thinking about you. If I close my eyes I can see you in my head. People have been talking to me all morning, but I can't concentrate, I can only think about you.'

'Sames,' she whispered.

He grinned. 'Is that your summary of the situation? I lay my heart and soul bare and I get "sames"?'

Meg nodded. A bubble of happiness stoppered the words in her throat.

Edd wasn't done. 'I didn't want to leave you this morning and I couldn't wait to get back to you now. I can't believe we only have a day and a bit. That can't be it. We need to make a plan. We will make a plan.'

'What does our plan look like?'

Edd exhaled. 'Truthfully? I don't know. Maybe you stay here or I come there or we emigrate to the Bahamas and go sit on a beach for a couple of years, living on a boat. I don't know! I'm not thinking straight, but there will be a solution, we just have to find it.'

Meg smiled and spoke slowly. 'A boat in

the Bahamas sounds good, especially today.' She cupped her hands to try and ward off the chill. 'Do they have baseball in the Bahamas? Just that I know you could never live anywhere that didn't.'

'Funny you should ask that – yes they do!'

'Well I never.' She laughed. 'Sounds like you've thought this through.' She stared at her toes. 'I have to go back, Edd. You know that, don't you?' She thought of Lucas and her heart lurched. She missed him. The guilt of separation was never very far from the surface.

He nodded. 'I do. And you know I have to meet my deadlines here.'

Meg looked up at him. 'I don't want to leave Lucas any longer than I have to, but I do feel the same. I haven't felt this way since–'

'Since your fiancé?'

Meg shook her head. 'No.' She took a deep breath and considered her next words carefully. 'Since never, actually. Bill was like something new and shiny and unbelievable in my very dull world, but I never felt like this. I never have.' She looked at the cold, grey pavement. 'That feels like a terrible thing to say. He's dead and it feels disloyal and he's Lucas's dad, but...' She searched her mind for the right phrase. *I feel like the sun has come up! I feel like everything is going to be okay!*

'But what?' Edd reached up and caught

the side of her face in his palm. He ran the pad of his thumb over the outline of her jaw as if committing the shape to memory.

Meg turned to look him straight in the eye. 'But it's the truth.'

Edd bent low and kissed her mouth. Meg raised her hands and placed them on his muscular back, happy to be in such close proximity to him once again.

'Ah! Oh God! Sorry! I just wondered ... err...' Juno coughed and spluttered behind them.

Meg pulled away and, despite the scarlet blush on her pulsing cheeks, tried to appear businesslike. 'Everything okay, Juno?'

'Yes! Yes! Everything is great. Wow!' Juno smiled, broadly, waving her pen in the air. 'I wanted to go through the display sheet with you, make sure I know how you want everything laid out on the main counter, but it can wait if you're busy...' She held her notepad to her chest and swayed on the spot, smiling.

'Right.' Meg didn't know where to put herself.

'Too cute!' Juno muttered as she skipped past them into the shop, which was now bustling with activity, one big step closer to opening.

'I need to go and check on the contractors, make sure everything is in place for the big installation later, but then I think we need to go off-site for a meeting,' Edd said. 'A very important meeting, just the two of us, and it might take some time.' He nodded, never losing eye contact.

'Right. Well, I better grab my bag and get my things together. See you back here in ten minutes?' she asked, with a tilt to her chin and a sparkle in her eyes.

Edd smiled his confirmation as he ran his fingers through his hair, then stepped inside.

Meg's phone pipped in her pocket. Fishing it out, she was delighted to see the word 'Home' flashing on the screen and a picture of Lucas, in his Gruffalo dressing gown, blowing a kiss. She'd taken it last year, one evening when he was fresh from his bath, his damp hair curled around his temples. Meg could almost smell his scent, a mix of talcum powder and baby shampoo. A quick glance at the clock told her it was early evening in London.

'Hello, Mummy!' he shouted.

'Hey! It's my boy! How are you, Lucas?' Meg held the phone tightly against her chin. The sound of his little voice sent a ricochet of longing through her whole being. She missed him so very much.

She heard Lucas take a deep breath. 'It's fifteen days until Christmas and Aunty Pru and Christopher took me to the winter wonderland in the park and I got a terrapin called Thomas and he is in my bathroom in a tank and I had a toffee apple and some candy floss and then I went on a ride and sicked it all back up on Christopher's leg. Bye!'

Meg chuckled down the receiver. 'Lucas? Helloooo?'

'Hello, love, it's me. He's gone, I'm afraid.' Milly had collected the phone from the floor where Lucas had abandoned it.

'Wow! That was informative and fast.' She laughed.

'My fault,' Milly explained. 'I've interrupted *A Bug's Life* and told him to give you his news. Which he did. I didn't specify that he had to make small talk, enquire about your day or tell Mummy that he loves and misses her. Which he does, incidentally – both, very much.'

'I love you for saying that, Milly, but I can tell he is as happy as Larry. As long as you are on hand to play pirates and feed him I know I'm entirely redundant. Is he sleeping okay?'

'Yes. I wish I could say he's pining for you and up all hours of the night, but the horrible truth is he's on great form, eating well, sleeping good and laughing lots.'

'I miss him.' Meg swallowed the lump in her throat that was stuck with glue made of guilt. There had been whole hours in the last day or so that she hadn't thought about him at all.

'For Gawd's sake, girl, you are only away

for a couple of days! Try and enjoy yourself a bit. He's more than fine, laughing all day and zonked out all night. And we still have lots to do. We have been eating all our meals inside the pirate ship, which I must say is a little cramped for comfort.'

Meg felt a fraction of her guilt slip away. If Lucas was happy... She closed her eyes, thinking about the rest of the day ahead and the man she would be spending it with. Enjoying herself was going to be easy. 'How fab that Pru and Chris took him out. Are they okay?'

'Yes, really good. We're all looking forward to Barbados for Christmas. Bit of sunshine won't go amiss. Is it cold there?'

'Bloody freezing!' Meg stamped her feet on the icy ground. 'And I believe we have a new addition to the household? Thomas the terrapin?'

'Ah yes, Thomas. Lucas thinks he's a baby dinosaur. I'm sincerely hoping he isn't – we just don't have the room and it would break his heart to have to send his pet off to a dinosaur sanctuary because we couldn't cope.'

'That won't happen, no matter how big he gets. We can just all budge up a bit and make space.' Meg laughed.

'It's lovely to hear you laugh. Are you positive you don't want me to book you and Lucas flights? You know we'd love to have him splashing around and it'd be nice for you to have a bit of sunshine.'

'Oh, I know he'd love it, but I'd rather we stayed at home, Mills. We'll be fine: days of pyjamas, pressies and the *Bug's Life* movie on a loop.' Meg let an image of Lucas and Edd flash into her mind. It was Christmas morning and they were all smiling. She shook her head. *Get a grip, girl, you only met him yesterday!*

'How are things there?'

'A lot better today than they were yesterday. Oh, Mills, you wouldn't believe the nightmare I've had. I'll tell you all about it on Friday.' Meg felt her breath catch as she realised she was flying home tomorrow. Torn.

'Blimey, sounds like a drama. Are the contractors cracking on?'

'Yes, finally. I can see light at the end of the tunnel. Should be back on track for opening just before Christmas.' Meg felt proud to report that things had gone well. Job done, or nearly.

'That's great news! I got the proofs through for the local flyers and PR – they look brilliant.'

Meg could hear the relief in her voice. 'It's all good, Mills. I'll give you a shout tomorrow. Tell Thomas I can't wait to meet him and give the boy a big kiss from me.'

'Will do, my lovely. Please take care of you. God bless and lots of love.'

Milly sounded motherly and concerned and, as ever, it left Meg with the warm feeling of being wanted, something she would never take for granted. An image formed in her head of the four-door saloons with the stench of fear ingrained in their velour upholstery that used to come and collect her from her mother's flat, taking her to whichever care home or foster family she was destined for. Her mum, with dark circles beneath her eyes and unwashed hair pushed behind her ears, would lean against the wall, barely able to meet her daughter's gaze, and mumble, 'I'll see you then...' between drags on her cigarette. Her cool delivery always halted the emotional out-pouring that threatened to spill from Meg, forcing her to match her mum's seeming indifference.

'God bless, lots of love, Mills.' Meg smiled as she folded the phone into her bag and looked up and down the street, feeling pulled and confused. Happy to be having this adventure in this city and yet feeling strangely like she was in someone else's shoes, living someone else's life. Things like this just didn't happen to her – only this time they had and she was loving it!

Meg turned and Edd was standing by her side.

'I want to take you on an adventure,' he announced.

She bit her bottom lip. 'Don't know if I

like the sound of that.'

'Well, this is my city. You have to trust me.'

I do...

'Taxi!' Edd stuck his arm out as a yellow cab swerved towards them and came to a stop. Opening the door, he ushered her in to the back seat before sliding in next to her. Juno waved goodbye from the shop window, giggling and winking as she did so. Leaning forward, Edd spoke beneath the plastic partition that separated the driver. 'Coney Island.'

'Coney Island?' the driver repeated, then muttered something under his breath. Meg got the impression he wasn't delighted about the fare – a bit like hailing a cab late in the evening in the West End of London and asking to go south of the river.

The cab pulled into the traffic. 'Is it an actual island?' Meg asked, picturing harbours, yachts and a ring of sandy beaches.

'It used to be,' Edd said, 'but it kind of got joined up.'

'What's there?' Her eyes were wide.

'You'll have to wait and see. It's the first part of our adventure. I told you to trust me, Mary Poppins. You do trust me, don't you?' He smiled at her.

Meg nodded as the butterflies rose in her stomach and fluttered joyfully in her throat. How many times during her childhood had she got all excited about the possibility of her mum turning up and whisking her off to the seaside? She used to keep her T-shirt and second-hand flip-flops in a carrier bag all ready. And now, just like that, Edd was making her dream come true.

'I love the seaside. It was the place I dreamt about when I was little. I never went, though, not properly.' She pursed her lips, wary of giving Edd too much detail.

'You never went on holiday?'

Ha! You don't know the half of it. 'I did once, to Clacton on the east coast, with a family I stayed with. We were in a musty caravan for a weekend and the dad, Len, set up a Swing ball that I loved. I remember we ate all our meals on a rickety pasting table that I thought would collapse with the tiniest puff of wind. It made it hard to enjoy my sausage sandwich. I played stuck-in-the-mud with the kids in the next-door caravan, three siblings from Newcastle who spoke funny.' She smiled at thc memory.

'That's funny coming from you, Mary!' He laughed.

'It's not me that speaks funny!' Meg swatted his arm. He caught her hand and kept it inside his.

Meg turned to look at the crowds of shoppers weighed down with festive-looking packages. She flexed her fingers. It felt wonderful to have her hand inside his. He tightened his grip. She hardly dared breathe;

the moment was so fragile and perfect. *Yes. Yes, she did trust him.*

The taxi trundled through the traffic and seemed to be heading out of town. Some thirty minutes later, Edd sat forward and reached for the wallet in his back pocket. The two had barely jumped out onto the pavement before the taxi sped away, still apparently less than happy, despite his hefty tip.

'Oh look!' Meg pointed. 'I can see a big wheel and a rollercoaster!'

'Not just any rollercoaster, that's the famous Cyclone!' Edd announced.

'Is it a theme park?'

Edd nodded. 'There are rides, yep, but it's not so much a theme park. Some of the best weekends of a boy's life are spent in Coney Island.'

Meg took in the red-brick towerblocks that sat behind the slightly rusty big wheel and the imposing bent track of the rollercoaster that looked fresh out of the 1950s. A mini Eiffel Tower stood in the foreground. She raised her eyes and looked it up and down.

'That's the parachute jump – fancy a go?' Edd nudged her with his elbow.

'No way!' She laughed, feeling a little faint at the idea. She cast her eyes over the slightly dilapidated fascias of the shops, cafés and gelaterias. The neon signs were unlit and tattered flags hung limply from stubby poles. Even at this time of year there were tables and chairs set outside for the more daring patrons and the hardened smokers. It looked like any other seaside resort that had been abandoned in favour of newer, shinier places. But it was still seaside and that was all that mattered. She was so ridiculously happy, she wanted to skip.

'I love seaside food! Greasy burgers, candy floss, chips!' Meg tried to ignore the rumble of hunger in her stomach.

'Candy floss? You mean cotton candy.'

'Do I?'

'Yes. And chips come in a bag from the supermarket. What you mean is fries.'

She shook her head. 'Yes, fries! And you know perfectly well what I mean – it's not my fault if you guys talk wrong!'

'Us that talk wrong? You are kidding me!'

'No, I'm not kidding you. You even drive on the wrong side of the road, for Gawd's sake!'

'What is this "gourd" you speak of?' Edd asked in an exaggerated tone.

'It's a mystic vegetable that we consult and it makes all the rules about driving, talking and eating in the UK. You could do with it over here to sort a few things out.'

'Oh, please, don't let it anywhere near our food. I can't imagine having all our prime beef, spicy gumbo and *the* best apple pie in the world replaced with over-boiled cabbage and tasteless potatoes. No thanks!'

'We don't all live off boiled cabbage. And I guar-antee nothing beats a good bacon butty made with thick white bread: four rashers fried to a crisp and a generous slosh of HP Sauce. You need to get the bacon grease soaked into the bread, that's one of the rules.'

Edd shook his head. 'That doesn't sound half as good as a Philly cheese steak! Thinly sliced steak oozing melted cheese and topped with fried onions, stuffed into a long roll, not too soft, not too hard.'

'What about British fish and chips? North Sea cod in a crispy beer batter, covered in salt and vinegar and eaten out of a newspaper.'

'What? In preference to a Maine lobster with garlic aioli? I don't think so!' Edd countered.

'Bangers!' she shouted. 'There's nothing better on a cold night than a good British sausage served with onion gravy and mash!'

Edd shook his head. 'Nope. No British sausage can come close to a good hot dog, eaten at a ball game with onions, ketchup and mustard.'

Meg was quiet, wondering whether to offer Devon scones with jam and cream next or a traditional Cornish pasty, when the idea of one of those hot dogs entered her head. She wanted one.

'Ketchup *and* mustard?' she asked. 'I usually opt for one or the other.'

'Both is the law. I shall take you to Nathan's later and get you the best hot dog you have ever tasted.'

'Yes, please.' Meg grinned. 'I do so love the seaside.'

'You do? I thought maybe being a city girl, you might feel a bit queasy when you see water,' he teased as they walked along the cold concrete of the almost deserted boardwalk.

'I *am* a city girl, but I think that's why the sea and beaches have always fascinated me. It's like a whole other world. They sound different and smell different, they're a place to escape to...'

'I get that. When my dad wasn't working weekends, he'd bring me here, give me a whole cup of quarters and I could stay till they ran out. I loved those days. I'd make those coins last for hours.' Edd looked at her and smiled at the memory.

'Where does your mum live?' she asked.

'Upstate, just under an hour away by train. About the right distance – not too close, but not too far either.'

'It must have been hard for her, losing your dad.' She hoped this wasn't too personal.

Edd swallowed. 'It was. It is. Thirteen years ago.' He sucked his teeth and shook his head. 'But there's not a single day goes by we don't miss him.'

Meg held his hand.

'Ah, it's strange, Meg. Meeting you, it's kind of stirred up all my emotions. Like taking a lid off. It's a very odd thing.'

'Odd in a good way?' she asked nervously.

'Oh yes, odd in a great way.'

They walked briskly, with Edd steering them.

'My dad would have loved you. Your accent and your funny little ways, so British.'

'I don't think I've got funny little ways!' She sulked in mock protest. Then she stopped on the pavement. 'Edd?'

'Yes?'

'I'm worried about something.'

'What are you worried about?'

Meg paused, trying to find the right phrase. 'I don't think we are meant to feel this way, this quickly.' She scuffed the pavement with the toe of her boot.

'No?' He looked at her.

Meg shook her head. 'No. When I met Bill, he kind of swept me off my feet, but even that was a million times slower than this. We've only known each other for a matter of hours, a little blip in terms of the universe. I think we are supposed to have time behind us and to have gone through things together before we start to feel like this.'

Edd looked skywards. 'Oh right.' He placed his hand over his heart. 'I'm sorry. I didn't know the rules. What are we *meant* to have gone through?' he asked, amused.

Meg sighed. 'I don't know... Things like ... having lots of sex, going to church at least once, going out to dinner.' She raised her arms and let them fall to her sides as she tried to think of more examples. 'Meeting family, sharing books and movies, letting you see me without my makeup... Dance! Nurse each other when we're ill. It's all those things that bind a couple and it's like we've taken a shortcut – bosh!' She chopped the air with her arm extended.

'Bosh?' He laughed. 'I think shortcuts are good. Look at the time we've saved!'

'You know what I mean.' She looked down at the ground.

Edd pulled her into him and whispered into her scalp, 'I *don't* know what you mean, but what I do know is that if anyone told me I might feel this way after knowing you for such a short period of time, I would have laughed at them. Things like this don't happen only it has. It has happened to me, to us and I couldn't turn back now, even if I wanted to.' He kissed the top of her head. 'I've been on this planet for thirty years without knowing you existed and that in my mind is thirty years too long. So I intend to continue at this pace and not waste a single day going forward. I can't change how I feel and I don't want to.'

'Sames,' she whispered back. She felt the

fabric of his shirt against her cheek and looked up along the deserted boardwalk.

Edd pulled away, holding her by the shoulders. 'Okay, we need to do everything in the next twenty-four hours, catch up to where the universe thinks we should have been before we took a shortcut! Bosh!' He repeated her arm chop from earlier.

'Can we do that?' She laughed.

'Absolutely! We can do anything. And incidentally, we have already had quite a lot of sex. Although not nearly enough,' he qualified.

Meg blushed.

'And I wasn't going to mention it, but you were sick outside my apartment last night, while I tried to find my keys.'

Meg slapped her hands over her eyes, splaying her fingers to look through the gaps. 'Oh God! I wasn't!'

'Yes you were. That's why you were in my baseball shirt. I took off your sweater and sponged it clean and hung it in the bathroom. I also held your hair away from your face while you threw up on the kerb. I didn't even mind that you were sick on my boots.' He raised the toe of his boot as if in proof. 'So I guess I *have* nursed you while you were ill. Can we tick that off the list?'

'I guess so. Thank you for looking after me.' Her voice was weak with embarrassment.

'No problem! You were even cute whilst

being violently ill, stopping between each bout to apologise, so very polite.' Edd looked at his watch. 'Come on!'

Walking rapidly hand in hand along West 10th Street and past the impressive Cyclone, they eventually turned left on to the Boardwalk. Meg trod with caution, not wanting to trip on the frosty wooden planking. Edd suddenly stopped and pointed ahead of them. His boyish enthusiasm was infectious. 'Here we are.'

Meg looked up to see the words 'New York Aquarium' set in the arc of a turquoise sign, with a variety of fish and other marine life picked out in gold. Edd bought the tickets and pulled her quickly past exhibits she would have liked to linger over. He steered her through the darkened corridors, between tanks whose fluorescent lights highlighted tropical fish that swum in mini shoals, darting back and forth with perfect timing as though choreographed.

Stopping abruptly at a large tank, he stood back and watched as Meg walked forward until her palms lay flat against the cool glass. She smiled into the depths, her eyes wide, misty with tears at the majesty and wonder of the creatures that hovered in front of her.

'Seahorses!' she breathed, turning to Edd and grinning over her shoulder.

He nodded. 'I thought you'd like to see them.'

Meg beamed, tracing the outline of one of them with her finger. 'Look at this little fella!' A dark seahorse bobbed towards the glass, his large eyes fixed. He had tiger-like markings that seemed to flex in the mild current of the tank as he swayed. He was anchored to a tall plant by his tail, which was curled around the stalk.

'He's come to say hello to me!' Fascinated, Meg bent low and placed her face inches from her new seahorse friend. 'They do look like fairy-tale creatures, don't they? Horsey faces and long, dragony tails. You can see why I got confused.' She tapped the glass.

'These are very special seahorses, rare pot-bellied sea-horses,' Edd said. He had read up on them.

'Oh yes, look!' Meg pointed at a soft, protruding tum. 'I can see them now, they look a bit like mine.' She rubbed her stomach beneath her woolly dress. 'They all look like they've had one too many pies or too much cotton candy.' She turned and smiled at Edd.

'Or like they are all carrying babies – isn't that what daddy seahorses do? Can they get pregnant? Or am I confused?' Edd asked.

Meg faced the tank again. 'They don't actually get pregnant. The mummy seahorse has the eggs and she puts them into his little pouch when they're mating and then he carries them until they are fully developed but still tiny and that's when he releases them. It's quite lovely really. When they meet, they dance, sometimes for hours, with their tails entwined. And when they mate, they do it snout to snout, spiralling up towards the surface. It's like they are ready to take on the world together.'

'That's quite nice, isn't it? Sharing the load, making the daddy feel more involved.' Edd contemplated this.

Meg flinched, thinking of Lucas's early months with no dad at all, let alone one who wanted to be more involved.

It was as if Edd had read her thoughts. 'It must have been tough for you having Lucas so soon after Bill died. I can't imagine it. As I said, it's been hell for my mum, still is, but at least I had my dad until I was older and I have a bucketful of memories. I'm so grateful for that.'

They stood in silence staring at the tank. Edd leant forward, resting his chin on Meg's shoulder. It made her heart skip; being so close to him was a thrill. Her thoughts raced. She would love Lucas to have a wonderful man in his life, a man like Edd. She pictured them playing and laughing as she prepared a Christmas lunch, to be served on a white tablecloth–

'I think it's time we made our way to the corner of Surf and Stillwell – it's hot dog time!' Edd clapped his hands and brought her thoughts to the present.

They retraced their steps, giggling like school children as they made their way back out into the cold December day.

Eight

Meg wound down the window of the cab that ferried them back to Manhattan, enjoying the cool air that rushed in.

'I've eaten far too much!' she wailed.

'I am almost speechless.' Edd shook his head. 'I have to say, I have some big friends – football players, firefighters, big guys with shoulders like this...' He gestured with his hands wide apart. 'And they would struggle to put away the lunch you just ate!' He shook his head again.

'Is that a bad thing?'

Edd laughed. 'It's an interesting thing. I keep picturing it: the chilli cheese dog with extra-large crinkle-cut bacon cheese fries, lemonade, bread and butter pudding.'

'With cream,' Meg added.

'Yes, with cream,' Edd acknowledged, raising his finger. 'I had forgotten the cream.'

Meg placed her hand on her stomach. 'I guess I was hungry. It was late for lunch, after all.'

Edd shielded her eyes. 'No, Meg. Uh-uh, I was hungry – people get hungry and when they do, they grab a sandwich or a banana. What you just demolished was award-winningly super-human. The equivalent chow fest of a bear after hibernation, a gannet at an all-you-can-eat fish-farm buffet, man versus food on a back-to-back challenge. It was ... impressive.'

'Mmmnn. You say "impressive", but you sound a little scared.' Meg felt more than a little self-conscious. Should she have opted for a salad and appeared a bit more ladylike?

'Most of the girls I know don't eat much, if at all, and certainly nothing like...' He thumbed towards the back window and the place they had just left. '...whatever that was!'

'Does Flavia not eat then?'

Edd shook his head. 'Nothing that isn't carb- and protein-free, weighed to order, carefully rinsed and picked fresh from organic soil within the hour.'

Meg considered this and smiled, imagining Flavia to be an activist type who wore hand-knitted jumpers and Ban the Bomb badges and never shaved her armpits. 'Do organic farmers ever grow crinkle-cut bacon cheese fries?'

'I don't think so.' He smiled.

'Then she is really missing out!'

They both laughed. Meg felt a flutter of happiness. It wasn't just the fries Flavia was missing out on; anyone that had let Edd slip through their fingers must want *her* head examining.

The taxi pulled up on Rockefeller Plaza off Fifth Avenue.

'Wow! Look at the tree!' Meg clapped as she leapt from the cab, feeling an excited buzz in her stomach that was nothing to do with the gargantuan feast she'd just consumed. 'It's so beautiful. There must be a million lights on it!'

Edd watched, delighted by the expression on Meg's face. He understood her reaction. No matter that he'd seen this tree countless times over the years, the magic never waned. He placed his hands in his pockets. 'This represents Christmas for me. This tree right here. My dad used to bring me up every year to watch them switch on the lights.' Edd shook his head and coughed, choked by the memory.

The vast Norway spruce stood majestically against the inky purple of the late afternoon. Its myriad lights dazzled and illuminated everything around it. On top of the tree sat a huge bright star. Meg vowed to bring Lucas to see this one day. Beneath the tree and in the shadow of the Rockefeller Center, set in a recess surrounded by buildings and walkways of dark marble and chrome, was a rectangular skating rink. Throngs of New Yorkers and tourists were cautiously circling the ice. Then the session came to an end and nimble-footed marshals in matching red polo-neck jerseys ushered the skaters to the exits, taking the opportunity to practise a quick twirl as they did so, or come to an elaborate stop with a kick, arms raised, all terribly artistic.

'Look! Poor chap.' From her spot on the raised viewing platform, Meg pointed at the green corduroy trousers of a middle-aged man. He was the last to leave the rink and was making his way very slowly, with legs bowed and arms outstretched, to the edge of the ice. His bottom was sodden, his trousers misshapen, weighed down with water and sludge.

'Oh dear!' She turned to Edd, burying her head in his chest as she laughed. The poor bloke could hardly take a step without faltering, wobbling and threatening to fall again.

'I shouldn't laugh really, that'd be me!' She grimaced.

'Are you not a good skater?' Edd asked. Meg felt the warm bass notes of his voice bounce down through her body. She liked listening to him very much.

'I don't know. I've never done it. But if my general balance is anything to go by, I think I'd be pretty rubbish! My best trick is falling up the stairs. I do that at least once a week, usually in a hurry to get to the loo after I've left it too long.' She looked at her toes; this was probably too much detail.

'Ah.' Edd pursed his lips. 'In that case, we might be in trouble.'

'Why? Have you got some stairs you want me to run up?' she quipped.

'No, not exactly, but I do have these.' Edd held up his hand in which sat two tickets to skate.

'What? No! I can't! I'll fall over, I know I will.' She laughed nervously into her palm.

'Meg, firstly, if you were a professional skater it would be very boring with you going ahead pirouetting around the place while I stood like a jerk watching you. And secondly, you have to trust me, right? We agreed. I promise I won't let you fall.' He bent forward and kissed her gently.

Meg tingled with the joy and novelty of it all. 'Okay,' she agreed quietly, her stomach lurching with nerves and half-digested chilli cheese dog.

Edd helped Meg into the black ice-skating boots, which were tight against her calves and around her ankles.

'Ouchy!' she said as he pulled at the long laces, looping them into double bows.

'They need to be snug to protect you,' Edd explained. He grinned up at her as he squatted on the floor, expertly lacing the boots as she sat perched on the edge of a chair, resting first one foot and then the other on his knee.

'I get that, but surely it's a fine line between doing their job and cutting off my circulation?' She winced.

'Ha ha!'

'Not that it matters, as you're not going to let me fall,' she reminded him.

'That's right.' He ran his hand up her calf, stopping at the back of her knee and only because they were surrounded by people. Meg felt a surge of warmth radiating from his touch. She couldn't wait to get him alone later. This desire was entirely new to her.

Edd took both of Meg's hands and helped her into a standing position from the chair. She swayed and he laughed. 'Meg, you are stationary on carpet and already you are wobbling – this is going to be fun!'

'I told you I'd be rubbish!' she countered. Taking hesitant steps, she tried to get used to walking on the thin metal bars of her boot. She felt tall, shaky and vulnerable as she gripped both of Edd's hands, tightly. He, however, seemed more than proficient as he walked backwards towards the ice, keeping his focus on her at all times.

Meg closed her eyes and swallowed as she trod with caution out on to the rink for the first time. She felt her feet slip on the unfamiliar surface. Her bottom jutted out backwards as she leant forwards, trying to find her balance.

'That's it, you are doing real good!' he encouraged, in just the way she sometimes talked to Lucas. 'Good work! Keep going.'

Edd moved from his position in front of her to her side, never letting go of her hand and arm. He stepped slowly, fluidly, repositioning himself with one arm around her waist, gripping her close against his body, and with the other holding her bent arm inside his. Slowly, slowly, he guided her across the ice.

'Don't let go of me!' Meg squealed, unnerved by those who zipped by at speed, making her feel even more useless as she teetered on the ice like a newborn fawn.

'I won't. Just relax.' He laughed.

'Relax? I'm going to hit the deck and if I go, I'm taking you with me.'

They both giggled. Meg's lapse of concentration caused her to tilt forward and then back, as though the ground were moving beneath her, before she came to rest in an upright position. 'Oh God! I'm as bad as soggy-bottom man!'

Edd laughed even harder and managed to push her towards the side barrier, which she eagerly grabbed with both hands. Sniggering, they both slipped and slid where they stood.

'I can't do this!' she sighed, her breath leaving a smoke trail that lingered in the chill Manhattan air.

'There's no such thing as can't. You can do anything if you put your mind to it. It's all about a positive mental attitude.' He tapped the side of his head with two fingers.

Meg groaned. 'I wish you'd tell that to my two left feet, who don't seem to be listening to my positive mental attitude!' She looked up, enjoying the sight of the couples, families and friends that whizzed around in pairs or individually, shrieking and chatting as they glided. It was wonderful to be part of it.

For the first time, Meg noticed a beautiful gold statue that sat on a plinth high above the edge of the rink. 'Wow! Who's that?' She shielded her eyes to better study the glistening, muscular man who seemed to be falling or leaping with his arms spread and his legs scissoring to the side of him.

Edd stood behind her, making a little cage in which to keep her safe, his arms braced against the barrier, with Meg nestling against him inside. 'That's Prometheus. He stole fire from Olympus and gave it to mankind. The gods weren't happy so they punished him by chaining him to a rock where he was pecked at by an eagle until eventually he was freed by Hercules.'

'Fancy,' Meg said. 'I thought he looked a bit like a goalie!'

'A goalie?' Edd laughed. 'Is there no educating you?'

'Apparently not! First I eat too much, now I can't skate and to top it all, I can't tell the difference between the bloke that brought fire to earth and Peter Schmeichel. What *do* you see in me?' Meg turned to face him. She was trying to sound cheeky, but there was more than a grain of truth in her statement. She winced as Piers' words jumped into her mind. *'I told them you're an orphan – thought that would be easier than mentioning the whole being in care thing.'*

Edd looked into her face, his expression serious now. 'Ah, well, that's an easy question to answer. I see my future, Meg.'

'Really?' Her voice was small.

'Really,' he confirmed, flicking his auburn fringe from his eyes.

'And what does that future look like?' She hardly dared ask.

'I don't know where or how, but I know I don't want to be away from you. I don't want to let you go.' His expression was sincere as he bent and pulled her towards him.

Meg looked over his shoulder, taking in the tall buildings all lit up against the darkening winter sky and the Christmas tree throwing its brilliance out like a beacon of hope. As she stared, she noticed something else – it was snowing!

'Oh, Edd!' She just stopped herself from

jumping up and down on the spot, remembering she was in skates and on an ice rink. 'It's beautiful!' Meg flung her arms wide and, tipping her head back, shouted at the sky, 'I'm in New York! And it's snowing!'

Edd lifted her by the waist and held her up against him as he ventured back on to the rink. He moved slowly, taking long strides as he sashayed across the ice.

Flakes of snow settled on their eyelashes and stuck to their hair. Meg looked at the man who held her, unable to quell the emotion that flooded her eyes and caught in her throat. 'I feel like Anna,' she whispered, as she pictured the two lovers atop Guy's magical cake in its snow globe on Curzon Street.

As they wandered arm in arm along Fifth Avenue, aching after their session on the ice, the two looked skywards, hypnotised by the fast-falling flakes of snow. The snow showed little sign of settling as it hit the ground, quickly becoming grey paste underfoot. The tyres of passing traffic seemed to stick slightly on the sludgy ice and the dirty gloop coating the pavement sent up a small arc of slush with each step. A policeman had donned a high-visibility vest, and a balaclava be-neath his hat and he stood in the middle of the road, directing the traffic with a whistle stuck in his mouth.

Meg beamed. Not even the inclement weather could wipe the smile from her face. She had glided over the ice in the arms of a handsome man and she had seen seahorses – it had been the most wonderful day she could have imagined. If Lucas had been there too, it would have been perfect.

'Shall we go and get a hot drink?' she said as they passed an A-board advertising Digby's on West 52nd Street, where apparently you could pick up the finest artisan sandwiches and homemade soup.

'You cannot be hungry!' Edd said, wide-eyed, recalling her lunch.

'No, more chilly than hungry.' She shivered. 'I thought it might be nice to go inside somewhere warm.'

'Don't worry, it's not much further to where a fine cup of tea awaits you.' Edd quickened his pace.

'Where are we going?'

'I want you to meet someone.' He spoke while looking ahead, not acknowledging her concerned expression.

'Oh! I'm not very good at meeting people. Who is it?' She tried to hide the nervous quake to her voice.

'You'll see in five minutes.' He squeezed her hand as he slipped it inside his.

Meg ran her fingers through her hair, which had become rather ratty at the ends, and wished that she had put lipstick in her pocket. If she was off to meet one of his mates, she wanted to look her very best. They made their way past the beautiful mannequins in Tommy Hilfiger and ogled the shining grandeur of Tiffany's, where an armed security guard eyed her with suspicion as she dabbed her sticky fingers at the window display, ridiculing the exorbitant cost. They giggled, breaking into a trot as they left the crowds behind.

'Here we are! The Plaza!' Edd announced. 'Everyone should have tea at the Plaza when they come to New York.' He shielded his eyes and looked up at the elegant façade. 'I love this place, its beautiful Renaissance symmetry. It's two hundred and fifty feet tall and there are nineteen storeys.' He pointed upwards. 'I came here in 2007, dragged some of my college buddies along for the hundredth anniversary celebrations. They had this amazing fireworks display. It was awesome – at least I thought so!'

Meg liked his enthusiasm for the building; he was clearly in the right job. She suspected that designing and constructing something that made a bold statement might be more his sort of thing than dealing with electrical jobs in a refit on Bleecker Street. She blinked through the snow flurry, trying to get a better look at the famous hotel with its enviable views over both Fifth Avenue and Central Park.

'This looks very posh, are you sure they'll let me in?' She brushed the snow from her tights.

Edd looked her up and down. 'I don't know. Don't speak or ask for bacon cheese fries and we should be fine.'

She lightly punched his arm and tutted. 'Is this where they came in *The Great Gatsby?*'

Edd nodded. 'Yes. And *Home Alone.*'

'Hey, *Home Alone,* that old classic!' She laughed.

'I know, right? It was in *The Great Gatsby* because F. Scott Fitzgerald and his wife used to hang out here all the time. Just think, lots of famous people have stood right where you are now. Truman Capote, Frank Sinatra, royalty.'

Meg stepped through the doors and it *was* like walking back in time. The marble lobby was opulent. Chandeliers hung like clusters of diamonds, sending rainbows of light across the pale, glossy surroundings. Oversized potted palms towered above overstuffed gold-brocade sofas, their coordinating cushions positioned just so. A magnificent cream marble staircase twisted away into the distance. Meg had an urge to run up the steps, her fingertips trailing over the wrought-iron railings, to see what sumptuous rooms nestled overhead.

'Come on.' Edd patted the damp snow from his shoulders and ruffled his hair as he reached for her hand.

'Do you come here a lot?' Meg asked.

Edd shook his head. 'I've only been inside once before and that was to meet the senior partners for a drink, just after I joined the firm. I always thought I'd love to come in and spend some time here. Maybe on a cold winter's day when I needed a warm drink after skating...'

'And here we are!' She beamed, childishly delighted that she would be part of his association with this place and not Flavia. But it felt churlish to enjoy such unnecessary point-scoring and she decided to try and feel sorry for Flavia instead of envious. After all, she had the prize, this beautiful, beautiful man.

Edd walked ahead, straightening his coat and stopping at a lectern to confirm their reservation. The mustachioed, white-gloved host of the Palm Court restaurant gave a small bow and with his hand outstretched steered them to the middle of the room. Couples and small groups were already nibbling on crustless sandwiches and biting into plump, warm scones that arrived in small baskets, hidden inside tightly wrapped white cotton cloths, like dough babies. Conversation hovered in the air like tinkling piano music, all trills and whispers.

Meg let her eyes wander over the ornate furnishings. The marble floor gleamed where it skirted the intricately patterned silk carpet and the tables dripped with fine linen, sparkling crystal and silver cutlery. Vast palms were dotted throughout, their enormous fronds fanning out above the diners. An elaborate display of Christmassy-looking red and green flowers on an oval stand was mirrored by smaller posies on each table, each bound with coordinating tartan ribbon, finished in a bow. Waiting staff wearing stiff white aprons and formal expressions glided across the floor in soft-soled shoes, delivering shiny silver teapots and dainty sugar bowls with tongs perched on the side. Others balanced three-tiered cake stands of delicate white china rimmed with a single line of pure gold.

Meg looked up and gasped. The ceiling was the most beautiful backlit stained glass, like a 1920s atrium ballroom. It was stunning.

'It's something else, isn't it?' Edd stared up at it too.

'The whole place is lovely!' Meg said. 'Very grand.' It had quite a different atmosphere to afternoon tea at a Plum Patisserie, where smoky jazz was likely to be playing, the daily specials were always hand-scrawled on blackboards, and ladies who lunched would periodically break into loud, relaxed laughter.

She beamed at Edd, reaching for his hand.

He nodded at her, a little nervously. 'I

wanted you to remember it.'

'I won't forget any of it, Edd. Today has been magic, all of it. I feel like I'm in a fairy tale and I don't want it to end.'

He smiled at her and took a deep breath. 'Meg–'

'No!' She placed a finger on his lips. 'I need to say this...' She coughed. 'I didn't think it would happen to me, but it has. I submit!'

'Meg, I–' Edd moved her finger and raised his palm to interrupt her.

'No. Please let me finish.' Meg raised her voice to make sure he heard every word over the chink of spoons against china and the polite chatter of the ladies in between nibbles of miniature sandwiches and sips of tea. 'In the short time I've known you, I feel like my socks have been knocked off and you've certainly got my knickers in a spin. You were right, we *have* had a lot of sex, but I want more. A lot more, in fact, as soon as we get back to my room this evening...'

Meg reached up to kiss him, but Edd placed his hand on her shoulder and with a little force turned her to face the woman who was sitting no more than two feet behind her. A woman whose teacup visibly shook in the saucer.

Edd stepped forward and gulped. 'Meg, this is my mom.'

Meg felt the colour drain from her face as

she silently prayed that Edd's mother was deaf. Judging from her tight-lipped expression and the two red spots on her cheeks, this seemed unlikely.

Meg moved cautiously forward, raking her hair and tucking it behind her ears as though a smarter fringe might help Edd's mother form a more favourable opinion of her. The woman was neat, bird-like and diminutive and nothing about her other than her fiery hair colour and the splash of freckles across her nose suggested she had produced the statuesque Edd. Meg put her in her early sixties. She was slim but had the furrowed brow and pale eyes of someone much older – or someone who had lived with heartache. Meg already knew which. She looked smart, in a round-necked taupe sweater with the Peter Pan collar of a pale blue shirt poking from beneath. Her hair was short and cut in quite a masculine style, which her elfin features and dainty demeanour more than balanced out. She wore little make-up apart from a coat of mascara on her pale lashes and no jewellery other than the thin gold wedding band on her left hand.

'Mom, this is Meg.'

'Hello, Meg.' She had an Irish accent that Meg had not expected. 'I'm Brenda.'

'Oh! You're Irish,' Meg observed, trying to lighten the atmosphere.

Brenda's expression remained tight, but

the chance to chat about Ireland was irresistible. 'Yes. I came here in 1974 from Blarney, County Cork. I only intended to stay for six months and I'm still here forty years later. What a waste of a return ticket that was.' She tutted, as though this fact still irritated her.

Meg loved her accent and lilting tone: soft New York with an Irish undercurrent that transformed 'i' into 'oi' and made her 't's sound closer to 'd's. 'Blarney as in the Blarney Stone?' she asked as she took up a seat opposite Brenda.

'That's the one. Have you been?' Brenda leant forward.

'No,' Meg confessed, 'but I've heard of it.'

'Oh.' Brenda sounded more than a little disappointed. 'My mammy used to say I hadn't just kissed the thing, I'd swallowed it whole! I like to talk a lot.' Brenda tutted again. 'But there are worse traits, I'm sure. I had to explain about the Blarney Stone to Fl–'

'Mom!' Edd raised his voice, interrupting his mother mid flow. 'We don't need to hear tales of the Old Country.'

'Suit yourself.' Brenda rolled her eyes mockingly.

'Do you ever go back?' Meg tried to imagine living this far from Pru and Milly, her family.

Brenda sipped her tea and shook her head. 'No, not for a long while. My life is here and

Ireland is so far away – and very expensive to reach.' She whispered the last bit as though this were a secret.

'She doesn't need to go back,' Edd said. 'There's a steady stream of relatives that come to stay, most of whom I have never heard of until they fly in and take up residence in her spare room. I thought Blarney was a small place, but it can't be because we've had at least a thousand people to visit.' He raised his eyebrows.

Brenda's face came alive for the first time as she bantered with her son and her voice took on a different tone altogether. 'You're wicked! You should be glad your cousins and sons of cousins and neighbours want to travel all the way here just to say hello.'

'I *am* glad, Mom. I just wonder if they'd be so keen if we lived in, say, eastern Utah?'

Brenda slapped his hand and smiled, clearly delighted by his words and humour. 'What difference does it make to you anyway, Edward Odhran Kelly? Sure you're never home, with your swanky flat that costs you an arm and a leg and doesn't even have a hook for you to place a wet coat on when you come in of a night! I don't understand how something can cost so much money and have so little space and storage. You couldn't even get a cat in that bathroom, let alone swing it!'

'I told you, Mum, it's all about living in

the right district.'

Brenda waved her hand dismissively. She turned her attention back to Meg. 'I don't need to leave the state – people come to me! I've got seven relatives coming over for Christmas.'

'Oh no! Remember, that subject is off-limits!' Edd shook his head.

'Well it might be off-limits for you, but I would like to hear your friend's opinion on a son that can't travel back to his mother's home for the holidays.' She turned to Meg and narrowed her eyes. Meg felt this was a challenge. She stared at Edd, not quite sure where to show allegiance in this mini domestic. She thought of Lucas, knowing she would want him to come home, always.

'I came home for Thanksgiving! And I've told you, Mom, I am working either side of Christmas. I've got so many projects on that I need to use those few days off to catch up. I shall eat takeout and work in front of the television. And it's not as if you'll be alone. You have half of Blarney coming to sit around your table, fighting over the turkey leg!'

'True,' Brenda conceded. 'I think there's no place like home.' This she addressed to Meg. 'Edward's daddy and I didn't travel, not really.'

Meg accepted the natty little cup and saucer that was placed in front of her, smiling at the waitress, who then poured her tea and set two slices of lemon on a tiny tray and a small silver jug of milk by the side.

'We lost him, you know. Thirteen years ago.' Brenda sucked in her cheeks, as if the news was still shocking, raw even after all this time.

'Edd told me.' Meg paused. 'I am so sorry.' She knew from experience that condolences from strangers often sounded hollow and yet the words fell from her almost automatically.

'He was a wonderful man, wonderful man. Edward looks just like him, which is comforting yet difficult at the same time.' She took a deep breath.

Meg nodded, thinking again of Lucas. This she understood.

'We were always very happy. Never had much, but we were happy. We got married on the eleventh of October 1974. I was a wee slip of a thing.'

You still are, Meg thought.

'And he died eleventh of September 2001. We nearly made twenty-seven years.' She sighed and twisted the gold band that was a little loose on her finger as she stared into the distance. 'He was missing for a long while and then they confirmed there were no more survivors, which I expected, but was still shocked. There was no body, of course, all they found was his battered signet ring, which made it harder and means that there is still a little bit of doubt as to what happened to him.'

Megan considered this, knowing that seeing Bill's dead body had been horrific, but had nonetheless given her finality, closure. She could only begin to imagine what it must have been like for Brenda, harder to grieve, harder to say goodbye.

'I still expect him to walk into the house of an evening. I buy his favourite food and I cook enough for two, when I do bother. It's the little things that get me. He knew how to make me feel safe like no one else ever could.' Brenda inhaled strongly and dug deep to find a smile. Patting the linen tablecloth, she tried to change the tone. 'He'd be so proud of Edward, of course. He's the first on both sides to go to college and get a degree, but he always was very clever. You could give him a box of random blocks and he'd build something nice – and now he's an architect!'

'Yes.' Meg sipped her tea. 'That's how we met.'

'Oh.' Brenda smiled. 'I must admit I was wondering what the connection was. Are you an architect too?'

'No, I was never that clever. I work for Plum Patisserie, in London. I'm here to help get the new store opened and Edd is running the project.'

'A baker then?' Brenda's words dripped with disapproval. She clearly did not see a baker being a good match for her architect son. 'How long have you known each other?'

Meg looked at her watch. 'Nearly forty-eight hours.' She smiled at Edd, who nodded his confirmation.

'Well I never. And you called me just this morning!' Brenda couldn't hide her astonishment as she arched one perfectly shaped eyebrow at her son, who blushed. She turned to Meg, trying to figure out the significance of this pretty young woman. 'And you live in New York now?'

'No, London.'

'So you are moving to New York?' Brenda was struggling.

'No. I'm only here until tomorrow.' Meg drew a sharp breath at this. 'I have to get back to my son, my little boy, Lucas. He's four.'

'You have a *son?* Forgive me, I didn't know you were married.' Her loaded statement was directed at them both. Her gaze went from Meg to Edward and back again as her lips formed a thin line.

'I'm not.' Meg placed her hand on her chest. *Ssssshhh...*

Brenda drew back in her chair and Meg watched as the shadow of disapproval crept across the woman's face. Her eyes were bright like chips of amber and her tongue seemed to be chafing at her teeth, desperate to launch the words that gathered in her mouth.

'Lucas's dad died while I was pregnant with him.' It was Meg's turn to look into the middle distance.

'I see.' Brenda's tone softened slightly as she leant forward. 'That must be tough. You're so young.'

'It is in some ways, but I have a lot of support. And, well … your normal is your normal, isn't it? You don't know any different, do you?'

'I guess not.' Brenda gave a brief smile. 'We were lucky to get Edward; he was our little miracle. We tried for years, but the fallopian tubes were blocked.' She pointed downwards with her forefinger, under the table to where her fallopian tubes lurked beneath the linen cloth.

Meg nodded awkwardly at the sudden detail revealed in this most fashionable of surroundings. She found it funny that the mention of money had warranted a whisper, yet Brenda was apparently happy to shout to the world about her medical condition.

'After nearly ten years we went to one of these fertility experts, which cost us a fortune. Edward's father said, "You've got one shot, if this doesn't work we'll be getting a puppy and saying no more about it!" Well, we got the puppy, but my treatment *did* work and we got Edward too.'

'And that right there is the story of my mother's fallopian tubes!' Edd laughed into his palm, shaking his head.

'Oh, it's only girl talk, isn't that right, Meg?' Brenda let a smile briefly flit across her lips, forming an alliance of sorts. 'Aww, he was a lovely little thing. Had a lazy eye and would widdle on the front-room rug, but he was so affectionate.'

'Just to be clear, she's talking about the dog, Meg, not me.' Edd winked at her.

'You were a special baby.' Brenda smiled at her son. 'And he's a special man. Just like his daddy.' This she directed at Meg. The tilt of her head made Meg feel she was being warned.

The next hour passed in a flash. Brenda wiped her mouth on a napkin, the only one of the trio to have indulged in a scone with jam and cream – which apparently wasn't a patch on the ones she made at home and for a fraction of the cost. When it was time to go, she held her handbag in both hands and leant backwards, meaning there was no possibility of a hug, handshake or, God forbid, a kiss. 'It was lovely to meet *another* of Edward's friends.' She nodded.

Meg stood and smiled, unsure if she was being told there were other friends just like her, so she was nothing special, or whether it was an acknowledgement that she and Edd were closer than colleagues. It was impossible to call.

She nodded. 'I've really enjoyed meeting you. I wish I was here for longer, we could do it all again!' she burbled.

'Hmmm.' Brenda lifted her coat from the back of the chair. 'Edward, you need to be getting straight home. You have a busy day tomorrow, I'm sure,' she said with a straight face as she stared at her son.

Edd waved his mother off into the cab that would take her to Grand Central Station. He turned to Meg and laughed. She followed suit. Both were embarrassed and euphoric, but for very different reasons.

'Let's walk for a bit!' Meg linked her arm with Edd's as he buttoned up his navy pea coat. 'Your mum's great. I really hope she didn't hear what I said to you – that was so embarrassing.' She hid her eyes behind her fingers.

'Don't worry about it, she likes you.' He pulled her hand from her face and kept it inside his.

'I don't *feel* like she liked me.'

'Aww, that's just Mom, right? A little overprotective.' He shrugged.

Meg made a mental note to always make Lucas's girlfriends feel welcome and accepted.

'Her bark is worse than her bite. She is very protective, but rest assured, she is going to like anyone that likes me.' Edd beamed. 'And you do like me, don't you?' he said as he nudged her with his elbow. It was part question, part statement.

Meg nodded, still feeling awkward, confused by the intensity of her feelings for this relative stranger. 'She obviously misses your dad.'

Edd slowed. 'She does. They were good together, great friends. He brought out the best in her, that's for sure. They did everything as a couple. I think she feels cheated; he worked long hours and they always talked about what life would be like when he stopped work. They made plans to move to a condo, go fishing. It's a shame they never got that. My dad always said he knew the first time he spoke to her that she was the girl he was going to marry. I was always kind of sceptical, I figured she was more like "the one at that moment in time" and then they just got lucky!'

'And what do you think now?' Meg asked.

Edd placed his arm along her shoulder and drew her against him on the busy pavement. 'Now? I think I know exactly what he meant.'

'You're a charmer, Edward Odhran!' She slipped her arm around his waist.

'I wondered how long it would take to get to that.' He sighed.

'It's the first time I've mentioned it!' She laughed.

'But not the last, am I right?'

'Probably not.' Meg threw her head back and chuckled as they walked into the oncoming crowds. A bubble of happiness formed in her stomach and spread to her throat.

The two stepped confidently along the streets, Meg guided by her native New Yorker. They stood on the opposite side of the road to the Apple building, admiring the vast glass box and the way part of it was visible beneath the pavement as well. The clean white logo shone brightly in the snowy darkness.

'Taxi!' Edd shot his arm out into the oncoming traffic.

'*Another* taxi?' she asked.

'All part of your magical mystery tour.' He smiled, shielding her from any snow spray as the yellow Lincoln Town Car pulled in towards them.

It was a full half hour later that their cab came to a stop on Broadway in Lower Manhattan, in front of St Paul's Chapel, Trinity Church. Edd opened the car door and helped her out on to the whitening pavement, where the snow flurries were now beginning to settle.

They stood and looked up at the impressive building. Meg ran her hands over the gilt-tipped, arrow-shaped railings that surrounded the beautiful portico and its four reddish stone columns. Light from a large arched window shone out into the darkness and spilled over a tall monument.

Edd stepped up close behind her. 'This is a very special church.' His voice was quiet.

Meg cast her eyes over the two ornate lamps that sat high on the wall above the doorways.

'George Washington prayed here.' Edd began. 'It's very close to Ground Zero and when the towers fell on 9/11 nearly everything around it was destroyed or damaged. But not St Paul's. It is incredible that it survived and not only survived but stayed completely intact, didn't even have a broken pane of glass, nothing. What do you make of that?'

'A miracle?'

'Maybe.' Edd ran his hand over her hair. 'Many of the rescue workers used it as a place to sleep and rest in while they were searching the wreckage. Volunteers came by without anyone putting a call out, pretty much 24/7. For months the rescue workers were fed and allowed to sleep on the pews. In fact the pews got scuffed and marked from the heavy boots they wore and the gear that they carried.'

Meg turned to see Edd swipe his eyes with the back of his hand. 'Like Mom said, they never found my dad, but this place ... it's where his colleagues came to think and pray. In fact they still come. Like I said, special.'

Hand in hand they went in. Meg relished the silence, a welcome refuge from the bustling city beyond the door. Once inside, they paused. Meg walked towards the fireman's uniform that sat on one of the preserved pews, which was scratched and marked just as Edd had described. The heavy cloth of the coat was thick with grey dust and grime, the once-bright high-visibility stripes now dull from smoke, soot and ash. She paused, wondering how Edd's dad might have spent his last moments.

'Do you come here a lot?' she whispered. It was odd being so close to it, the tragedy that changed the world. She had seen the footage on TV, of course, but to be here within feet of where so many had perished was intensely moving. She felt a wave of emotion ripple through her body.

Edd shook his head. 'Not often enough. But when I do, it means something. I feel like a part of my dad is here.'

He walked ahead. Meg followed him into the main body of the church. She looked up, awestruck by the majestic white columns supporting the arched blue ceiling from which hung chandeliers that looked like they were suspended in heaven itself.

'Shall we light a candle for Mr Redlitch?' Edd asked.

Meg nodded. At a small table they lit their small tribute. She looked at Edd and smiled, thinking of Nancy in her loud, floral blouse. 'For Gabriel, Mr Redlitch.'

They stood in silence, bewitched by the flickering stumps that danced in the cool air of the chapel, sending wispy black messages up into the roof space, hoping that the silent prayers they offered went beyond. Meg could feel the ghosts of the thousands that had stood before her in that exact same spot offering similar words of condolence and hope. Closing her eyes, she prayed for Bill, something she hadn't done for a very long time. Then she watched as Edd opened his, the message to his father repeated, she suspected, with far more regularity. He took her hand and led her out into the cold New York evening.

An hour later, Salvatore squared his shoulders and eyed the man who stood by Meg's side with thinly veiled suspicion.

'Thank you.' Meg smiled sweetly as she retrieved her key from his miserable grip.

'Well, hey, Meg! Is that you?' Elene swooped down the stairs and into the reception area.

Meg gave a long, slow blink. She had been hoping to avoid scrutiny, but no such luck.

'Oh, you're not alone!' Elene, mistress of stating the obvious, looked Edd up and down, desperate to know the details. 'I didn't realise it was a room for two you wanted.'

'This is Mr Kelly, the architect for the new store.' Megan blushed.

'Well fancy! Did you two meet here?' She patted her leopard-print turban, checking it was still in place. It hid her thin hair and provided just the right amount of theatricality for her simple black outfit.

'Yes we did! Sorry to arrive so late,' Edd gushed. 'We hate to be apart, but sadly our schedules clashed this week. Anyway, I am here now and that's all that matters? Right, darling?' He grabbed Meg and kissed her on the mouth.

'Yup.' She nodded, pulling away from him and willing the scarlet stain that was creeping up her neck to stop spreading.

'Well, that's lovely.' Elene clapped. 'And how's that new store coming along? Got a date for the big opening yet?'

'Oh, not too much longer now. We'll be open before Christmas!' Meg spoke over her shoulder as she made her way to the staircase, eager to be gone.

'Don't forget the invite for me and Stella, we are looking forward to it!' Elene called after them as she wagged her finger.

The two fell inside the room, laughing as Meg twisted the key in the lock behind them.

'Jheesh, they are something else!'

Meg roared. 'Oh, don't be mean! They're really sweet – if a little eccentric,' she conceded.

'A little? How did you find this place?' Edd flopped down on top of the bed, ruffling the counterpane and throwing his coat on to the floor.

'I found it by chance online when I was looking for places near Plum's. It's homey and I like it.'

Edd took in the chintzy drapes, dated furnishings and rather eclectic artwork that cluttered the walls. 'I can see why!'

'Plus it's a great spot, close to everything. And just think, if I hadn't stayed here, I would never have gone out for a sandwich on my first night and we would have started off very differently.'

'Listen, if this is the place that brought you to me a whole eighteen hours sooner than fate intended then I love it too.' He winked.

'Those two are hilarious, aren't they?' Meg jerked her head towards the hallway as she pulled off her boots and wriggled her toes before clambering up next to him on the bed. She felt suddenly shy, the bravado of earlier had long gone. 'Today has been amazing.' She spoke to the ceiling as she lay back and placed her hands behind her head.

'I knew you'd like the seahorses.' Edd lay back alongside her and mirrored her pose.

'I did. I liked all of it, especially meeting

your mum, even if she was a little scary. And St Paul's Chapel.' She meant it.

'Well, that's a few things we can tick off the list: church, obviously, and you've met my family...'

Meg rolled on to her stomach and propped her head on her hands. 'I can't believe I'm going home tomorrow.'

'What time's your flight?' He ran his thumb over the pale inside of her forearm.

'I need to check in at two o'clock, mid afternoon.' She felt guilty as she pictured Lucas, knowing that she would give anything for one more day with Edd.

'Good, that means we get three quarters of the day together.' Edd reached out and pulled her towards him, until she was squashed up against him, their legs entwined.

'And then what?' Meg whispered, almost fearful of his response.

'And then our adventure really begins.' He smiled as he raised his head, seeking out her mouth with his and pulling her even closer. 'And I do believe you promised me lots of sex!' he breathed into her hair.

Meg rolled on top of him, laughing as she shed her dress and twisted her hair into a bun, from which it quickly fell loose. 'Well, if you insist. A promise is a promise, just don't tell your mother...'

Nine

'Do you think we should arrive separately?' Meg asked nervously as they hovered on the kerb of Bleecker Street, waiting to cross. She rubbed her hands together and pulled her pixie bobble hat over her ears. There was a cold wind blowing.

'What, like you hide in a doorway until I give the secret sign?' Edd laughed. 'I could do this.' He placed his cupped hands to his mouth and squawked like a bird.

'No, I don't think that's a good idea. And actually,' Meg sighed, 'I was thinking *you* hide in a doorway until *I* give the secret sign.'

Edd grinned. 'Think it's a little late for that.' He raised his hand to wave at Juno, who stood on the pavement smiling and laughing at the two of them.

Meg rushed forward and practically jumped from the road to the pavement, trying to avoid a particularly large slush-filled pothole.

'Morning! How are we doing, Juno?' Meg wanted to keep things on a professional footing.

'Great, come see!' She inclined her head

and stood back to allow Meg entry into the premises.

Edd followed closely behind. Meg looked up at the tangle of wires and loops of flex that had been taped and gathered into bundles. The contractors had been working hard.

'And that's not the best bit!' Juno beamed as she walked to the wall. 'Ta da!' She flicked the brass switch and clusters of lights shuddered to life under vintage glass cloche shades positioned at regular intervals around the bakery walls. 'We have light! And more importantly, we have insurance!'

'That's brilliant. They look great.' It was an effect that was much commented on in all the Plum branches. Meg was relieved and delighted to see the progress.

'They said they'll finish off the wiring by lunchtime and then start on the new ceiling.' Juno clapped her hands under her chin. 'We are officially back on track.'

'Another satisfied woman!' Edd commented, winking at the two of them with his hands on his hips.

Meg glared at him in pretend annoyance, praying that this was the last contentious thing he was going to say.

'And are the team happy? No dissenters in the ranks?' Meg turned her attention back to Juno, hoping there was calm among the staff, not wanting the rest of her day to be hijacked when she could be spending it with Edd.

'Everyone is fine. You were right about getting them started; once they had dates it was all good.' Juno cast her eyes over the tables piled with boxes, their contents waiting to be put in place. 'I think this is going to be one helluva place, Meg.'

'Me too.' Meg smiled; Juno's excitement was infectious.

'When you heading back?' Juno asked.

'Today.' Meg looped her sleeve back with her index finger and checked her watch. 'In about five hours, in fact.' She exchanged a furtive look with Edd. Their clock was counting down; it sent a shiver of panic through her.

'But you'll be coming back soon, right?' Juno felt sad that this new fling might be thwarted before it had properly got going.

'I'm sure I will be.' Meg gave a tight-lipped smile.

Meg nudged Edd with her elbow as they slid into the back seat of a waiting taxi. '"Satisfied woman" indeed!'

'Well I don't remember hearing any complaints.' He smirked.

Meg laughed as they laced their fingers together and let them lie on the seat between them. 'You know we don't have that long?' she reminded him, not wanting the day to spiral away from them and end with a mad dash to catch her flight.

'Don't you worry. I have everything planned to perfection.' He lifted their joined hands and grazed her knuckles with a kiss.

Meg raised her eyebrows as they passed the Apple store again; surely they weren't heading back to the Plaza? She craned her neck as the cab pulled up outside the hotel.

'Are we going to see your mum again?' Meg half joked, remembering the judgemental Brenda and her fallopian tubes.

'No! I don't want to share you with anyone today. I intend to make the most of our last few hours together.' He was serious.

'I don't want to leave you.' She hesitated after this stark admission. 'Well, I do and I don't...' she confessed, staring at the floor and picturing Lucas and the sticky-lipped welcome she would un-doubtedly receive.

Edd placed his thumb under her chin and tilted her face upwards until she was looking directly at him. 'And I don't want you to leave. But what did I tell you last night? Hmmm?'

'That our adventure is just beginning,' Meg offered in barely more than a whisper.

'That's right. Don't ever forget that, Meg. I mean it.' His tone was solemn.

'Okay.' She nodded and fell into step alongside him as they crossed the street and headed towards Central Park.

'Oh no!' she wailed as Edd approached the horse-drawn carriage that was waiting by the entrance. She covered her eyes with her hands, but when she removed them it was still there.

'Oh yes!' he countered, dragging her along the path.

'Are we really getting in that?' Meg felt elated and embarrassed at the same time.

Edd took her hand and pulled her towards the shiny white carriage. The dappled grey mare flared her nostrils, breathing steam out into the chilly Manhattan morning as she swished her beautiful thick creamy mane over one eye. She dipped her head and pawed at the tarmac with her front hoof, shaking the stiff wooden rods and leather harness that tethered her to the carriage.

Meg approached the horse. With her palm flattened, she ran her hand over the mare's warm flank. 'Hello, beautiful. What's your name?'

'She's called Storm.'

Meg looked up for the first time at the bearded driver, who was sitting on a bench at the front of the carriage. 'Hello, Storm. She's a real beauty.'

'She sure is.' The man repositioned his hat and sat back on the padded leather seat, his long whip curled against his thigh and his knee-high riding boots resting against the wooden frame, ready for the off.

'Your carriage awaits, Mary Poppins!' Edd gave an exaggerated bow and stood back, waiting for Meg to get in.

She climbed up onto the step, gripping the sides of the carriage as she ducked beneath the red leather canopy and settled herself on the red leather seat. Edd got in beside her, then reached over and wrapped a thick red tartan rug around their legs. He pulled a second blanket around their shoulders and scooted across the seat until their thighs were touching and her body nestled against his.

The driver clicked his tongue and pulled the reins and slowly Storm started to move. She found her rhythm in a dull plod as she made her way into Central Park.

Meg stared from the open carriage, looking up at the trees that passed overhead and the landscaped spaces of the park. 'This is quite possibly the most romantic thing I have ever done.'

'Good,' Edd said, adding smugly, 'That was the idea.'

Meg turned to the man who had her anchored in the back of the carriage. 'I can't believe this is happening to me, Edd. It's like every movie I've ever seen, every story I've ever read. You are Mr Perfect. You are good-looking, funny, kind, generous, romantic, sexy...'

'I'm assuming those are in no particular order?'

Meg shook her head. 'I'm serious. You are almost too good to be true. In fact you *are* too good to be true. What's the catch?'

Edd raised his palms upwards. 'There isn't one.' She ignored the twitch that flickered under his left eye. 'This is as much a surprise for me as it is for you. You were the last thing I was looking for, the last thing I expected. The situation with Flavia has been...'

'Tricky?' she offered.

Edd smiled, 'Tricky is an understatement. I've just been concentrating on my career; there hasn't been room for anyone or anything else, not really. The only thing that's distracted me has been the same thing that got me my less than impressive grades in Junior High and that is an unhealthy obsession with the Yankees.'

Meg smiled. 'Are you sure? There's got to be something dark about you. I think you must be a master criminal or gay or married!'

'You've got me! I'm a gay master criminal, with a wife, in fact several wives, who all visit me during my regular incarcerations, but at the moment I am one step ahead of the law and out on bail, g-dang-g-dang!' He snapped his fingers.

'I knew it!' She narrowed her gaze at him.

'You've met my mother, for God's sake!' he countered, as though this were proof enough.

'Well, she *said* she was your mother. For all I know, she was hired for the day as part of your elaborate plan.'

'Trust me, if I was going to employ the services of a fake mother, I would have chosen one that didn't drink so much tea at eight dollars a cup and didn't give her medical details to my new girl at a volume slightly louder than the pianist could play.'

Meg smiled and wriggled back against his arm; she liked being his new girl. 'Trust is the most important thing for me.' Her mum's words floated into her head. *'It'll only be for a night or two and then you can come home and maybe we can go to the pictures or out for the day. You like the seaside, don't you? Maybe we could go there, have a paddle...'*

'I won't let you down, Meg. You have to trust me, remember?' Edd's words returned her to the present.

She nodded. 'I know, but I've been let down a lot...' She bit her lip, thinking how to phrase all that she wanted to say. She looked out of the carriage; opening up like this did not come easily. She drew breath to continue. 'I've told you how I grew up and I don't know how many more times I can bounce back from having the rug pulled from under me, Edd.'

'I know that, Meg, and you don't have to worry. You are amazing. I don't know how you've coped.' Edd leant forward to kiss her.

Meg placed her hand on his shoulder, keeping him at bay. 'I don't want you to feel sorry for me. I just want you to be honest with me.' She thought of Bill's promises, whispered against her naked shoulder and laced with deceit, his plans wrapped in dishonesty and his words unfaltering. 'It's the most important thing for me, to know where I stand.'

Edd nodded, this he understood.

The sound of Storm's hooves clip-clopping along the path filled the air. They passed the zoo and then the pond, where people stopped to watch and wave. She felt quite regal and thought once again of Anna dancing in the arms of her Dimitri. The carriage veered left around a bend and there was an ice-skating rink. The people on it looked like little penguins as they waddled and spun, all going in the same direction around the ice, with the towering sky-scrapers as their backdrop.

'I'll always try and be honest with you, Meg.' His voice was steady.

'That's good, because I can cope with separation, I can cope with just about anything, but not dishonesty. Promise me that you will never, ever lie to me, Edd. Never.'

Meg was studiously looking away from him. Edd's heart gave a little squeeze at the sight of her. He swallowed. 'I promise.'

Meg tore her eyes from the rink and

looked at him. 'Okay then, be honest right now. Tell me exactly what you are thinking.' She tilted her chin.

Edd took a deep breath. 'Apart from thinking that my butt is a little numb and I can't feel my toes, I was thinking that despite having known you for only approximately sixty hours, I love you. I love you, Meg.' He looked up at her from beneath his fringe.

Meg smiled, forgetting that in a few hours she would be on a plane heading nearly three and a half thousand miles in the opposite direction. 'Do you?' She needed to hear it confirmed.

'I do. Meg, I love you.' Edd stood up in the back of the carriage, holding on to the side so he didn't fall. He brought his right hand to his mouth and spoke as if through a megaphone. 'I love Meg Hope! I love her!'

Meg slipped down the seat, giggling, and tried to hide under the blanket; she felt delighted and embarrassed in equal measure. She closed her eyes and couldn't remember a time when she had felt happier.

The two collected Meg's luggage from the Inn on 11th and walked around the block.

Edd checked his watch. 'We have exactly an hour and a twenty-three minutes before we need to leave for the airport.' He held her hand and quickened his pace.

Meg teetered behind him, wishing she hadn't chosen her black heels. To hell with being sexy; trying to keep up with him on these icy pavements was proving challenging. She smiled when she saw where they were heading. The Greenwich Avenue Deli, of course.

The place was busy as usual. Edd opened the door and stood back to allow her in first. She was immediately engulfed in the smell of food, spice and coffee.

'What'll it be, buddy?' The sandwich guy tapped the sharp knife on the counter, marking time, impatiently.

'I'll take a hoagie with pastrami, pickle and sauerkraut, coupla slices of Swiss and tomato, lots of black pepper, hold the mayo.'

The guy nodded as he slit the bread, reached for the meat, pulled spoons from tubs, separated thin slices of cheese, sprinkled pepper and with nimble fingers reached for the waxed paper. 'And for the lady?'

'Who? Mary here? She'll have the same.' Edd smiled at her.

Ten

Meg settled back, glad of the window seat. She pressed her nose to the pane and watched the city getting smaller and smaller as the plane climbed higher and higher. The powdery snow made the Big Apple look like it was dusted with icing sugar. She swallowed the sadness that sat in her throat, unable to fully reconcile what had happened within such a short space of time with how she felt. Her stomach muscles clenched with excitement at the memory of their carriage ride around Central Park just a few hours earlier.

He loves me. Edward Odhran Kelly, he bloody loves me! She had to stop herself squealing with happiness. This was almost instantly superseded by a wave of longing. They had agreed to meet in the New Year – he would come to London but that was weeks away. Meg giggled into her palm. *Blimey, girl, you've got it bad. You have been on the planet for nearly three decades without knowing he existed and you managed just fine, so what's a few weeks in the grand scheme of things?* Edd's words of reassurance filled her head. *'This is the beginning of our adventure. Trust me...'*

Meg smiled as she closed her eyes and lay back in the chair, touching her fingers to her cheek where his palm had rested in goodbye. She did trust him. She sniffed the edge of her scarf, which held the faintest trace of his scent, and felt herself drift into the dark abandonment of sleep. When she woke, the bright sky of a British dawn beckoned her home.

Meg sighed as she stared from the window of the taxi. London looked grey, the cabs bland and sombre compared to their bright yellow New York counterparts and the drizzle no match for the fluffy white snow. It was 8 a.m. and Curzon Street was slowly coming to life; shutters were being raised and curtains drawn, and office workers strode along purposefully, clutching their free copies of *Metro* and cups of takeaway coffee. Meg paid the cabbie with a flutter of anticipation in her stomach at the prospect of seeing her little boy. She smiled as she stood in front of the Plum Patisserie display window. Her thoughts flew to her wobbly performance at the Rockefeller Center ice rink and the solid feel of Edd's arms on her waist, keeping her steady. She studied Anna and Dimitri, who continued to loop, twirl and smile on the ice, just as they had before she'd left them. 'I take my hat off to you, Anna, that skating lark is much harder than it looks.' She winked at the duo as she ferreted through her handbag for her key.

'Mummy!' Lucas, still in his pyjamas, charged down the hallway of Milly's flat and collided with Meg's legs. He wrapped his arms around her knees.

She bent down and gathered him up into her arms, kissing his face and hair, inhaling the scent of him as she hugged him tightly into her chest, feeling his hot cheek against her own. Her tears gathered in sweet relief at the joy of reunion. *I'm sorry I was happy without you, Lucas; you know I love you the most, don't you? Always.*

'I missed you. I missed you so much!' Meg leant back to study her little boy who she hadn't seen for four whole days. 'Goodness me, did you get bigger? You look like you have grown!'

'Did you get me a present?' he asked, hopefully.

'I did. I got you some pirate Lego to add to your collection!'

'Yaaaaaaaaaay!' Lucas punched the air, signalling his approval, before wriggling free and plopping down with a thud, eager to be free of his mum's grip. 'I made you a present!' He scampered off to the sitting room as Milly popped out from the kitchen.

'Here she is!' Milly wrapped Meg in a hug and kissed the top of her head. 'Welcome home, love. Tired?'

'No. Actually, I feel great.' This was true. Seeing Lucas had boosted her flagging energy, but also the thought of Edd kept her adrenalin pumping and her brain wired.

Milly stepped back and admired her from the kitchen door. 'You're right. You don't look tired. In fact you look great! Glowing!'

Meg nodded as she grinned.

'Anything you want to share?' Milly smirked, her hand on her hip.

Meg rolled her eyes and indicated Lucas, who had just reappeared. Her news would have to wait. Lucas was holding a robot made of empty cereal boxes, loo-roll tubes and a couple of coat hangers.

'Wow! Look at that! It's amazing and huge!' Meg bent down to receive the rather unwieldy sculpture.

'It's a robot,' Lucas confirmed.

'I can see that. Did you make it by yourself?'

'No.' Lucas shook his head. 'Mills helped me.'

Meg glanced at her friend, employer and mentor, who chuckled into her fist. The robot was vast, at least two feet high. 'I think as Mills helped you, this robot should probably live in her flat, where she can see it every single day! I'd feel mean taking it upstairs.'

'No!' Lucas was adamant. 'I made it for your bedroom.'

'Nice try,' Milly mumbled as she went off

to put the kettle on.

Despite the tiredness that pawed at her late in the afternoon, Meg was determined to observe Christopher's rule and go to bed when everyone else did. Adrenalin, excitement and the first flush of romance were her fuel for the day. That evening as she watched her son's tummy rise and fall in sleep she smiled at his chubby baby cheeks and his little fists, closed now on the edge of his blanket and with dimples of fat above each knuckle, yet to flatten and stretch into the hands of a boy. Meg smoothed his hair and blew a final kiss as she closed Lucas's bedroom door and retreated into the hallway. Then she slumped down on the sofa next to Milly, who looked marvellous in her ageing tiger onesie.

'So come on, let's have it! And I don't mean the whole dead-body saga – I don't want to hear any of those details again.' Milly grimaced. 'I mean, what's really going on? I know you, Meg Hope, and you are up to something.' She folded her arms across her orange-striped chest.

Meg sighed, wondering how to begin without the whole thing sounding corny.

'It's unbelievable, but I met someone.' She bit her bottom lip.

'I bloody knew it!' Mills thumped the cushion beside her. 'You've got that vacant, dewy-eyed stare going on. So come on, who and where?' She twisted herself round so the two of them were facing each other on the wide squidgy sofa.

Meg lifted her hair and bunched it on top of her head with a covered elastic band. 'His name is Edd, Edward Kelly. He's an Irish New Yorker and works for the architects that are overseeing the new shop.' She closed her eyes and pictured his smile, his face.

'What's he like?' Milly leant forward.

'He's lovely. Funny, spontaneous, thoughtful, kind.' Meg nodded at the truth of this. 'He took me to the aquarium and showed me seahorses!' This, she felt, illustrated exactly what sort of man he was.

'Real seahorses?' Milly winked.

'Yes, *real* seahorses! And he knows my seahorse shame.'

'Well if that didn't put him off, love, you might be on to a winner!'

'He's really looked after me – even though I don't need looking after.'

'No, of course not.' Milly smiled and patted the leg of the girl she would always feel responsible for. 'What does he look like?' She was curious, having never seen Meg in this much of a spin over a man, certainly not the lovely but dull Piers Parkinson-Boater who had kept her occupied for the last couple of years.

Meg looked past her to a space beyond the

window. 'He's got red hair, auburn.'

'He's a fellow ginge!' Milly laughed, tossing her head so her own natural auburn streaks glinted in the lamplight.

'He is. I'll show you photos tomorrow.' Meg giggled. 'Oh God, Mills, he's lovely, gorgeous!' She paused, trying to find the right words. 'We met and it was just like...' She exhaled, blowing a slight raspberry. 'He's...'

Milly sat up straight, her expression now serious. 'Bloody hell, girl, look at you, all in a tizz. Do you *like him* like him?'

'I don't know.' Meg felt her eyes mist over.

'You *don't know?'*

'I mean I do know. Yes, I *like him* like him. I just don't know how to say exactly how much I like him without it sounding cheesy or fake.' She swallowed the lump in her throat. How could she explain the longing she felt for this man whom she had only known for a matter of hours, or the way her mind raced ahead into the future. It sounded ridiculous and rushed, even in her head. 'He is magic, he's everything!'

Milly needed to pursue this further. 'Did you spend a lot of time with him?'

Meg nodded. 'Yes. We did a lot of things – I even met his mum!' She smiled at the memory of afternoon tea at the Plaza.

'You met his mum?' Milly repeated. This was really motoring. 'Did she like you?'

'Hard to say. She was a bit frosty. Wary of

me, probably. But I understand that. If Lucas turned up with a girl in tow I think I'd be a bit protective.' Meg tried to picture her little boy dating and couldn't.

'You didn't like her, did you?' Milly asked.

'It's not that I didn't like her...' Meg bit her nail and wondered how to phrase it. 'She just...'

'What?' Milly pushed.

'Okay, I didn't like her that much, but it was our first meeting and so...'

'Oh my God! You're defending the battle-axe mother-in-law already! You have got it bad, girl.'

Meg laughed, remembering the comments Brenda had overheard. 'I think she was a bit shocked by me, a Brit who was only visiting and seemed to have hijacked her son. He was keen for us to meet. We tried to cram as much as we could into our time together and we did quite well!' She pictured them strolling around Manhattan, drinking wine, falling into bed and kissing on the top of the Empire State Building. 'I know it sounds crazy, Mills, but I think he could be the one.' Meg lifted her shoulders and grinned, looking like a little girl who had been given a wonderful gift.

'And does he feel the same?'

'Yes. He told me he loved me. And I believed him.' She couldn't recount this without almost laughing as the happiness bubbled from her.

'And do you love him?'

Meg looked her friend in the eye and thought about not seeing Edd for a few weeks. Her tears gathered and her heart sank. 'Yes. Yes, I do.' The admission left her beaming. It was the first time she had admitted this out loud. She did, she loved him. 'I don't know what's happened to me! I don't believe in things like this. It's total crap – only it isn't!' She laughed.

Milly laughed too. They sat as if in shock at the state in which Meg found herself. It was a few minutes before Milly gave voice to the thoughts that spun inside her head.

'So here's the thing. If he is the one...' She paused, not wanting to pour cold water on the excitement that sparkled in Meg. '...how is it going to work with him being in New York and you being here?'

Meg lifted her feet and placed them on the sofa cushion until her knees were up under her chin. She covered her hands with the long sleeves of her pyjama top and hugged her shins, staring at the window as though an idea might present itself. 'I honestly don't know.' Her tears came without warning as if the enormity of the barrier that sat between her and Edd suddenly came into view. Meg sniffed and wiped her eyes on her sleeve. 'Sorry, Milly, I think I'm tired.'

'That'll be it, love. Get yourself off to bed.

I'll stay here in case Lucas wakes up so you can sleep through. You need a good night.'

'Thanks, Mills.' Meg stood and stretched.

'He sounds very special, Meg, and as we all know, special don't come along that often. You've got to grab it, my girl, and run with it.'

Meg bent down and hugged the woman who made everything feel better, who had a solution for everything. Although she had to admit that even Milly was going to struggle to build a bridge that spanned nearly three and a half thousand miles.

Their texts flew back and forth and though it wasn't the same as being close physically, it certainly kept the flame and enthusiasm burning. Every time her phone buzzed, Meg's heart flipped and her pulse raced. The reverse was also true: she sometimes forgot about the time difference and would find herself checking the blank screen with a heavy heart and a feeling of loss, when in fact poor Edd was only sleeping and wasn't guilty of neglect.

Somehow it was easier for Meg to be open about her emotions, hopes and fears when text-ing than it had been face to face. She felt like a teenager, asking questions like, *Would you like to be a dad?* and hiding her head under the duvet as she held her breath, waiting for the reply. When it came, she yelped with happiness. *Only if you are the mom. Would Lucas prefer a brother or sister? Or both?*

Her head was full of Edd, which made eating and concentrating difficult. She was, to put it mildly, distracted. It was two days since she had last seen him, two days that felt like months. Meg yawned as she trod the stairs and buttoned up her cardigan, thankful that she didn't have to venture out onto the streets. Today she was in the Plum office in Curzon Street, where she and Guy would catch up and look at sales figures for the new stores. Meg silently prayed that there were no site visits looming; she didn't relish jumping on a train and leaving Lucas again, even if it was just for the day.

She was tired but happy – not nearly as tired as Edd must be, though. Since she'd got home, he had stayed up all hours to talk to her. He had watched her fall asleep via Skype and today had waited up until about 2 a.m. his time so that he could speak to her before she went work. What had he said? *'Have a nice day, Mary Poppins.'* Then he'd walked the phone around his apartment, showing her the view from the window. It looked snowy and beautiful, with the lights from the surrounding buildings illuminating Greenwich Village. She yearned to be with him, wrapped in his arms. Wondering again how it was she could so desperately miss something that she had only had for such a short time.

Meg heard the familiar laugh before she walked into the office that nestled behind the bakery kitchen. It was Pru's deep, throaty chuckle, emitted at regular intervals whenever she and Guy chatted. Meg realised how much she had missed it as she pushed the door open and beamed at her dear friend.

Pru smiled at the sight of her. Jumping up, she embraced the girl whose life she had saved and kissed her on the cheek. 'Hello, my lovely.'

'Oh, Pru, you look fab!' Meg took in her shiny, sleek bob and the high-waisted navy trousers, cream silk blouse and string of pearls that looped down to her waist. Pru at seventy was still one beautiful, classy lady.

Pru waved her hand to bat away the compliment. 'Now, I think we need to have some tea, is that right? A little bird tells me you might have some news?' She sucked in her cheeks, trying to look clueless.

'Was it a little bird? Or a big bird who likes to dress like a tiger or a pirate?' Meg asked.

Pru dissolved again into laughter.

'I knew she'd tell you!' Meg thumped her thigh and laughed, knowing the two cousins would share in her joy.

Guy threw a chunk of wood from the basket in the hearth into the log burner of the cosy office. The two women took up comfy seats either side of the flickering fire, and Meg filled Pru in on every detail that came to mind about Edward Odhran Kelly; some she repeated for good measure. They sipped at cups of strong tea and bit into warm, spiced Plum Patisserie teacakes that dripped with melted butter.

When they were full and Pru was fully informed, she sighed and rubbed her forehead. 'Well, you've certainly got it bad, just like Milly said.'

'I have.'

'And you're sure he feels the same?'

Meg nodded. 'He does. We speak all the time and, if anything, our feelings just get stronger and stronger. It's a bit scary though, Pru; it's all happening so quickly.'

'Some of the best rides do,' Pru offered, wisely. 'So what's the plan? When are you going to see him again?' She sipped her tea, fearful of the response. As much as she wanted Meg to be happy, both she and Milly dreaded the thought of her moving to the States; the thought of her taking Lucas to live in New York was enough to send them into a blind panic. Especially so for Milly; that child was the centre of her world.

Meg shrugged. 'I don't honestly know. My home is here; my job, my family.' Pru knew this meant her. 'And Lucas is so happy, which has to come first. I know how much you both love him. And Isabel, too.' Meg thought of Bill's mother and the lifeline she had been thrown by Lucas's arrival. 'But Edd's life is there – his job, his mum, his baseball...' She sighed and covered her eyes. 'Sometimes it feels too big a muddle to sort out.'

Pru didn't confess to the relief she felt at hearing that Meg had no immediate plans to jet off to the U S of A. 'It will all come good in the wash, darling, you'll see. These things have a funny habit of working out, if they are meant to.'

'Will it, Pru? I really want it to, but when I say it all out loud it sounds complicated and I don't see how. I just wish I could see him, confirm that it's real, because it was so perfect. Sometimes I think I might have imagined the whole thing!'

Pru sat forward and turned to Meg. 'You know, that's not a bad idea. Why don't you go back out, talk things through with him, make a plan and go from there? It can't be easy conducting this new and exciting love affair via a computer. I remember when I first met Christopher, I couldn't sleep, waiting to see him again.' Pru closed her eyes at the memory and with the underside of her thumb twirled the gold band on the third finger of her left hand. The novelty of being someone's wife had not waned.

'It's the same for me,' Meg confirmed. 'It isn't easy, but a computer is better than no communication at all. And I don't see how I can go back. It's Christmas in less than a fortnight and there's just too much to do.'

Pru let this settle. 'Guy has everything under control here. And what if Lucas came to Barbados with us and you went off to New York? He's only little and he doesn't know exactly when Christmas is. You could celebrate with him when we get back. I don't think he'll mind or even remember whether he opened his pressies and had a bit of turkey on December the twenty-fifth or at the beginning of January.'

'Oh, I couldn't. That'd be cheating! And I'd know, even if Lucas didn't!' Meg bit her bottom lip.

Pru stared at the girl who was like a daughter to her. 'Meg, I love you, you know that. And what I would like more than anything in the world is to know that you and Lucas are tucked up here in Curzon Street, where your lives are steady and out of harm's way, and where you can keep an eye for me on Mills and Plum's. You're an amazing girl.' Meg smiled to hear this, brimming with love for the Plum cousins. 'But that's just me being selfish, fearing change,' Pru continued. 'And what I really want more than anything is for you to be happy. Happy is the goal, it has to be.'

Meg nodded. Happiness. It was what she wanted too. Who didn't?

Pru wasn't done. 'And if that means you packing up and going to live with some dashing red-haired New York architect who is smart enough to take you to see sea-horses, then that's exactly what you should do. As long as he treats you properly and loves Lucas, then if it's right for you it will be right for us because you will be happy and that–'

'...is the goal,' Meg finished.

'Precisely.' Pru smiled.

'God, it feels a bit premature talking about packing up and going there to live when all we have had is a couple of days together.'

'All the more reason to go back and double-check. Otherwise, how will you know?' Pru's voice was soft, reasoning.

Meg shrugged. 'I guess I won't.'

'I tell you what: I'll get your ticket and it can be your Christmas present!' Pru clapped.

'I don't know how I can not see Lucas for Christmas. I just can't imagine it.' Meg stared at the glowing embers of the log burner, trying to figure out how to appease the two men in her life who were so very far apart.

'Of course you could take him to New York with you?' Pru threw this suggestion into the mix.

Meg considered this and shook her head, rejecting the idea. 'No, I think it would feel odd and a little forced, like trying to play happily families. I think Edd and I have to be more settled and have more of a plan in place when I introduce them. Don't you think?'

'It's not about what I think, darling, it's about what you think.'

'Oh God, why is nothing ever straight-forward? Why didn't I meet a bloke who lives up the road?' She sighed.

Pru smiled, thinking of her own journey and the obstacles that she and Christopher had faced. She was thankful that their deep and unshakeable love had triumphed in the end. 'Because, Meg, you meet who you are meant to meet and once that fuse is lit, it's really out of your control. They say you can't help who you fall in love with and I think there is some truth in that.'

'So you are saying I'm sunk!'

'Pretty much.' Pru nodded.

'Do you think Lucas would miss me while he was away?'

'Of course he'd miss you!' Pru tutted. 'But in the future, when he's old enough to understand, he'll be very glad you sorted yourself out, one way or another. It's the most important thing, Meg. He's very much like us in that regard: if you are happy, then so is he.'

Meg smiled, picturing herself arriving back in New York and falling into Edd's arms on that wide bed in his tiny, flashy apartment without a hook for a wet coat but in the right district. 'I'd love to see Edd's face if I just pitched up. I could call him, couldn't I? Make out I was in London and then knock on his front door!' She squealed, imagining his response, scooping her up into his arms and smothering her with kisses.

'It sounds like you've made the decision,' Pru said.

'I think I have.' Meg smiled. 'You are right, Pru. Lucas and I can do Christmas when you get back from Barbados and I could leave when you guys do!' Her cheeks flushed pink with excitement as the idea grew into a possibility.

Pru's eyes twinkled. 'Have you got any plans today?'

'Only working. Guy and I are going through some figures.'

Pru stood and smoothed her navy trousers with her palms. 'I think a day out might be in order – go get your glad rags on, girl!'

Eleven

Sir Christopher Heritage was Bill's uncle, the brother of Isabel, Bill's mother, which made the connections within this little family unit even more intricate. When his Jag pulled off the motorway, Meg knew they were getting close to Mountfield, Isabel's vast Queen Anne mansion. It was undeniably a beautiful house, boasting the obligatory Aga, boot room, kennel and stables, all set in sweeping grounds; these days, however, it had become a rather grand prison, holding too many memories for Isabel to walk away from and yet also, following the loss of her husband and son, now little more than a shell with the heart ripped from it.

'Do you think Isabel will mind Lucas and me not being around for Christmas?' Meg asked from the back seat.

'Knowing Isabel in the way that I do, I'd say that she will definitely mind.' Pru turned to face her and rolled her eyes. 'But the thing is, Meg, it's about what is best for you and ultimately Lucas, not what's best for Isabel or anyone else.'

'I do love you, Pru!' Meg felt the need to share this, a rare and open admission on her part.

'The feeling, my darling girl, is entirely mutual.' Pru reached backwards over the gear stick and patted her calf.

The car eventually swept up the drive of Mountfield, Bill's childhood home.

'I can see some reindeers!' Lucas screamed as he bobbed up and down on his booster seat, pointing excitedly at the display on the lawn.

Isabel had for once thrown good taste out of the window in her effort to delight her grandson and she had truly outdone herself. Six illuminated garish plastic reindeer, harnessed in pairs and wearing red collars and wide toothy grins, pulled a sled that bulged with gigantic plastic presents and oversized candy canes. The whole thing was lit from within and in the gloom of the December day it shone like a beacon at four-year-old Lucas. He was already beyond excited. His uncle Christopher had given him a steering wheel and he had 'driven' all the way from London. Thankfully his engine noise, achieved through a form of raspberry blowing, had exhausted itself before they hit the motorway. He did however manage to raise his fist and shout, 'You bloody idiot!' at the car ahead that had braked and turned without warning on the A40, perfectly imitating his uncle in the front seat. Meg had snickered while Pru had glared at her husband with a look of thunder.

'Is it going to fly up into the sky?' Lucas asked, wide-eyed, pointing to the majestic sleigh.

'I don't think so, mate.' Meg stifled her giggles. As if the display wasn't impressive enough, he wanted flight as well.

'You need to tell Granny Isabel that you would really like to see it fly!' Christopher encouraged Lucas.

'Don't be mean!' Pru dug her husband with her elbow, knowing he wouldn't miss a chance to wind up his sister and take the gloss off her efforts.

The shiny green double front door with its lion's-mouth knocker opened and Isabel trotted from the grand hallway on to the circular drive, wiping her hands on her cook's pinny as she crunched across the frosty gravel in her tan suede loafers. She hurried to the side of the car and was pulling Lucas from the back seat before Christopher had a chance to cut the engine.

'Hello, darling! Oh, look at you! You have grown, Lucas William! You look wonderful! I've made you some lovely Santa biscuits with icing and magic wish glitter.'

Pru smiled. She always felt Isabel went out of her way to prove that she too could bake. She and Milly did nothing but praise her brittle meringues, dense scones and rather stodgy sponges. Lucas, however, wasn't always quite so guarded with his feedback.

Isabel peppered his face with kisses that he immediately wiped off with the back of his hand.

'I don't like yucky kisses, Nan!' Lucas scowled. 'Can you take me to see the reindeers?'

'*Grandma* can't help kissing you, Lucas. You are too gorgeous to resist!'

Meg inwardly sighed as Isabel emphasised

the word 'Grandma'. She was never best pleased to be referred to as 'Nan' – the moniker apparently left her feeling like 'that dog creature from *Peter Pan!*'

'Do you like the reindeer, darling?' Isabel set him on the ground then tucked her tweed skirt under her haunches as she dropped to a crouch and continued her chat face to face.

'Can we watch them fly now?' Lucas jumped up and down on the spot, thrilled at the prospect.

'Well, no, they don't fly. They just look pretty!' Isabel blinked rapidly as her balloon deflated a little.

'But Christopher said they would!' Lucas turned to look at his uncle, who was suddenly preoccupied with hauling bags from the boot of the car.

Meg laughed, which helped ease the flutter of concern in her stomach. She was apprehensive about telling Isabel about Edd, certain that it would be all too obvious that he had succeeded in taking Bill's place in her affections, where Bill's friend Piers had clearly failed.

'Meg?' Christopher called to her as he slammed the boot shut.

'Yes?' She held back, thinking he might want a hand with the bags and boxes as Pru, Isabel and Lucas had abandoned him.

'Pru has told me all about your chap.' He

gave a small cough.

'Yes. It's early days, Chris, but it's exciting!'

Christopher looked her in the eye and Meg sensed his hesitation. 'I want nothing more than for you to be happy and I want stability for Lucas; you know that, don't you?'

She nodded. Christopher was a good man.

'But you know next to nothing about him. I know Pru and Milly are very excited, carried away with the idea and romance of it all, but at the risk of sounding like an old fart, I would say, be careful, Meg. Take it slow and make sure everything is as he says it is. In my experience, young men when faced with a pretty girl will say and do just about anything to win them over.' He looked worried.

'I know you are right and thank you for caring about me.' Meg was genuinely grateful for his concern. 'But I am absolutely confident that Edd is not like that. He is genuine and lovely.' She hunched her shoulders.

'Well, I hope you are right.' Christopher gathered the handles of the carrier bags into his palms. 'Because anyone that messes with our Meg will have me to deal with.'

Meg laughed, trying to imagine Christopher, in his cords and tweed jacket, squaring up to the young, fit Edward Kelly. Thankfully, she knew this would never happen.

After their delicious, filling lunch of fish pie topped with mountains of fluffy mash, Christopher was nominated to take Lucas for a ramble round the garden, stopping on the way back at the reindeer with a pocketful of carrots. It was his punishment.

'What do I do with the carrots?' he had asked.

'Feed them to the reindeer!' came the unanimous reply from the women at the table, leaving him utterly perplexed.

'Ready?' Isabel looked at Meg as she finished stacking the dishwasher and set it whirring.

Meg nodded and reached for her coat. No need to ask where they were heading.

Sitting in the passenger seat of Isabel's car, Meg waved at her son, trussed up like a snowman in layers, scarves and a bobble hat as he raced ahead of his uncle and tramped wellington boot prints all over the crisp lawn.

'I'm so glad you came today, Meg; I wasn't expecting you until Christmas. You can of course come any time – you don't need an invite. You do know that, don't you?'

'I do. Thank you, Isabel.' Meg swallowed her guilt. She avoided visiting too often – Isabel could be hard work, a bit intense.

'I miss you both dreadfully. It's wonderful to have Lucas running around the house; there really is nothing like the sound of his little feet in the corridor. It takes me right back. He looks the image of William, don't you think?' Isabel spoke from the side of her mouth as she navigated the ancient Mercedes estate out of the gates and towards the village.

'Yes. He really does.' Meg bit her lip and stared out of the window. This lie was the kindest thing. She had no intention of confessing that Lucas was in fact the image of one of her brothers at the same age and bore more than a passing resemblance to her cousin. Nor would she ever tell Isabel that she had forgotten much of the detail of Bill's face; she could recall the idea of him, but not the finer points or his expressions. He had been dead far longer than she had known him alive. She had to study the few photographs she owned to try and crystallise him in her mind. It saddened her that the father of her child was blurring with each passing year. But as the image of him faded, so did her grief.

The indicator ticked at the entrance to the church. It was what they always did: made a mini pilgrimage whenever she visited. This was part of the reason she chose to stay away. Meg found this grief and contemplation on demand a little forced.

Isabel pulled the car up in front of the church and ratcheted the handbrake before turning the key in the ignition. The old diesel engine fell eerily silent. The two women sat quietly as a crow screeched overhead.

'I come here a lot,' Isabel confessed. 'I like to be close to him. And I know it's hard for others to understand, but I feel like part of him is still here.'

Meg thought of Edd's similar words, spoken at St Paul's Chapel. She looked up at the sound of Isabel sniffing up the tears that threatened to fall.

'It doesn't get any easier, does it?' Isabel warbled into her handkerchief.

Meg shook her head. *Not for you.* She pictured Lucas and her heart constricted at the thought of losing a son. It was unimaginable, horrific. Meg knew she needed to make more effort with Isabel, had to find a way to overlook her pushy nature and funny old ways. She was Lucas's nan after all and there could never be too many people on the planet that had got his back.

'Come on, let's go!' Isabel announced with false bravado as she swung her legs from the car.

They made their way up the winding gravel path towards the spreading cedar tree at the top of the hill. The grave was well tended; a jam jar half buried in gravel sat on top of the grassy patch with a generous bunch of holly poking from it.

'They are from the garden.' Isabel pointed at the sprigs bursting with red berries. 'I always try and bring him something seasonal and from home.' She nodded.

'They look lovely.'

Meg tried not to let her eyes stray to the gravestone that sat alongside Bill's. It was for Roberta 'Bobby' Plum: Pru and Milly's niece and the woman who, unbeknown to Meg, Bill had become engaged to. All the while Meg, ignorant of being the 'other woman', had been quietly growing their baby and planning for a future that was never going to happen.

'Just popping to the vestry!' Isabel added brightly, as though she was off to the shops or the loo.

Meg knew this was an excuse to leave her alone and she was grateful. She bent down and ran her hand over the arc of his grave. The stone, having absorbed some of the sun that shone directly on to it, felt surprisingly warm to the touch.

'I haven't been here for a while, I know,' she began. 'I'm sorry. I've been working like a loon and when I'm not working Lucas takes up every second. He's amazing, Bill. By far the best thing we ever did. You and I might have been flawed as a couple, but Lucas ... he's perfect.'

She paused and glanced at Bobby's grave, feeling the usual mixture of confusion and sadness. Bobby had been young as well, killed alongside Bill in the crash that had changed everything.

'It's funny, you know, love. I don't feel angry about the way it all happened, not now. Life's complicated enough without hanging on to anger or looking for someone to blame.' She sighed and straightened, continuing with her hands in her pockets. 'I didn't know how I'd cope when I lost you. I felt like I had a lump in my throat that I couldn't shift. But it's not like that now. I talk to Lucas about you all the time; he knows you're his dad and you are watching over him. He says goodnight to you and he knows he has the same hands as you, which he does.' She smiled at the thought of her little boy drawing around his splayed palm with a stubby crayon.

'The thing is, I've met someone, Bill. He's a good man – at least I think he is. It's very early days. But I want to make a go of it. It's the first time I've had thoughts like these since you and it doesn't scare me. You will always, always be Lucas's dad, but I think it would be good for him to have a man in his life, don't you? I can't imagine what Isabel will say. She is broken without you. I promise to always keep bringing Lucas up to Mountfield and as he gets older, he can come and stay.'

Meg sighed and kicked at the frosty brown soil. 'I'm dreading telling her, I don't know what she'll say–'

'She'll say, what's his name?'

Meg turned abruptly to find Isabel standing not two feet behind her.

'Wh ... what?' Meg stuttered, wondering how much she had heard.

'What's his name? The man that you've met?' Isabel gave a small smile and adjusted her fingers inside her gloves.

'Oh, Isabel, it's very early days...'

'I know.' She stepped forward and threaded her arm through Meg's. 'But I can tell you like him.'

'I do.' Meg nodded, looking up shyly to gauge Bill's mum's reaction. She was smiling softly. 'His name's Edward.'

'Edward,' Isabel repeated. 'That's a fine name.'

Meg placed her hand over the back of Isabel's. She knew that she had liked her seeing Piers as it was another link to Bill, though they'd both been far too nervous of the topic to say so.

'Piers is a lovely bloke,' Meg offered.

'But not for you,' Isabel said.

'No.' She shrugged. 'Not for me. And the more I think about it, Isabel, I'm not for him either, not the real me.'

'And you think Edward might be the one? It's none of my business, of course.'

'Of course it's your business, you're our family,' Meg shot back. 'And yes, I think he might be.'

The two women turned and wandered through the graveyard, making their way back to the car.

'I understand how William let you down, Meg. It's difficult as a mother to see faults in our children, but I can see that it was a bloody mess.'

'It doesn't matter, not now, not in the scheme of things.' Meg stood by the car. 'All that matters is what's right for Lucas.'

Isabel nodded as she fished in her bag for the car keys. 'And you are right, you know, Meg. I am broken without him, completely and utterly broken. It's a waste of a life, which is why you must go and live yours, live it to the full. And if Edward is the means to that, then you have my blessing.'

Meg rushed around from the side of the car and wrapped Isabel in a warm embrace. 'Thank you! We are lucky to have you, Isabel.' She meant it, thinking of the argument and kerfuffle she had feared her announcement might cause.

The two women stood like that for a moment or two. It was healing, conciliatory and comforting.

'There is one other thing,' Meg whispered into the woman's shoulder.

'Tell me.' Isabel pulled away and smiled at the mother of her grandson.

'Edward is an American. A proper American, living in America.'

Isabel blinked slowly and frowned. 'Oh, Meg,' she sighed. 'I can see why you kept that quiet. How utterly, utterly ghastly.'

Twelve

'Lucas, this is for when you are on the aeroplane.' Meg held up a Monsters, Inc. colouring book and a new set of pens. 'I'll pop them in your rucksack and if you get a bit fed up or bored, you can have a colour-in. I think there are puzzles to do as well.' She tried to sound jovial, ignoring the catch in the back of her throat as she tidied his bedroom, placing his clothes into piles destined for either a suitcase or his chest of drawers.

'I won't need that book, Mum.' Lucas was quite clear.

'Oh, why not?' She hid her disappointment. When she was little, that would have been the best treat imaginable.

'Because I am going to watch a movie and when that's finished I'm going to play on my new iPad that Christopher and Pru have bought me, but it's a surprise and they are going to give it to me before we get on the plane to Barbarbados and I can play with that instead. It's got lots of games!'

Meg put her hands on her hips. 'How do you know they have bought you an iPad if it's a surprise?'

'Because Milly and me said we'd tell each other what we got for presents if we found out and we wouldn't tell anyone else. So she told me that and I told her about hers.'

'I see. And what present has Milly got that you know about, Lucas?' She admired his guile.

'Her talent lessons!' He beamed.

Meg laughed into her palm. She had indeed booked Italian lessons for Milly, which would start in the New Year. It made her chuckle that Lucas hadn't quite managed to spill the beans. She knew that it would drive Milly crazy trying to fathom just what a 'talent lesson' might be. Ha! Well that would serve her right for trying to get information from a small child.

'I'm going to have the Barbarbados Christmas and then the proper Christmas when I get back here, aren't I, Mum?' Lucas peered up at her as he kicked his little leg against the bed.

She nodded. 'That's right. But I'm going to really miss you over the next couple of weeks, pal.' It was going to be the longest they had been separated.

'I'm going to miss you too. Are you going to 'Merica to work?' He held his red wooden car against his chest.

Meg sat on his bed and looked him in the eye. 'No. I'm kind of going on a holiday, going to see someone and I can't wait to get back and tell you all about it!'

'Is it a lady?' Lucas asked as he ran his car over the track printed on his rug. This kid was astute.

'No.' She gave a small cough. 'It's a man.'

'What's his name?' Lucas looked at her now.

'His name is Edward, but he likes to be called Edd.'

'Edd,' Lucas repeated.

This one syllable sent an immediate rush of love for her child into her stomach. Hearing her little boy testing out the name that she hoped would become familiar to him was quite a moment.

'I love you, Lucas. I love you so much.' Meg enveloped him in a tight hug, from which he immediately tried to wriggle free. 'I want you to take lots of photos of yourself in the pool and of everyone enjoying themselves in Barbarbados and you can send them to me on your iPad. Christopher will help you.' She kissed his hair, which smelt of sweet shampoo.

'Having second thoughts?' Milly asked from the doorframe on which she leant.

'Yes and then no and then yes again immediately after,' Meg confessed as Lucas climbed down from the bed.

Milly snorted. 'Look, it's easy. If you change your mind, just jump on a bloody plane. You'll be with us in no time!'

'You can bring your friend!' Lucas did a little jig on the spot.

'He's right.' Milly smiled. 'You can. And do me a favour, Meg, go check on Juno and the new site, make sure there are no more D.E.A.D. B.O.D.I.E.S. lurking behind the counter or in the cupboards. I think that might be off-putting while people are trying to tuck into their tarte tatin.'

'I will.' Meg smiled.

Early the next day, after a flurry of kisses and last-minute hugs, Meg waved Milly and Lucas off in the back of their luxury taxi bound for Gatwick. She sat in front of her laptop and read the latest email from Juno – who was apparently being stalked by Elene, getting daily reminders not to forget her invite to the big launch party! Meg laughed out loud. She could just imagine it.

Edd's email was less funny, more moving: *I'm wondering how I get through the festive season without you. This separation thing doesn't seem to be getting any easier…*

Meg closed the lid and squealed with anticipation, thinking, *You don't have to, my love. I'm on my way!* She clenched her fists and closed her eyes, beyond excited.

After retrieving the post and booking her

cab for the airport, Meg was in the front hallway when she felt a wave of panic wash over her. Sitting on the step, she ran her fingers through her hair, still damp from the shower.

'Oh God! What am I doing?' she muttered at the floor, her head hanging down.

'Morning, chérie. All okay?' Guy bent down and lifted the curtain of hair that covered her face, then let it fall again once he was confident there were no tears.

'Oh, Guy, am I doing the right thing? I can't believe I'm doing this. What if I am about to make the biggest mistake of my life? I waved Lucas off earlier.' She couldn't help but think of the nights she had spent in care, away from her family. She had to admit that this was very different, in that he was off to stay in a lovely villa in the Caribbean where he would be doted on morning, noon and night, but still, Meg felt like she was abandoning him nonetheless.

'Lucas will be spoilt rotten and have a ball. He told me he was getting an iPad!' Guy laughed.

Meg giggled, wondering who else he had told. 'It's not only that I'm worried about Lucas. I know nothing about this man really and I am about to jump on a plane and turn up, declaring my undying love and wanting to stay for Christmas! Am I mad? Is this insane?' She glanced up for the first time

with a look of panic.
'Yes. You are a little bit mad and yes, it's insane...'
'Please tell me there is a "but".'
'But, you know, Meg, when you first came here, all beated up and pregnant and grubby...'
Meg screwed her nose up; she hadn't realised this was how he saw her.
'...I would never have imagined how you would have bloomed like a flower in front of me. You are beautiful, Meg, and so young still. You have to live this life and if that means following your heart and taking a risk...' Guy raised his palms and shrugged. '...then that's what you should do. If you don't, you will regret it forever. Anyway, one look at you and anyone can see that you have already fallen; it's too late to reverse your heart.'
She smiled at him and his lovely expression. He was right, it was too late to reverse her heart. 'Thank you, Guy.'
'Mon plaisir. And don't forget, chérie, if it's not what you think it is, you can always come home to those who love you. We'll be here.'
'Thank you,' she said again, thinking of Christopher's similar words of support. It was so lovely being loved.
'Now!' He clapped his hands. 'Are you rushing off to the airport or do you have

time for a warm frangipane aux framboises with thick cream and a strong cup of coffee?' He inhaled. 'I can smell them from here!'

Meg stood and dusted down the back of her jeans. 'I'm not flying until eleven and besides, I've always got time for warm frangipane aux framboises!'

Guy placed his arm across her back and ushered her inside. 'Your French accent is terrible, we need to work on that.'

'I'll try harder.'

'Bon.' He beamed.

'I wasn't grubby, Guy,' she whispered as they stepped into the café.

'Oui, chérie, you were grubby,' Guy murmured.

'Is that because your English isn't too good? You don't mean "grubby", do you?' She looked up at him.

'My English is perfect and you were grubby.'

Meg checked in and took a seat in the departure lounge. Nerves and excitement swirled around inside her stomach. She pulled out her phone and devoured the latest text from Edd.

6 a.m. and already been for my morning run. Impressive, huh?! Gotta keep in shape, I have a hot British girlfriend who I have to impress. Kinda wish she was closer right now...

Sames, was Meg's succinct reply.

She held the phone to her chest and blinked slowly. *She will be closer, and sooner than you think!*

As she watched the planes coming and going at the various gates, her head was with Lucas, way up above the clouds. He was probably playing with his new iPad, if everything had gone according to plan. Lucky boy! She smiled at the thought of him.

She patted the small square package that sat snugly in the front pocket of her handbag. She hadn't considered buying a Christmas gift for Edd. Ironically, even though she was in love with him, she didn't know him well enough to buy for. What was his taste in socks, music, books? She decided on no present, but maybe a spontaneous gift if they spotted something on their wanderings. Her stomach clenched in excited antici-pation at the prospect. She pictured the two of them perusing a flea market before stopping for coffee and a cake at the Doughnut Plant, where she would happily demolish their famous crème brûlée doughnut, one of the finest things she had ever tasted. Fate, however, had had another idea. As she'd made her way along Curzon Street a couple of days before, with an armful of fresh vegetables and an apricot-stuffed loin of lamb, she'd felt drawn to the window of Amy Bauer the jeweller. There, sitting proudly on a little raised glass plinth, was a pair of silver cufflinks. Not just any cufflinks, but cufflinks with seahorses engraved onto them. The flat silver discs, displayed side by side, each carried one of the creatures and they were facing each other, as if they were about to link tails, snout to snout. Perfect.

Thirteen

The taxi queue at JFK Airport was long and snaked back into the terminal. Meg bounded towards it and took her place; as this was the second time in as many weeks that she had been here, the routine now seemed quite familiar. She heard the beep of a horn and the bark of a cabbie and grinned: she was back in New York and within the hour, assuming her man wasn't at the Yankees stadium or visiting his favourite deli, she would be in his arms. A jolt of happiness fired through her body and ricocheted along her limbs. She twitched with impatience. Edward, Edward... Isabel was right; it was a fine name.

'Move it along now! Move it along!' The guard rolled his hand, keen to get this line of passengers off the rank, ready for the next wave of arrivals.

It was busier than it had been last time. Everyone was trying to get home for the holidays, weighed down by luggage, gifts and an extra carrier bag or two of airport-shop booty. The wind had dropped in the six days since she had left and it felt all the warmer for it. Six days, was that all? This was a crazy life she was living, nipping back and forth across the Atlantic like she was a film star. Truth was, she felt like a film star, with the world at her feet.

Meg looked out of the taxi window and narrowed her eyes to better glimpse the Statue of Liberty.

'Your first time in New York?' The cabbie leant into the middle of the car to speak through the gap in the grille.

'No! I've been once before. I love it here...' *I do now.* 'And my boyfriend lives here, so I've come for Christmas!' She giggled, still feeling a swell of joy at the idea of her boyfriend, the most perfect man on the planet.

'You got much planned?' he asked as he navigated the three lanes of traffic leading towards the city.

Meg shook her head. 'Not really.' She pictured them on the sofa, her wearing his Yankees shirt and him in his red and yellow plaid pyjama bottoms. 'We are just going to eat takeout in front of the television; he has a lot of work to catch up on.'

She smiled out of the window as she

mentally formalised the plan for the holidays. Edd could work and she would drag him out to the Greenwich Avenue Deli for a treat. Truth was, she would be happy never to leave the apartment. As long as they were together, that was all that mattered. Uninterrupted time with no alarm set – bliss!

As they got closer, Meg pulled her make-up bag from her holdall and removed the faintest smudge of mascara from beneath one eye. She applied her nude lipstick and then kissed the excess into a tissue. A quick spritz of her favourite fragrance, Calvin Klein's Eternity, and she was all set.

The taxi driver was delighted with his generous tip, a direct result of her buoyant, heady mood. 'Happy holidays!' he boomed.

After straightening her hemline and taking a deep breath, Meg flicked her hair from her collar and walked to the front door of the block on East 12th, pushing the button for apartment 18. She swallowed her nerves, her mouth dry, wondering what her first words should be. She decided to go with 'Delivery for Mr Kelly!' and then stand quietly, allowing the penny to drop. She would then place the cufflink box on the flat of her palm and simply stand with her hand out. She almost squealed with excitement.

'Hello?' The voice was slightly muffled over the intercom.

'Oh, sorry! I think I've buzzed the wrong

apartment!' Meg released the button and gave a small laugh with her hand over her mouth. The woman didn't sound too happy at having been disturbed. Meg checked her watch; it was early afternoon, surely not too early.

She ran her fingers over the panel and this time determinedly pressed the circle numbered 18.

'Hello?' It was the same voice; this time her tone was more questioning.

'Oh God, I'm really sorry. I've done it again!' Meg racked her brain, trying to remember Edd's apartment number; she had clearly got the wrong one.

'Who is it you are trying to reach?' The woman's manner was a little clipped, impatient.

'Oh, no one, I'm sorry. Well, I mean, yes, someone, obviously! But not you. I was after Edd, Edward Kelly.' Meg cringed as she hopped on the spot. This was no way to endear herself to his neighbours.

'Oh, right. Well, you have the right apartment, but he's not here right now.'

'Oh?' Meg stood still; the wind blew her hair across her face. Her voice was small. Who was this? A cleaner? Friend? Cousin? She mentally ran through the possibilities.

The woman continued in a brisk New York accent. 'He's shopping right now, but should be back any time. Was he expecting you?'

She sounded puzzled and was far too informed and asking too many questions for a cleaner.

'Not really, no.' Meg heard her heart beating loudly in her ears. 'Sorry, but who am I talking to?'

'Flavia, Edd's girlfriend. And you are...?'

Flavia. Carb- and protein-free, organic Flavia. Meg placed her hand on her chest. *Ssssshhh.* Her head swam and her legs felt like lead. Her chest heaved with dry sobs, her tears yet to catch up with the tsunami of sadness that engulfed her. I should have known. *I should have known.* She replayed Christopher's words of advice: *'Make sure everything is as he says it is. In my experience, young men when faced with a pretty girl will say and do just about anything to win them over.'*

'Won't they just,' Meg muttered.

'Excuse me?' Flavia strained to hear.

'Oh, nothing. I was just...' Meg swallowed the sob that was building in her throat. She pictured herself at nine years of age, walking into the sitting room of yet another foster family on Christmas Day. It was a house that smelled of dog. The mum had a purple paper crown on her head that was ripped and clashed with her bright red hair and she was talking to a fat aunt that had appeared. She remembered the way they all stopped talking, staring at her as though expecting a performance. She had stuck out her chest, clenched her palms, slick with sweat, and twisted her foot inside her black elasticated plimsolls. 'I'm Megan,' she had announced and they gazed at her in silence as if to say, so what? And she had realised in that second that she was nothing special.

'I ... I'm Meg. I work for Plum Patisserie.' She cursed herself for having given too much information. It was an automatic response, given as she tried to control the wobble to her voice and attempted to steady her legs, which swayed beneath her. 'I'm sorry, I...' Meg tried, but there were no words for how she was feeling.

'Hello? Are you okay?' Flavia's voice brought her firmly to the present and she realised that nothing had changed, she was still Megan, arriving unannounced, unwanted and surplus to requirements. Nothing special.

Looking up and down the street, she was struck by the appalling thought that she might bump into Edd as he returned home to his girlfriend, laden down with goodies for the festive period, which they would spend on the sofa in his apartment. Even the idea of that was more than she could stand. Meg picked up her small suitcase and ran. At the first turning she came to, she found herself on First Avenue. Placing her luggage on the pavement by her feet, she leant against the wall and clutched her stomach as if in pain. Picturing Lucas, she felt a very, very long way from home.

A howl escaped from her and she bent forward, trying to contain the noise. Great gulps of distress rippled through her body. She didn't care that people stared, she didn't care that a couple laughed. She didn't care about much. Her heart ached in her chest and the thud of a headache throbbed behind her temples. Wiping her tears as fast as they fell, she smeared make-up onto the sleeve of her coat and sniffed, loudly.

'Oh God! You stupid, stupid cow,' she muttered, running her hands through her hair and trying to catch her breath between sobs.

Eventually her crying slowed and her breath found an almost natural rhythm.

'Are you okay?'

Meg recognised the voice from the intercom. She looked up at the woman standing on the pavement. She was holding her silky, patterned, kimono-style top closed over a tight, pale blue vest, her long legs were encased in skinny jeans and cowboy boots, and she had short dark hair, wide, almond eyes and a large, fabulous chest. She reminded Meg of a vintage-styled doll; she was perfect.

'Is it Meg?' The woman approached, bending slightly to get a better look at the crumpled mess in front of her.

Meg nodded as she stared at beautiful, beautiful Flavia. Not a badge of protest or a hemp shoe in sight. No wonder Edd wasn't seriously interested in her – how could he be?

Meg knew she could never measure up. She placed her arms across her flat chest, feeling stupid for thinking she might have been able to.

'I was talking to you via the intercom but getting no response.' Flavia pointed back towards her home. 'I came to find you to say if it's a work thing then come on up to the apartment and wait. I could make you a coffee?'

I've already had a coffee in your apartment, made in that flashy coffee maker. I drank it from your plain white mug and I sat on the sofa before falling into your bed. Oh God!

'You seem really upset – what's wrong?'

Flavia's concern made Meg cry even harder. It would have been easier if she'd been a cow.

'Oh!' Meg swiped at her tears. 'It's just because we are so pushed at work and I need to get a few things sorted. I think I'm just very tired.'

Flavia let her eyes widen and her mouth twist in irritation at any woman that could get in such a state over something so seemingly trivial.

'Do you want to come up and wait for

Edd? The offer's there.' She splayed her fingers, which Meg checked for an engagement ring. There wasn't one, although this was scant consolation in the grand scheme of things.

Meg shook her head. 'No. No, it can wait. I think I'll get back to the office and get a grip!' She tried to laugh. 'But thanks.'

She straightened her back and gathered up her bag as Flavia sauntered back along the pavement to the apartment she shared with Edward Odhran Kelly.

Meg looked up and down the street and tried to think what to do next. She needed a base from which to make calls, use her computer and wash her face. Thankfully, she knew just the place.

As the taxi headed west, Meg ducked down to avoid any last views of East 12th and Edd's apartment block, pretending to fumble in her handbag on the floor, until it was nothing more than an upscale pile of bricks in the rearview mirror.

The cab bumped the kerb on Bleecker Street outside Plum Patisserie. Despite her broken heart, she felt warmed by the logo that always made her feel at home.

The outside of the café looked beautiful. The windows were sparklingly clean and well lit, bursting with panniers of baguettes and crusty golden boules de campagne. Ornate glass stands displayed a sumptuous array of baked goods that shone like pastel-tinted jewels. They had done it! In just six days since she had last visited, Juno and the team had pulled it off. Meg was glad of this for two reasons. Firstly, all their hard work had been worth it. Secondly, she was confident that Juno would make a great success of the place; and if things at Bleecker Street ran like clockwork, there would be no need for her to come here again – ever. That thought brought a small amount of calm to the rising tide of panic inside her.

Meg hovered outside and used a wet wipe, normally reserved for Lucas's sticky mitts, to remove the residual mascara that clung to a lash or two. She pinched her cheeks in lieu of blusher and blew her nose. Smiling, she pushed on the door. What she found wasn't quite what she expected.

'Yay! I don't believe it – you came! I'm stoked!' Juno shouted as she rushed over and grabbed Meg by the arm.

Juno looked stunning in her signature tight bun and high-necked white shirt and black skirt. Today she'd added a generous amount of pillar-box-red lipstick, which accentuated her full mouth. Meg noted the mix of staff and customers. One or two people in black jeans and oversized black-framed glasses – food journalists, she assumed – made notes and swooped on the silver platters being passed around, keen to sample everything.

The launch party. Meg had had no idea it was today; her heart sank at the realisation. *Oh no, please not today.*

Juno looked ecstatic. 'I sent the invite but I thought, there's no way she'll come at such short notice, plus she's only just gone back,' she gabbled. 'But I sent it anyway. It was important that you knew we wanted you here. And here you are. I can't believe it!' Juno gave a delighted giggle before looking Meg in the eye and gesturing at the space. 'What do you think?' Her eyes were wide. 'Are you happy?'

Happy? I don't think I'll ever be happy again. I thought he loved me, but why would he? I'm so stupid.

Meg wanted to hide away in a dark corner and book a flight; instead she was going to have to socialise. The very idea felt like torture. She looked at the clusters of wall lights and remembered her last visit and what they had had to go through to get things finished. She thought of the photograph of Mr Redlitch with his arm around the waist of the girl he loved, lucky girl. 'I really am. It all looks amazing. You've done an incredible job, Juno, all of you.'

'It wouldn't have been a proper launch party without you. I'm so glad you came, and you kept it a surprise. You are totally rad, Meg.' Juno lightly punched Meg's shoulder.

Meg nodded, feeling far from rad, assuming that was a good thing.

Christmas carols were being piped via the speakers and a small Christmas tree sat in a red china pot on the counter top. In lieu of baubles and tinsel, stars and angels fashioned from baked golden salt dough hung from each branch; they were covered in thick royal icing and edible glitter and threaded with red and white gingham ribbon. They were perfect.

Scanning the bistro tables, which were crammed with people, Meg tried to keep smiling, fighting the temptation to sob loudly. There were some faces she recognised, including those of Elene and Salvatore. They were busy gorging themselves on tiny crème-filled caramelised choux buns from the impressive St Honoré gateau on the table in front of them. The St Honoré was a Plum Patisserie staple, filled with vanilla-bean cream and topped with Chantilly and they were clearly enjoying it. Meg smiled. Elene's badgering had obviously paid off.

On the wide wooden counter sat mille-feuille stacks: three layers of pastry, crème pâtissière and confiture de fraises topped with thick fondant icing and combed through with threads of chocolate. Dainty pyramids of macaroons in flavours that ranged from pistachio to rose were arranged in a rainbow of colours. Mini tartes au citron were interspersed with tiny glazed lemon frangipane tarts. Eclairs oozing fresh cream and topped with glossy blankets of shiny chocolate jostled for space alongside tiny sugar-dusted beignets that were garnished with sugar-paste sprigs of green holly and red berries.

The patisserie looked and smelt fantastic and the assembled New Yorkers beamed as they let the delicacies melt on their tongues, washing everything down with fragrant teas, chocolat chaud and chilled champagne. Everyone clearly loved the ambience and fare of this new kid on the block.

The blackboard on the back wall was written up in Juno's neat script: 'Join us at Plum Patisserie every morning from 7 to 9 a.m. to enjoy the Bleecker Street Breakfast – a flat white coffee, two giant fresh-baked golden croissants and pots of confiture d'abricots and organic honey for dipping. See you in the morning!'

'I hope you don't mind.' Juno pointed at the board. 'Nancy said it was Mr Redlitch's favourite and he was so looking forward to popping in each morning for his breakfast. We thought it would be a nice thing to do.'

Meg nodded. 'I think it's a great thing to do.' She widened her eyes and blinked away her tears. *Poor Mr Redlitch…*

Juno gave her a small hug. 'I know. It's been an emotional journey getting to here.'

Meg smiled; she didn't know the half of it.

'Hey, here's Victor!' Juno released her grip and went to greet the building superintendent.

He had spruced up for the occasion and looked older somehow in his pale slacks, long-sleeved shirt and Christmas sweater. Meg noticed how he reached for his belt loops, searching for the keys and torch of his uniform, props that he didn't have at hand to rely on, not today. Meg felt so weakened; it took super-human effort to raise her hand and wave at him from across the room. He beamed back, any misdemeanour on her part now clearly forgiven.

'I just need to go and freshen up, put my slap on,' Meg called after Juno, indicating the back offices and kitchens, below stairs, before rubbing her make-up-free eyes, still gritty with tears.

'Yes, sure. You look beat, actually. This jet-set lifestyle must be taking it out of you,' Juno called back over her shoulder, touching her hand to her own heart as if noticing for the first time her boss's less than sparkling demeanour.

I am beat. Beaten. 'Shan't be a mo!' Meg smiled with false bravado and picked up her bag, trying to make her way across the room without having to stop and chat. She could feel a sob building in her chest and didn't want it coming out there on the café floor.

'Meg! Hey, Meg! Over here, sweetie!'

Elene gestured wildly from her table.

Meg had no choice but to acknowledge her. She raised her hand and made her way over.

Elene beamed and with her crimson nails elegantly pulled the choux bun from her fingers and placed it on the table. This enabled her to lay her sticky, sugar-coated palm on Meg's coat.

'Honey, this is my friend Stella, the one I told you about.' Elene gestured at the diminutive elderly lady beside her with grey set hair and a heavy palette of make-up smeared over her crêpey jowls.

'Pleased to meetchoo.' Stella nodded graciously to the side.

'Yes, you too.' Meg indicated the detritus of pastry, cream, crumbs and droplets of icing on the table in front of them. 'How are the cakes?'

Elene clapped her hand on to the pussy bow of her leopard-print blouse. 'Oh my word. They are the finest cakes I have ever tasted – ever! I said to Sali, I thought I could bake, but oh my, these are somethin' else. Isn't that right, Sali?'

'Sure.' He shrugged.

'Ignore him.' Elene pointed at her husband with her thumb as though he were deaf. 'He can't give a compliment in case his face cracks.'

Stella let out a wheezing laugh, which set

Elene off. They were having a good time.

'I didn't know you were in town. Where you staying, Meg? With lover boy?' Elene smiled. 'Ah, don't look so worried.' She batted the air with her hand. 'I didn't expect you to stay with us, not now you and Mr Kelly are so close. I'm pleased for you. I really am. Hopefully we'll be seeing a lot more of you in the Village now?' she fished.

Meg simply nodded and prepared to walk away, but Salvatore placed his hand over the back of her palm, which rested on the table. 'You did good, kid,' he murmured. And he winked at her with the beginnings of a smile that quickly faded.

Meg felt the tears rising at his unexpected gesture and words of kindness; it was enough to push her over the edge. 'I must go and freshen up.' She pointed towards the back door, trying to smile; it was becoming harder and harder.

'Hey, talk of the devil! Here he is!' Elene pointed over Meg's shoulder.

She felt her blood run cold and her heart jump. *Oh please, no!*

She heard Juno's voice echoing with excitement. 'Monsieur l'architecte! You made it!'

Turning, Meg instinctively felt her face wanting to smile at the sight of him. He looked wonderful in his crisp white shirt and navy jacket over jeans, of course. Not that she had expected him to change in any way; it had been less than a week since she had seen him in person, only a couple of days or so since he had watched her fall asleep across the miles. Meg felt anchored to the spot. Her legs shook and her heart thudded as she saw his stricken expression.

Without acknowledging anyone or anything, he made his way over to her. She watched his hands twitch in her direction, wanting to take hers, but deciding against it, thank goodness.

'Ma... Me–' he stuttered.

'It's Meg,' she assisted. 'I understand it must be hard to keep track.' She spoke quickly but quietly, not wanting to bring her domestic disaster to work on this day of celebration.

'I know it's Meg, Meg! I was going to say Mary, but I didn't think you'd find it funny.' His expression was doleful.

'I never did,' she lied. 'And incidentally I'm not finding anything very funny right now.' She was aware of her shallow breaths and that her chest was heaving with all that it contained.

'I get it. I dumped the grocery bags and came here as quickly as I could.' Edd scanned the crowds around them, looking for a quiet spot.

'Oh, well, thank you so much for coming.' Her sarcasm wasn't lost on him. 'I hope your girl-friend puts the groceries away. I can't stand to think of you two love birds having spoilt milk.'

Edd grabbed her arm and steered her more forcefully than she was comfortable with towards the back of the shop. He led her down the service stairs and out into the small courtyard at the back of the kitchen. She was irritated that he had taken control and had marched her so determinedly out of the café and doubly irritated by the way her body folded and sang at the touch of his hand on her arm. Flavia's words floated into her head, *'Flavia, Edd's girlfriend...'*, and her tears finally broke their banks, falling down her cheeks and splashing from her nose and eyelashes.

'Oh God, please don't.' Edd placed his hand over his mouth as his own eyes misted over. He reached for her, but hesitated as he watched her shrink from him. Finally he placed his hand inside his jacket, resting it on his hip as he paced in circles in front of her. 'I can't bear to see you cry,' he whispered.

Meg stood in front of a trio of large metal bins and folded her arms across her chest. She let her head hang forward and her hair dangle over her face; she was glad of the veil.

'We need to talk,' he said.

'No. *You* need to talk!' Her words when

they did come were fired from lips contorted with anguish; they were delivered quickly and with anger. She tucked her palms under her arms. Her muscles ached with the effort of trying to stop herself from trembling with distress and cold.

Edd exhaled and raised his hands as if in submission. 'I love you.'

'Don't start with all that bollocks!' she shouted.

'It's not bollocks. I love you, Meg. I do. And even though this is a mess, I am so pleased to see you. I hated every second of being away from you.' His tone was pleading.

'Is it true? Is Flavia your girlfriend?' She cut to the chase, unable to cope with the sugar-coating when they were yet to establish the fundamentals.

'Yes.' His voice was calm, directed at the floor.

'Oh God. There was still a tiny space in my head that was hoping it wasn't true, that it was some kind of horrible mix-up.' Meg shook her head. 'I don't believe it. I am so fucking stupid.'

'You're not, you're not stupid.'

'I must be, don't you get it? You made me the other woman again! And yet again I wasn't given the choice because I didn't know. So yes, I must be fucking stupid.'

'You didn't know...' Edd offered.

'No, I didn't. Not that it makes it any

easier. You lied to me and you promised you wouldn't and like an idiot I believed you.' This she uttered through clenched teeth. 'I can't believe I fell for it!'

'I never lied to you. I never said Flavia and I had finished.' He caught her eye.

'No, you're right, clever Edd. You didn't quite, did you? And you might not have lied outright, but there are many ways to be dishonest and lying through omission is one of them.' Meg felt a swell of anger inside her. 'I met her, Edd, and she was lovely and beautiful and she has big boobs and I had to look her in the eye, knowing that I had slept in her bed, with her man and it was shit! You put me in that position.'

'It's not her bed, it's my bed. She doesn't live with me.' He shook his head.

'Oh, well, that makes it okay then!' Her words dripped with sarcasm. Meg pictured the mauve sequined cushions, at odds with the masculine design of the apartment. A woman's touch.

'I know it doesn't make any difference and I can't imagine what it was like to turn up and find her there. I'm sorry. I'm so sorry.' His voice was quiet.

'Well, sorry is easy, too easy and doesn't mean fuck all. I'm sorry for assuming you were single. I can't think where I got that idea.' She placed her finger over her lips as though in contemplation. 'Oh, actually, thinking about it, it might have been something to do with the fact you picked me up, we had sex in your apartment and then you took me to meet your mother. Oh, and the church visit, that was a nice touch, completely reeled me in. Don't even get me started on the fricking million texts and messages all telling me about our fantastic fucking future!'

She watched what could have been a look of hurt flash across his face, but that was too bad, she wasn't done. 'I have flown around the bloody world to see you, to spend Christmas with you.' As these words left her mouth, she thought of Lucas and hearing him saying the word 'Edd' and the joy it had brought her. 'I have waved my little boy off for Christmas without me! Something I said I would never do and I did it because I believed you. I thought I was paving the way for our glorious future, the one you told me we would have. I'm such a fucking idiot!' She banged her clenched fists against her thighs.

Edd stepped forward with his arms wide, wait-ing to encircle her, comfort her.

'Don't you dare touch me! Don't you dare. You're a fake and a liar and a bastard!'

Edd shook his head. 'No. I'm not. I'm really not. I love you, Meg!'

'Stop saying it. Just stop it. It doesn't mean anything. Not now,' she howled.

'Well it means something to me,' he countered. 'I have never lied to you. It's just that it has all happened so fast and it's not straightforward. Things are not what they seem between Flavia and me. And they haven't been for a very long time.'

'Oh well that's good because she seemed like your girlfriend and you seemed to have been stringing me along with your bullshit!' she shouted.

Edd sighed, 'She's, she's fragile.'

And I'm not?

'I've known for a while it wasn't right, maybe always, but I didn't do anything about it because I was chicken and working such crazy hours that I hardly ever saw her. I admit I avoided the conversation because I hate hurting people and I was waiting for the right time. I feel sorry for her. She lost her mom this year and she hasn't got anyone else. I didn't want to add to her hurt.'

'Have you slept with her since you met me?' Meg looked him squarely in the eye, picturing the beautiful girl in the kimono top who had offered her coffee.

'No, we've shared a bed a couple of times, but nothing happened,' he admitted. This made her tears fall afresh as she recalled his words, after her night in his bed, '*...just a little making out. But no more than second base, I swear!*' She pictured him and Flavia together and her gut twisted with sadness and jealousy.

He took a step closer to her. 'And the only reason she stayed over was because I couldn't figure out how to get her to leave.' He closed his eyes. 'I can hear how shit that sounds.'

'You think?' she managed between sobs.

'I don't love her in the way I should. I don't think I ever have. We were just friends to start with and we supported each other through some tough times, me missing my dad and her mom dying. After a while we drifted into bed with each other and I haven't had the heart or the guts to admit that I wanted out. I've just avoided the discussion, but then I met you. I love *you*. *You*, Meg. You haven't been out of my head for one second, not one single second since we met.'

'What, even when you were snuggling up to Miss Carb-Free-Organic?' she quipped, wanting to dislike Flavia, but finding it almost impossible.

'Yes, even then.' He whispered his admission.

'Fucking hell. You are the limit!'

'I know how this sounds, how it looks, but, Meg, just let me say–'

'No. I will not let you say anything, because nothing you can say will change this. You're just like all the others.' Meg turned around and banged the bin with the heel of her hand; it gave off a loud, metallic thud that rattled around the courtyard. She thought of Bill, of her dad, thought about everyone that had let her down, lied to her or abandoned her. 'I don't want to see you ever again. Ever. And I wish to God I'd never met you; you turned my world and my son's world upside down for nothing. That's a cruel trick to play.'

'It's not a trick. I love you.' It was as if he could think of nothing else to say.

Meg straightened her back and pushed her hair behind her ears. She sniffed and wiped her eyes. 'Fuck off, Edward. Go back to your needy girlfriend and your controlling mother.'

Edd opened his mouth to speak but thought better of it. Turning, he reached for the handle and opened the door that would take him from the courtyard and out of her life.

'Incidentally,' Meg called. He looked back and she was shocked to see the tears that fell from his eyes, turning them instantly bloodshot. 'If what you're saying is true, which I don't believe for one second, then why are you still with her? If you've been waiting for the right time, why wasn't the right time when you met me?'

Edd looked up as the sky clouded over and it began to snow, just as it had when she had skated in his arms at the Rockefeller Center and when they had kissed for the first time on top of the Empire State Building. Flakes settled on his eyelashes and his thick auburn fringe.

'Because it's Christmas,' he managed, before slipping through the door.

Fourteen

Without adrenalin and excitement to counteract the fatigue, Meg felt completely exhausted. All she wanted to do was close her eyes and go to sleep. She had little memory of the flight home, conducted in the dead of night with an eye mask on and a blanket over her head. She rejected both meals and movies as she cried across the time zones. Every time she closed her eyes, she pictured him standing in the courtyard as it began to snow. *'We've shared a bed a couple of times...'*

It was midday when the taxi dropped her off and exactly a week before Christmas. Judging by the groups of men in sharp suits and women in sparkly tops and heels, it was office party time and some seemed to have started the celebrations earlier than others. She dodged a cluster of women of various ages and sizes, linked arm in arm and talking loudly, laughing open-mouthed without restraint as they teetered along in a cloud of wine fumes. Most were revealing ample amounts of cleavage, wearing tops that paid no heed to the cold bite of winter. They clutched coordinating handbags that were too tiny to contain much other than their lipstick of choice, a slim phone and a travel card. Meg hovered on the kerb with her suitcase by her feet, waiting for them to pass, her eye trained on the front door that would mean a soft pillow and some privacy.

'Cheer up, princess, it might never happen!' a dark-haired man in a navy pinstriped three-piece suit shouted at her, drawing a smile with his index finger from cheek to cheek.

If only it were that simple. She gave a little nod, trying to join in, but the truth was it had already happened.

'Leave her alone, Ricky, she's well out of your league, mate!' His friend slapped an arm across Ricky's back and moved him along the pavement.

Placing the key in the lock, Meg trod quietly up the stairs to her flat. Without putting on the lights or opening doors to other rooms, she slipped into her bedroom and after pulling off her boots, still in the clothes she had been wearing for countless hours, slid between the sheets. No matter that it was lunchtime. *'Cheer up, princess!'*

The man's words echoed in her mind as she fell into a slumber of sorts.

Meg was jolted awake by a horrible dream, but when she sat up and glanced at the clock on her bedside table she realised it wasn't a dream at all. Screwing her eyes shut, she thought of Lucas, thought of the seaside, anything other than the reality of the situation in which she found herself. Laying her head back on her tear-soaked pillow, she forced herself back to sleep, welcoming the dark escape it offered.

When she woke again at three o'clock in the afternoon, her arm immediately snaked along the cushions, searching for the reassuring warmth of her lover's skin. But he was in a different country, in a different time zone and he was not hers to love. The future that she had envisaged had gone for good. This caused her tears to pool again. In her jet-lagged, sleepy state, confusion reigned and she didn't know if she was crying for Bill or Edd or the fact that Lucas was so far away from her so close to Christmas. And even though she had heard it from the horse's mouth, she still found it hard to believe that Edd was a fake and a fake with a girlfriend. She loved him – well, she thought she did; at least the beginnings of love.

It was as if the anguish and hurt she felt on account of Edd had reawakened her grief at losing Bill. Her head was a jumble of facts and dark imaginings; the deep pain of rejection she'd felt at Bill's infidelity had been soothed by Edd, who had made everything feel better, but now it was more agonising still because he too had let her down. And so it went, a desperate, endless cycle of sadness, within which she could see no light.

Meg crept from her room and halted in the hallway, standing on the slightly sticky marble floor; the stickiness was partly her own fault – she could afford to be a bit more liberal with the mop – and partly down to Lucas, who tended to swing his cup and spray the area with juice. She pictured his face and smiled; he really was her greatest achievement. She was certain that at that precise moment he would be enjoying the mid-morning sunshine on a beach, with Milly, Pru and Christopher dancing attendance.

She swooped down to collect one of his stray socks from the floor. There was something about his little socks and the feet that went into them that always sent a jolt of love right through her. 'Oh, Lucas.' She sighed, thinking of him and trying not to jump ahead to Christmas, a Christmas that her baby would spend over four thousand miles away from her. It wasn't anything like what she had planned.

Meg was, as ever, extremely grateful to the Plum cousins for scooping him up and giving him this amazing adventure. She thought back to the time soon after Lucas was born. She was still in deep mourning for Bill, but Milly and Pru had insisted that she go out at least once a week, even if it was only for a walk; anything to get her out of the flat. She had been reluctant at first, preferring to spend her nights tucked up on the sofa with her son asleep in the adjoining room. But Milly had been adamant – what had she said? *'You're in your twenties, not your eighties. You need to go out, make a life and have a life. I can assure you, Meg, the way to meet a man and move on is not to sit in your pyjamas watching* Corrie. *Brad or Leonardo ain't going to come and knock on your door during the break and see if you fancy sharing a bag of chips. You have to go out into the big, wide, scary world!'* Meg sighed; she had given things a go with Piers and had been prepared to jump for Edd. But that was enough trying now. She would simply go back to her nights on the sofa. That way she wouldn't suffer further upset or inflict upset on others. Much better. As long as Lucas was happy, she didn't need no Brad or Leonardo.

Meg studied the coconut welcome mat with its pink and red floral pattern, blobs of mud, tangles of hair and three toy cars lined up on it as if parked. On close inspection it was quite disgusting. She decided that over the next few days she would get on with all the household chores so that when her boy came back the place would be sparkling. She would tackle the hall floor and she would finally get round to scrubbing the stained laminate of her spice shelf, which had got surprisingly grubby. She would sort Lucas's playdough into single colours from the multicoloured lump that it had become and pop it back neatly into its various tubs. She'd clean the windows and wash and iron all the bed linen. It would be good for her and would fill the waking hours while she was alone.

Her phone buzzed on the hall table. She flipped it open to see the first lines of twenty text messages, all from Edd. One swipe of her fingertip and they were deleted. Easy.

Meg flicked the switch on the kettle. In her experience most things, from a hangover to a busy workload, could be eased if not cured with several cups of Earl Grey. Today though, even the fragrant brew could do little to lift her spirits.

With several productive hours still left in the day, she showered and did what she always did when times got tough. She went to work.

Guy did a double-take as she came in the back door from the hallway that led to the bakery, abandoning the order he was writing. 'Meg! What are you doing?'

'I'm coming to work, Guy.' She ran her palms over her Plum apron and black skirt. 'I hope you need a waitress until closing time, because what I need is to ferry cakes and teacups up and down the stairs without having time to think. Is that okay?'

'Of course. But I meant, what are you doing *here?* I thought you were in New York – what happened?' He shook his head, perplexed.

Meg felt her shoulders sag. She knew this was only the first of many times she would have to repeat the story and her heart sank at the prospect. It was humiliating, having to admit that she had got it so wrong.

'I was, but it didn't exactly work out how I'd planned.' She paused.

'What happened?'

'I went to his apartment...' Meg pictured herself hovering eagerly on the pavement with the cufflinks in her hand. 'And a girl was there – his girlfriend, to be precise.' She looked up as Guy tutted loudly in horror and flung his fingers over his open mouth.

'Non!' he gasped.

'Yes,' she countered. 'I pretty much just spent an hour or two at Plum's Bleecker Street launch party and then waited at the airport for a flight back. It was bloody pointless, tiring and expensive. I feel sick.'

Guy fluttered his palm around his face as

though trying to alleviate a hot flush. 'Oh, mon Dieu. I don't believe it. Are you sure she was his girlfriend? Maybe she just said that...'

Meg shook her head. 'No, he confirmed it, Guy; didn't deny anything. He even shared a bed with her while I was back here. I'm such a mug.' She pushed a stray lock of hair behind her ear.

'You are not a mug. He is a fool, letting you slip through his fingers. And he clearly isn't worth getting upset over. You need to find a nice English boy who is close enough for us all to check out.'

Meg twitched her nose and thought of Piers, whom they had indeed all checked out and whom she hadn't loved, not even a little bit. 'I don't think I want any boy at the moment, English or otherwise. I'm going to concentrate on Lucas for a while; I feel I've neglected him a bit recently.'

'Rubbish. Lucas is fine and taking a week or so for yourself is no crime. Look how much you have missed him – it's good for you both.'

He made her feel better, he always did.

'Okay!' Guy clapped his hands together and made her jump. 'To work! Put this sign out the front, we have a few afternoon tea specials.' He pointed to Curzon Street.

Meg rolled her eyes. 'Oh God, I had forgotten how bossy you are to work for!'

'You see, a few years of management and you have gone soft.' Guy winked at her as he skipped down the stairs to the kitchen.

Meg lifted the side of the heavy A-board and slipped the poster into it, before repositioning it and placing it on the edge of the pavement. She ran her hand over the top and pictured the day she had turned up here all those years ago. How had Guy put it? *'All beated up, pregnant and grubby.'* He was right.

Turning back towards the shop, her eye caught the cake in the display window. Dimitri and Anna, she had quite forgotten them. She walked over to where they whirled and skated. Placing her hands against the cold glass, she felt her tears gather. 'I knew it was too good to be true and I told him so. He denied it of course. But deep down I knew: no one can be that perfect, not even you two. But I was so happy. I've never been that happy.'

'And you will be again, chérie.'

She hadn't heard Guy follow her out. He pulled her towards him and gripped her in a hug while she cried.

'Of course, you could always jump on a plane to Barbados. Maybe that would make you feel better, a week in the sun?'

Meg shook her head against his chest. 'No, I thought about it, but I don't want to tell Milly and Pru just yet. I'm going to sit here with my sadness and get it out of my system and when they come back I will have come out the other side. I will never have to mention or hear his name again and we shall have the Christmas we deserve, albeit a little later than billed.'

'That sounds like a plan.' He nodded.

'I'll be fine here, Guy; it's only a week or so. I'm going to work, catch up on paperwork, clean the flat and shut myself away from the world.'

'Or you could come to France with me? Make out to my mother you are my girlfriend, stop her nagging me about settling down and making her a grandmère!' He shrugged his shoulders theatrically, then placed his hand on his hip.

His admission made her laugh, despite her tears. 'Do you think she'd fall for that, Guy?'

'Yes, of course. I can be very masculine when I try!' He pouted. 'Plus mothers only see what they want to see.'

'Ain't that the truth.' Meg thought of the Plaza and Brenda's words, uttered through her scone-filled mouth: *'He's a special man.'*

Special, my arse, thought Meg.

At the end of a long day that had seen her deliver twenty pots of tea, nineteen coffees, thirty assorted cakes and numerous platters of everything from eggs Benedict to croque-monsieur, Meg was shattered. Emotional and physical tiredness seeped from every pore. Her feet throbbed and her back ached. She rubbed at her eyes and pulled her ponytail loose from its band. A hot bath and an early night beckoned and even the thought of her soft pillow and warm duvet was enough to make her smile.

She plodded up the stairs at a snail's pace, hoping she had the energy to reach the top, wondering if she might stop for a nap on the first twist of landing. The doorbell to their apartments rang. She sighed and turned, looking at the four steps she had climbed as though they were a mountain she now had to descend. Then she heard the voices: carol singers. They started singing 'Oh, Come, All Ye Faithful'. It was sweetly sung and achingly beautiful and it rang out down the street. Meg sank down onto the step and started to cry. It was as if the dam had been lifted on a river of distress. Once she started, she couldn't stop.

Fifteen

Meg shifted to get comfortable on the sofa as the pixelated image sharpened on the screen. There they all were, against a backdrop of azure blue. It looked stunning and she felt warmed simply to see them. Their relaxed demeanour, makeup-free smiles and sun-kissed shoulders told her they were in full Caribbean mode. Pru held an ice-filled glass of something sparkling in her hand. Clad in a vibrant hot pink sarong, she looked beautiful, stylish as ever. Even Christopher had made a concession to the weather and was wearing a polo shirt with the collar open! Milly was in a T-shirt, but with a pirate eye patch nestling on her forehead and a bandana over her hair; clearly there was no let-up in the great pirate adventure that she and Lucas had embarked upon a while ago. And at the front of the group, with a toothy grin and an enlarged hand waving very close to the camera, was Lucas. He had caught the sun already; freckles peppered his nose.

'Hey!' Meg swallowed the lump in her throat. 'Look at you all! Hey, Lucas! It's so good to see you, little man.'

'Look what I've got!' He held a bucket up in front of the laptop camera and tipped it to reveal an impressive array of shells.

'Wow! They look awesome. Are you having a great time?'

Lucas nodded. 'I went on a water slide that was higher than our roof!' He stretched up as far as he could with his arm. 'And I did it twice and Christopher nearly got stuck and I went on a boat and I caught a fish and I was going to bring it home to live with Thomas but it died and we threw it back in the sea. But I'm going to try and get another one today if I go on the boat.'

'Oh my goodness, you've been so busy. The water slide sounds a bit scary, but amazing.' *It all sounds amazing and I am here without you, and it's my own stupid, stupid fault.* 'Are you looking after Milly and Pru for me?' She smiled.

Again Lucas nodded enthusiastically.

'Well, that's good. I miss you, Lucas, and I can't wait to see you and hear all about your adventures.' She tried to keep the quiver from her voice.

Lucas took a deep breath. 'Tomorrow I am going to a waterfall and then we are going to have a day by the swimming pool because Christopher is knackered.'

Meg roared with laughter at hearing the word so clearly uttered. She could imagine Christopher using it all too regularly as he was dragged from one adventure to another.

'I'm fine really.' Christopher coughed. 'The little chap's having a ball.'

'I can see that, Chris, and how kind of you to try and bring more pets home! That's just what we could do with – a great big fish to live with Thomas the terrapin!' She gave a double thumbs-up.

Lucas disappeared from view as Milly leant closer to the microphone. 'Shouldn't worry, love, they don't last five minutes. Lucas has caught two, but then he takes them out of the water to check on them, have a little chat with them – boy to fish, that kind of thing – and surprise, surprise, they aren't too fond of it!' She grimaced.

'How's New York?' Pru asked.

Meg sat forward so her face filled the screen and obscured the background. She smiled. 'I'm fine! Yes, fine.' It wasn't exactly a lie, more an evasion of the facts. She didn't want to spoil their holiday or cause them to worry. Lying through omission...

'Did you get to the launch party at Bleecker Street? Or were you otherwise occupied?' Milly smiled.

'No, I went, of course, and it was great.' She was happy to give the details: she had been there, no lie this time. 'Juno and the team have done a really good job. The café looks incredible and it was packed to the gunnels. There was a decent turn-out from journalists and the local press and I heard nothing but good things. The patisserie went down a storm.' *I heard good things, apart from what came out of Edd's mouth: an honest account of his life with his girlfriend that ripped me in two, leaving me stunned, shattered.* 'I have the review from *The Villager*, would you like me to read it to you?' she asked.

'Ooh, yes, read away!' Milly and Pru drew themselves even nearer to the screen so they could hear better.

Meg held the article that she had printed

off from Juno's email and coughed to clear her throat. '"Make a stop at Plum Patisserie, our very own slice of Paris in New York! Sumptuous, moist, mouthwatering patisserie and authentic artisan loaves are served by smiling, knowledgeable staff that sure know a thing or two about baking. And with the Bleecker Street breakfast special of two giant croissants, a flat white coffee and pots of confiture d'abricots and organic honey for dipping, why wouldn't you make it part of your morning routine? I know I will be. Five stars."'

'Oh, that's wonderful!' Pru exhaled. 'Well done, you. And well done, Juno!'

'Yes, brilliant,' Milly added.

Christopher beamed in the background.

'Have you heard from Guy?' Pru enquired as she sipped her drink.

'Yes, today. He's on good form. I think they've been quite busy, but he's great, gearing up to go home for Christmas.' She nodded.

Milly glanced left and right. 'It doesn't look like Lucas is coming back to the camera.'

'That's okay,' she lied. 'Just tell him I love him and thank you all!'

'We'll say bye-bye, poppet. And tell Juno and everyone a massive well done!' Pru enthused.

'Will do. Bye, everyone. Speak soon!' Meg blew a kiss to the camera and received two in return and a brisk wave from Christopher.

A chorus of 'God bless!' could be heard as she clicked and they disappeared into the ether.

Meg sat and stared at the blank screen. The silence filled the room and wrapped her in a veil of loneliness. Lumbering from the sofa, she decided to seek solace in her bed.

It was to be a restless night: not being straight with Pru and Milly felt alien to her. She woke several times, imagining that Lucas might be calling her. Stumbling into the darkness to find the flat empty and noiseless did little to ease her disquiet.

She woke early, which gave her plenty of time for a long shower and a large, restorative cup of strong coffee. After tying a clean apron around her waist, Meg went downstairs, planning to respond to a few emails and make her weekly calls to the branches. It was her responsibility to check all was well at this very busy time of year. Then she would be ready for another day of running up and down between kitchen and café, numbing her brain until she could fall into bed.

'Hello, Plum Patisserie Cheltenham. Can I help you?' The voice was chirpy.

'Linda?'

'Uh-huh. Is that you, Meg?'

'The very same. How's everything?'

The shop in Cheltenham had been open

for six months and was a roaring success. This was in no small part down to Linda, who as a keen amateur baker had turned up for a job in the kitchen and had been shocked to be asked to run the place. Milly and Pru loved her passion and eye for detail and had instinctively felt that she was the right person to head up the team. Her skill in baking and wonderful motherly nature soon proved them right.

'Everything's great! At least I think it is. I'm so busy I haven't had time to look too deeply. I knew things would ramp up over Christmas but I had no idea we'd be this popular. My boys are disappointed on a daily basis, no "spare" cakes to bring home; we're cleared out by closing time. How's your little one? Getting excited, I bet.'

'Yes, he's good.' *Excited about fish and boats and shells and not with me right now, and I miss him very much…*

'I saw that New York opened. How was it? Did you go over?'

Without warning, Meg drew breath and began to cry. She'd kept her tears at bay since waking, but this was an outpouring that she couldn't control, triggered by the smallest of things, the mention of the city where her heart had been broken.

'Oh, Meg! Are you okay? What's wrong?'

Meg gripped the phone with both hands. 'I'm sorry, Linda, I think I'm just tired. I'll call you back.' She replaced the receiver and sat with her head in her hands until her distress had exhausted itself.

The day passed quickly. As Linda had noted, things were so busy that there was no time to think about anything too deeply. This suited Meg fine; she was simply getting through the days until Lucas returned and they could have 'Christmas' together.

The weather had warmed slightly, the wind had dropped and it was one of those beautiful winter days on which you could get away with wearing sunglasses. Customers in coats and hats had occupied the outside tables for most of the day, sipping hot drinks with faces lit by the last rays of the December sun. The heavier puddings and pies were selling less well; instead, people were ordering crumbly shortcrust tartlets filled with layers of fresh strawberries and crème pâtissière, served with a generous dollop of Chantilly cream. This was always a sign that the sun was out.

Guy was fussing. He was flying to France for the festive season in just two days and as usual was starting to panic about leaving Plum Patisserie without his hand on the tiller. The bakery closed on the twenty-third of December, meaning they would have to cope for a whole forty-eight hours without him. Meg assured him they would be fine, but he wasn't convinced. He spent much of the morning writing copious messages on post-it notes and sticking them on people's telephones, computer screens and work stations. He even stuck one on her forehead that read, 'Be happy!' She wished it was that simple.

Hovering on the stairs, Meg re-did her ponytail, which had worked loose. She sat on the step, taking a breather, and gave a long, slow yawn. She rather liked this dark little space, it reminded her of when she was young and she would take refuge from life's ills by sitting in the bottom of a cupboard.

Guy was checking the little drawers in the counter for till rolls and order pads. He didn't want them to run out during the couple of days that he was away, even though that was extremely unlikely.

The little brass bell above the door rang and in walked a woman laden with shopping bags and puffing loudly with effort, as though the Plum Patisserie café was actually at Everest base camp and not in a quiet, flat corner of Curzon Street. She sported a slick of bright orange lipstick on her thin, puckered lips and a band of bright blue eye shadow sat on her crêpey lids. Her blonde shoulder-length hair was wild, slightly matted at the back and looked like it needed a good dollop of conditioner and the attention of a hairbrush. She was in her late forties and was wearing a leather miniskirt and matching leather jacket, black cowboy boots and tights, but no coat, scarf, jersey or anything that looked substantial enough for December, however sunny the day.

'Good afternoon!' Guy greeted her.

The woman gave a brief nod in his direction, eyeing him suspiciously, and slumped down into a chair, spreading her plastic bags around her seat, making it nearly impossible for anyone to pass via the gap between the tables.

Guy said nothing; it was a quiet spell and the woman would probably be on her way before the place got busy again. He walked over to her. 'What can I get for you today?' he asked with his biggest smile. His mantra was that everyone should be made to feel comfortable.

'Well, how should I know? I haven't seen a menu yet! Give me a minute.' She rolled her eyes.

'Yes, of course,' Guy said. 'Today's patisserie menu is up on the wall.' He used his pen to indicate the blackboard behind the counter. 'I'll pop back in a sec.'

'No, don't bother, I only want a cup of coffee.'

'Certainly. And which coffee would you like? We have a list here.' Again he used his pen as a pointer.

The woman squinted at the list of coffees that started with French roast breakfast blend and ended with decaffeinated frappé.

She turned to Guy, who stood with his pen poised. 'Two pound eighty for a bloody coffee? Are you having a laugh? I can buy a jar of coffee for that! Who in their right mind would pay that for one cup of bleedin' coffee?'

'It's very good coffee.' Guy smiled.

'Very good? I'd want it to do the ironing as well for that price!' The woman sucked at her teeth.

'Did you want to leave it then, madam?' Guy kept the smile on his face, trying to remain as polite as possible.

'No, I'll take one. A normal coffee with milk and two sugars.'

'Coming right up!' Guy gave a slight bow and turned to head for the kitchen.

'And while you're at it...' she called to him.

'Yes?' Guy looked at the lady from over his shoulder.

'I'd like a word with the owner, Plum whatshername, the big boss.' She clasped her hands on the table. The sleeves of her jacket made a sticky noise as they stuck to the surface.

Guy walked back over. 'I'm afraid Madam Plum is not available today. I am the manager here and am happy to assist in any way, Ms Plum's assistant is also here, Miss Hope.'

The woman looked at Guy through narrowed eyes. 'Miss Hope, eh? Yep, get her, she'll do.' She laughed.

Guy skipped down to the office, not liking this woman one little bit. He came across Meg sitting on the stairs.

'Meg, there's a lady upstairs wants a word with you. She's a bit off, was moaning about the price of the coffee. She wanted to talk to Pru. I told her the two of us were here and she has asked for you specifically. Lucky you.'

Meg sighed. 'No rest for the wicked, isn't that what they say? I reckon I must have done something really bad in a former life because I've been pretty good in this one.' *Apart from sleeping with Flavia's boyfriend...* She dismissed the thought, rose and dusted off her skirt.

She approached the table, trying to adopt an expression that was both welcoming and confident, the look of someone who would not be intimidated, even though her insides churned a little. If someone wanted to speak to the management team it was usually either to heap praise or register a petty complaint; by the look of the back of the woman slouched at the table, Meg doubted it was praise.

'Hello there, I'm Meg. I believe you wanted to see me?'

The customer turned and looked her up and down. It was a full second before she spoke and another full second before Meg recognised her as the woman she had waited for on more cold nights than she cared to remember. Meg felt her bowel spasm and her mouth open. Her knees weakened and her stomach flipped as she steadied herself on the back of a chair. She had aged, of course – ten years was bound to have taken its toll. She looked like someone to whom life had been less than kind, but the slanted smile, the deep furrows from mouth to nose and the pale blue eyes were all the same.

'Hello, Meggy. Well, don't you scrub up nice.' Her smile was fixed.

'Mum! I ... I don't believe it!' Her voice was forced and quiet as the breath failed in her throat. It was a shock.

Lorna Hope drummed her fingers on the tabletop. 'I don't believe it either – two pound eighty for a cup of bloody coffee? You're having a laugh! No wonder you're based in Mayfair, it's daylight bloody robbery.'

Meg beamed and chuckled, remembering her mum's sour view on life and feeling a wave of nostalgia wash over her. Lorna smiled too, happy she could still make her daughter laugh. She took it as a positive sign, that all was forgiven. Meg shook her head; it was typical of Lorna: no running through the doors with arms wide, no practised apology with watery eyes, just the trademark blunt delivery and almost aggressive humour. She had to admit that anything else would have unnerved her even more.

'I've missed you, Meggy.' Lorna addressed her fingers, which tapped the table. It was a phrase offered casually, as if it had been weeks not years since they had last seen each other.

'I've missed you,' Meg confessed. No matter how much hurt she had suffered because of Lorna's indifference and inability to cope, Lorna was still her mum.

Meg opened the front door and ushered her mother into the hallway.

'Come in, come in!' She tried to put Lorna at her ease, remembering how intimidated she'd felt stepping into such grand surroundings for the first time, four years earlier. 'Where are you living now?' she asked, sounding like a stranger making small talk. It saddened her.

'I was up at Crystal Palace, with my partner Don – well, ex-partner now.' Lorna raised her eyebrows. 'And before that we were in north Wales, in the middle of bloody nowhere, but I hated it, all that fresh air, fields and mountains...'

'Yeah, sounds horrible.' Meg smiled. She couldn't imagine her mum anywhere but in a city.

'You know what I mean.' Lorna lifted her head and turned three hundred and sixty degrees, her eyes wide. 'Nice place you've got, you must sell quite a few buns. Mind you, if they're as expensive as your coffee, I guess you wouldn't have to sell that many.'

'This way.' Meg ignored the comments and gestured towards the stairs.

'Think I'll leave my stuff down here.' Lorna dumped her many bags and her one holdall against the wall before following her daughter up.

Meg closed her eyes as she stepped ahead, feeling a strange mixture of elation and nerves. It was wonderful to be showing Lorna how she lived, but she was slightly embarrassed by the luxuriousness of her surroundings, proof of what a privileged life she now led. She had a sudden vision of the lounge in her childhood home, with its ill-fitting curtains held together by pegs.

She pushed open the door to her flat. 'Come in, come in!' She was excited by her mum's presence, a stranger in so many ways.

'Well this is *very* nice. I'd say you've fallen on your feet here, girl.' Lorna scanned the pale marble floor, the muted tones of the walls and the spacious square hallway with its console table and oversized mirror.

Meg nodded. She had. And not one day went past when she didn't reflect on her very good fortune to have found love, warmth and security with Milly and Pru.

'You look tired,' Meg observed. It was true; Lorna had two large dark circles beneath her eyes.

'Charming! Tired? Is that the welcome I get after not seeing you for God knows how long?' Her sharp response suggested she was entirely free of blame for the lack of contact. Meg tried to imagine a situation where she would think it okay not to contact Lucas or even Milly or Pru for months or years. She couldn't.

Lorna wasn't finished. 'I've schlepped all over town trying to find you.' Her tone was almost scolding as she stepped forward and grabbed her daughter in an elaborate hug.

Meg inhaled her scent of cigarettes and musk, a familiar fragrance that was repellent and intoxicating in equal parts. It was the smell she had tried to recollect on many a night as a child, stranded in an unfamiliar bedroom, her toes tucked into the hem of her nightdress as she watched strange shapes loom like monsters in the corners.

She looked anxiously over her shoulder into the hall mirror, feeling ill at ease. It had been a long time since her mum had touched her and she'd certainly never greeted her in this most exuberant way. She bit her lip, swallowing the questions that nagged. *Schlepped all over town? Blimey! It's been nearly ten years since I saw you last; just how hard were you looking?* Instead, she chose to say nothing. Why spoil this lovely reunion?

'How *did* you find me?' Meg cringed as soon as the words left her mouth; it sounded as if she had been hiding. She was, however, curious, having lost contact with Lorna after her last move. Unaware that her mum had relocated, she had travelled to Hackney and stood face to face with a Polish man and his wife who shook their heads, no they didn't know Mrs Hope and no, they definitely didn't know where she was living now. If they did, they would have told the gas, electricity and cable companies, who were all keen to have their accounts settled.

'Our Liam told me. I went to his flat. Shit-hole, isn't it?'

Meg thought about her cousin Liam's flat. It was grim, true, but had provided her with a roof over her head when she had needed it most.

'He's a shifty little bastard, that one,' Lorna continued. 'He said you'd got yourself some fancy new friends.' She waved her hand in the air as if proving the point.

Meg's cheeks flushed scarlet. Liam was sweet and kind and he loved her. Despite his rough exterior, he would walk over hot coals for Lucas and that was all that mattered. She knew that any 'shiftiness' in his demeanour would have been due to suspicion at Lorna suddenly appearing after all these years.

'You look nice and skinny. *I* was always like that, mind.' She rubbed her hand over the generous stomach that sat above her thin legs, giving her an almost barrel-like appearance. 'I had you and was in my jeans by the next day, out clubbing the day after that!'

Out clubbing when I was only two days old – I believe you. Meg shook her head to erase the image; her mum had found her and this was to be celebrated. No point trawling through the past, what would that serve?

'Where's the boy?' Lorna had never met her grandson, but had been informed of his birth via a text message to which she hadn't responded. Meg knew that Liam's mother had bumped into Lorna in Wembley and had shown her one slightly out of focus photograph taken on her son's phone.

'He's in Barbados.' Meg spoke without a filter, then realised how surreal that probably sounded to her mum. To her knowledge, Lorna had never left the UK and holidays were almost unheard of. It was yet another jolt of realisation that the world she now inhabited was very different from the one into which she had been born.

'Barbloodybados? Well I never. What's he doing there? Who's he gone with, his mates?'

Meg laughed again; another refreshing reminder of just how funny her mum could be. 'No, although at the rate he grows and the way the years fly past, it won't be long until he does.' Again she worried that this might be seen as a veiled dig at her mum's absence.

Maybe it was. She wished she could relax and wasn't so guarded.

'When's he back then?' Lorna asked.

'In about ten days' time. He's there with Milly and Pru, who I work for and live with, obviously.'

'Blimey, that's all a bit cosy, isn't it?' Lorna seemed to be insinuating something.

'Well, it just works. They are lovely to me and always have been. It was tough when Lucas's dad died.' She let this hang in the air.

Lorna chose not to pursue it. 'It's a nice name, isn't it, Lucas?'

'Yes. I love it.'

Meg walked over to the console table and picked up a silver-framed photo of Lucas. He was on his red truck and had his thumb in his mouth as he looked up into the lens. It was one of her favourite photos of him. She handed it to his nan.

Lorna studied it briefly. 'Don't know who he looks like, not our lot that's for sure.' Lorna placed the photo back in its place, running her finger over the frame.

Meg smiled and thought of Isabel, who fixed on even the remotest family resemblance in her grandson. According to her, Lucas had William's eyes, her father's nose, her brother's smile... And yet Lorna could see none of her genes in Lucas.

'He's beautiful, isn't he?' Meg beamed. No

matter what their history, she, like any other girl, wanted her mum's approval, wanted to show off her greatest achievement.

'They're all beautiful until they grow up and start giving you lip.' Lorna sniffed. It wasn't quite the response Meg had hoped for.

'Come through, Mum, and I'll make us a cup of coffee.' Meg led her mum down the hall.

'Gawd blimey! Look at this! It's like a mini Downton Abbey, isn't it?' Lorna was clearly taken with the grand sitting room. She walking over to peer through the floor-to-ceiling Georgian windows, just visible behind their heavy drapes.

Meg shrugged. 'It is lovely to see you, Mum. A bit strange after all this time, but lovely.'

'It is, love,' Lorna confirmed as she reached into her bag for her cigarettes.

Meg opened her mouth to protest as Lorna pulled at the French doors that led on to the Juliet balcony. This, Meg knew, would make little difference, but it felt churlish to request that her mum didn't smoke. After all, she was her mother and instructions and reprimands usually flowed in the other direction. Plus she didn't want to make her feel any more uncomfortable than she already might be.

Meg balanced the tray as she walked back

into the sitting room. Lorna was still smoking her cigarette by the open balcony door; the smoke blew back in and circulated around the room, filling the space with its toxic fumes. Meg's nose twitched.

'It's funny, isn't it, you think you know a city and then you're shown a different view, a different postcode and it's like a whole other world. I think if I lived here, I'd sit and watch the world going by below me, all them people with their fancy handbags and posh haircuts. I bet they've never had to struggle. How is it that some of us struggle our whole lives and others don't? That's weird, isn't it?' Lorna turned to look at her daughter as she took a long, deep drag on her dwindling fag, before turning her head to the window and blowing the smoke out. She flicked the butt from the pad of her thumb with her forefinger. Meg gasped, praying it didn't land on some unsuspecting passer-by, especially not a Plum Patisserie customer. The seconds of silence told her Lorna had probably got away with it. Her heart skipped a beat nonetheless.

Placing the tray on the coffee table, Meg twisted her hands together. 'How long are you here for, Mum?' She felt oddly nervous around her mum and struggled with what to say next, which made their conversation a little stilted.

'What, you trying to get rid of me already? I've only just taken me shoes off!' Lorna gave a wheezing giggle that turned almost immediately into a cough.

'No!' *The exact opposite. I'm wondering how long I've got you for. Who knows when I'll see you again?* If *I'll see you again.* 'I was just thinking about what to get for us to eat tonight and stuff. That is, if you've got time. If not, then that's okay too, but it would be really nice.' Meg recognised the neediness in her tone.

Lorna smiled. 'You was always a good eater. I remember when you were little, you'd eat anything I put in front of you. Not like Jason or Mel.'

Meg winced at the mention of her older siblings, the ones who got to stay while she had to go. She could only picture them as surly teenagers; ghost-like figures whose names were engraved in her memory but whose substance and characters were missing.

'They were fussy little bastards. I spoilt them.' Lorna nodded.

Meg looked at her mum and wondered if she had ever actually indulged any of them. She was not able to remember a single example. She pictured Lucas, who knew only the exact opposite.

'Do you ever see them, or Robbie or Janey?' Deep down, Meg hoped the answer was no, that she wasn't the only one who'd been cut out of her mum's life. But then she felt bad for wishing her same sad situation on her siblings.

'Nah, all grown up, living their own lives. I think Mel's up north somewhere, Yorkshire or something like that, I don't know. If I have to go north of the Watford Gap I get a bit jittery.' Lorna made it sound like this was the norm, as though her children were like chickens that had flown the coop or bears that after the first hibernation were set free to roam and fend for themselves.

Meg thought of her brothers and sisters scattered across the UK and beyond and wondered how many nieces, nephews, brothers- and sisters-in-law she had never met, how many cousins and family celebrations Lucas would be denied. They were a family fragmented like a broken mirror and just as dysfunctional. It made her sad that even if it were possible to glue all the pieces back together, the whole would still be riven with blemishes, cracked and useless.

'Yeah, I'll stay for tea if ya like, that'd be lovely.' Lorna took up a seat on the sofa and picked up her mug of coffee. 'Is this free or are you going to charge me an arm and a leg? Just that I'm skint, might only be able to afford half a cup.' She winked. 'I'm not stopping you working, am I, love?'

'No. I pretty much work every day, through choice, not because I have to. It's easy to catch up on emails when Lucas is playing and I go down into the café when he's at nursery. So when I take a few hours or a day to myself, no one minds.'

'That mincey gay bloke said you was Miss Plum's assistant, is that right?'

Lorna's summary of Guy hit Meg in the face as surely as any sting from a raised hand. 'Guy's one of my best friends,' she retorted. 'And Lucas's.'

Lorna seemed indifferent. 'Yeah, him. Is that right then? You're her assistant?'

Meg nodded. 'Yes. I'm still learning the business, but I'm like the eyes and ears of Pru and Milly.'

'What, like a grass?' Lorna gulped her coffee.

Meg snorted her laughter. 'Yes, Mum, I'm a grass.' She giggled again, thinking of all the patis-serie training, the hours spent watching, reading and learning everything she needed in order to try and step into Pru's shoes.

'Do you earn a lot of money?' What might be a taboo subject in other families was to them quite ordinary. They both recalled counting coins into palms to cover the cost of a pint of milk, and searching down the back of the sofa to try and gather enough for a bus fare.

'Yes, I suppose I do. It feels good to know that I can provide Lucas with a great future. If he wants to go to university or travel, then he can. To give him that freedom... That's all I want really.'

Lorna yawned. 'University, eh? Blimey. Well, it's good to know all them afternoons with Uncle Frank paid off – he was your dad's brother, he was a grass too.' Lorna tucked her leg underneath her bottom, making herself comfortable.

'I don't really remember him,' Meg confessed.

'No, you wouldn't. He went inside when you were quite young, been in and out ever since, so I hear.'

Meg smiled as she imagined how Isabel would take this news.

With each hour that passed, the two relaxed into each other's company. Having polished off a large bowl of shepherd's pie, peas and carrots, washed down with a bottle of plonk, they were slumped on the sofa. The Christmas lights of Curzon Street sparkled beyond the window and a small lamp lit the room from inside. The soft half-glow made it easier to talk with honesty. Meg, like her mum, had kicked off her shoes and they now sat facing each other.

'...So that was that.' Meg let her palm fall into her lap. 'I came back to London and have been ignoring his texts and missed calls. I can't believe I fell for it, but I did, hook line and sinker. He was lovely, nice-looking, kind, successful. The full package. Or so I thought.'

'You're probably better off. I don't trust Americans.' Lorna pursed her lips and narrowed her eyes.

'Do you know any?' Meg was curious.

'Yes, loads, of course I do! There's that OJ Simpson – didn't he bump off his wife and then get away with it? And what about *Breaking Bad*? That's how they actually live; making drugs and living in a trailer.'

Meg smiled. It wasn't quite what she had meant by 'know'.

'Nah, America's no good. You're better off, love. They're all either God-botherers like Tom Cruise or they've got guns, shooting each other every five minutes and eating nothing but doughnuts. And don't get me started on *Jersey Shore*. I've seen it, whole place looks like shite.' Lorna shook her head in distaste.

Meg didn't bother to try and put her right. Her mum was correct about one thing: she was better off without Edd, no matter how much it hurt to admit that. A liar in her life was one complication she didn't need. Her tummy tightened as she recalled Flavia's voice on the intercom: *'Edd's girlfriend. And you are…?'*

Meg glanced at her watch. It was nearly seven o'clock. 'Do you have to head off soon, Mum? Or shall I open another bottle?'

'I don't have to be anywhere, love. You

open another bottle,' she said graciously.

Meg jumped from the sofa and bounded into the kitchen, feeling a rush of love for this woman who had given birth to her and was in no hurry to disappear, not this time.

The wine loosened Meg's tongue and gave her confidence. 'I'm happy you are here.'

Lorna raised her glass. 'Yep, me too.' Her head lolled a little against her chest.

'It's especially lovely because it's Christmas!'

'It is. It is.'

'It was never the best time of year for me when I was growing up,' Meg admitted. Then swiftly she added, 'But not because we didn't have any presents.'

'Didn't have any money for bloody presents!' Lorna's interruption was sharp.

'No, I know, and as I said, it wasn't about that, not for me. It was more the expectation of what Christmas *should* be and the fact that it was always a bit disappointing.'

'Welcome to my life. That about sums it up – a bit disappointing.' Lorna laughed once.

Meg looked at her mum, checking it was okay to proceed. Lorna was listening calmly. 'I think I had an idea of what it should be like, the family all together.' Meg paused, this was hard to talk about. 'I guess being away from you at that time of year was harder than any other. Every advert and picture I saw told me I should be at home with you, waiting for a cake that you'd popped in the oven, or decorating the tree–'

'You'd have had a bloody long wait! Don't think we ever had a tree and me and cake baking don't exactly go together. Any rate, you've more than filled that gap – you live in a sodding bakery!' Lorna wheezed her laughter.

Meg nodded. This was true. 'What are your plans for the next week or so?'

'Plans?' Lorna laughed. 'Blimey, girl, who makes plans? Not me.' She sniffed. 'Truth is, I'm going through a bit of a rough patch, Meggy. I wasn't going to mention, not with us having such a lovely time, but as I said, me and Don have split up. My fault, but what can you do? You can't turn the clock back, can you?'

'No, you can't.' *Although I often wish I could. Back to before I agreed to go to New York, back to before Bill died and back to before you put me into care.*

'He's chucked me out, bastard.' She reached for another cigarette. 'Takes the word of some bloke in the pub over me!' Lorna jabbed at her chest. 'Mind you, the bloke wasn't lying. But even so.' She gave a wry laugh.

Meg leant forward and placed her hand on Lorna's arm. 'You can stay for as long as you need to, Mum. We can have Christmas together, just the two of us. Would you like that?'

There was a pause before she responded and Meg held her breath. *Would she like that?*

'I'd like that more than anything, love.'

'We can just stay at home. I'll cook a lovely turkey and we can eat it on our laps and watch rubbish on the telly.' Meg couldn't help thinking that her Christmas had been salvaged.

'That sounds perfect, just what the doctor ordered.' Lorna smiled.

Meg beamed back. It did sound perfect.

Lorna wasn't done. Her words, when they came, though a little slurred were not unconsidered. 'I do sometimes think of all them Christmas days with you lot spread to the four winds. Didn't know where you all were. I used to just go back to bed and sleep till it was all over. I struggled back then, Meggy. I had a lot of demons.'

Meg nodded, she understood. And the wonderful thing was that it wasn't too late to forgive and forget.

'I get it, Mum. And I think about it a lot, especially at this time of the year. It can't have been easy for you.'

'It wasn't,' Lorna confirmed, reaching into her bag for her lighter.

Meg wriggled on the sofa to get comfy. 'I remember me and Liam going through the catalogue one year. I don't know how old we were, but we were little. We sat in our pyjamas and went through every section, picking out all the toys and things we wanted Santa to bring us. We made a list with little descriptions. Pages and pages of it.' She smiled at the memory of the two of them meticulously copying the reference numbers and chosen colours with a stubby pencil gripped between their fingers. 'We both knew we weren't going to get any of it, but it was brilliant to pretend. I kept that list under my pillow for a long while and every night I read it before I fell asleep.' She recalled packing the list into her carrier bag along with her clean pyjamas. 'By the time Christmas came, I didn't need any of the stuff on that list because I'd played with it all in my head for hours and hours. It's funny, isn't it, the things you remember?'

Lorna nodded as she sipped her wine.

Meg looked at her own glass and swilled the contents from side to side. 'I used to wait for you to come and get me and take me to the seaside.' She felt her cheeks flush at this very private confession.

'The seaside? Why the bloody hell the seaside?' Lorna laughed.

Meg shrugged. 'Don't know, really. I thought we'd have a lovely day out, just the two of us.' She twisted the stem between her fingers.

'As you said, Meggy, it's never too late. We

could go to the seaside if ya like?' Lorna sat forward and sparked the flint, then puffed blue-tinged smoke into the atmosphere.

'Could we?' Meg was conscious of how eager she was, her eyes wide and her muscles tense.

'Yeah!' Lorna waved her cigarette in the air. 'We can do anything we want, we're free spirits, right? No bloody Don or bloody Yank telling us what we can or can't do.'

Meg nodded. Maybe things did happen for a reason, maybe this was why she was here alone on December the nineteenth; it was fate's way of placing her at home, ready to receive her mum, ready to make things good. 'When shall we go?' She was as excited as her six-year-old self, but without the flip-flops under the bed.

Lorna considered this. 'How about Boxing Day or the day after? Depends on the trains.' She drew on her cigarette. 'We can go to Southend, walk along the pier, go and have a nice fry-up in a café. A proper café, mind, where a bacon sarnie costs less than one of your fancy cups of coffee!'

'We could go to the cinema and get popcorn!' Meg gushed. This was another activity on her wish list of things to do with her mum.

'The cinema it is. The cinema in Southend, we'll make a right old day of it.' Lorna nodded, drowsily.

Meg laughed, loudly and without restraint. She was happy. She was finally going to the seaside with her mum. 'I love you, Mum.' It took every ounce of her courage to say the words out loud. Looking up, Meg smiled at Lorna, who, with her head tilted back against the cushions and mouth open, slumbered like a baby. She removed the smouldering cigarette from between her mum's fingers and stubbed it out in the water glass, along with the others.

Sixteen

Meg woke the next morning with a headache throbbing behind her temples. She wandered into the kitchen and ran a long glass of water. Lorna was already on the sofa, scrolling through the channels and enjoying her second or third cigarette of the day, if the additional stubs in her empty glass were anything to go by. The smell of lingering tobacco smoke made Meg retch. Despite the chill of the December morning, she walked over to the balcony doors and opened them a crack, mindful today more than ever that this was Milly and Pru's flat. Although she knew the flat was hers for her lifetime – yet more proof of just how loved she was by the Plum cousins – she still didn't want anyone, including her own mother, not appreciating it.

'Blimey, what are we, bloody penguins? It's freezing with that door open!' Lorna balanced the cigarette on her bottom lip and squinted to avoid the smoke as she thrust her arms into a cardigan she'd found in the spare-room wardrobe.

'I just thought some fresh air in here might be nice.' Meg bent to retrieve the glasses and empty wine bottles that littered the table from the previous evening. Her headache intensified a notch as she handled the bottles; the sharp crack of glass against glass a reminder of how much they had drunk.

'Fresh air is what you want in the summer, not in the bloody middle of winter.' Lorna feigned a shiver.

'Did you sleep all right?' Meg was already mentally locating extra blankets in case her mum had been too cold in the night.

'Who wouldn't in a room like that?' Lorna laughed. 'It's the flashiest place I've ever slept, Meggy. I opened a cupboard door and walked into a bloody marble bathroom! How the other half live, eh?' She drew on her cigarette. 'I felt like Kim Kardashian.'

Meg laughed, thinking how Pru would wince at her interiors being compared to theirs.

'So, I was thinking, if we're going to have our little Christmas here, just the two of us, why don't we jazz the place up a bit? It needs a bit of Christmasifying, don't you think?'

Meg looked at the luxurious furnishings and heavy drapes. Lorna was right; it could be any time of the year, there was certainly nothing to suggest it was Christmas. She thought of Elene and Salvatore, who had made the effort with their rather gaudy tree in the reception of the Inn on 11th. Her heart twisted at the memory of Edd; how she had arrived at her rented room with him in tow and the night they had spent, a blissful night, skin to skin under the counterpane. She never had found out what his most treasured thing was after his baseball shirt and his dad's badge. Not that it mattered, not now.

'Yes, let's do it! I was going to get a tree and bits and bobs for when Lucas gets home, but you're right, we should do it now.'

'Tell you what, love. You have your shower and wake up a bit and I'll go out, get us a tree and pick up a nice breakfast, what do you say?' Lorna stood and Meg noticed for the first time that she was fully dressed.

'Oh, okay!' This was new to her; the mum of her childhood had never taken control, been proactive or considered the purchase of a 'nice breakfast'. She rather liked it. She liked it a lot; it was proof that people could change.

Lorna rifled in her bag and turned to her daughter. 'Couldn't lend us a few quid, could you, Meggy? Don owes me some money, said he'd settle up when he got some cash from his daughter who owes him, but I'm a bit strapped till then.' She looked her daughter in the eye.

'Yes of course. Tell you what, take my card. I want to pay for the tree; it's Lucas's tree after all.' She tore a corner from an envelope on the mantelpiece and wrote the PIN number on it. 'Here you go.'

Lorna placed them into her purse. 'What shall I get us? What do you fancy to eat?'

'Oh, anything. Bacon, eggs, I don't really mind. I definitely need something to soak up all that wine! You can always see if there is anything you fancy in the bakery downstairs – we *are* the best in London!'

'They've got you brainwashed, my girl. Mind you, I reckon I wouldn't mind a bit of brainwashing if it got me a bedroom like that.' Lorna jerked her head in the direction of the spare room.

Meg's phone buzzed. She gathered it to her chest and swiped the screen, erasing Edd's latest text with the brush of a fingertip.

'I'll be off then.' Lorna buttoned up the cardigan.

'Don't get lost!'

'Cheek! I know this city better than most and if I do get lost, I've always got a tongue in my head to ask directions. You always were a worrier, Meggy.'

I wonder why. Meg smiled.

Two hours later and Meg was pacing the sitting room, wondering where her mum had got to. She trod the stairs, and walked into the bakery via the side door from the hallway. She heard Lorna's voice before she saw her.

'So you might want to watch your tone, matey. My daughter is practically the boss around here, after all.'

Meg darted forward to see Guy behind the counter, looking both mortified and furious.

'Mum!' she yelped. Embarrassment bent her double. Guy – her friend, her mentor and the biggest asset that Plum Patisserie had – deserved to be spoken to in any way other than this.

'Oh hello, love. Was just trying to get hold of some cakes and he was trying to make me pay for them!'

'I ... I...' Guy stuttered, speechless. It was never an issue; Meg could help herself to any baked goods she wanted and bar the odd croissant with her morning coffee or grabbing a loaf at the end of the day for

Lucas, she never took advantage.

'Meg, I...' Guy tried again, looking from Lorna to his friend standing in front of him.

She rushed forward and placed her hand on his arm. 'I'm sorry, Guy. It's my fault. I told Mum to pop down and take what she needed. I should have come with her. She is going through a bit of a rough patch, she's upset – aren't you, Mum?'

'Not so upset that I don't know when someone is giving me a load of old flannel!' She scowled. 'I'll wait outside. Think I need a fag.' Lorna gathered up the two shopping bags from beside her feet and gave Guy a withering look as she stomped out of the bakery.

'Have you always apologised for her?' Guy turned to Meg as the door closed behind her mother.

She sighed and looped her hair behind her ears. 'Pretty much.'

'Well, maybe it's time you stopped. She's a grown woman.'

'Yes she is, Guy. A grown woman who happens to be my mum and who I haven't seen for a very, very long time. And I am very glad that she is back in my life, in our lives!' She pictured her mum and Lucas strolling in the park, catching up on lost time.

Guy sighed and placed one hand on his hip; with the other he swept his brow. 'I understand. But I didn't know what to say to her, Meg...' He avoided her gaze.

'Well, no harm done. We only wanted a bit of breakfast, although it's nearer lunchtime now!' She laughed, trying to lighten the mood.

'C'était plus que cela...' He rubbed his chin. 'It was a misunderstanding, I'm sure.' He smiled at his friend.

Meg shifted from one foot to the other. 'Thanks. She can be a bit blunt. It's just what she's like. But she's quite harmless.'

Guy gave a tight-lipped smile but didn't doubt for one second that Lorna could cause a lot of harm. 'I'm glad you are having a nice time and it's great that you've had some company – a good distraction, non? Is she leaving today?' He hoped his question didn't sound too loaded.

Meg avoided eye contact. 'No. In fact we are going to spend Christmas here together.'

'Oh.' Guy frowned.

'She and her partner Don have split up and he's chucked her out, so she's a bit stuck.' Meg shrugged, still unable to look her friend in the eye.

'Have you told Milly?' Guy was direct and for the first time ever, Meg felt a flush of anger towards her loyal friend.

'Have I told Milly what?' She was aware her tone was quite sharp.

Guy decided not to press further. He took

a deep breath. 'I'm heading back to France tomorrow.'

'Right.' Meg hesitated. 'I'd rather you didn't tell Milly that I am back or that Lorna is here. I don't want to spoil her break. She'd only fuss or cut the holiday short and I don't want to be responsible for that.'

'No, of course, I won't say a word. Anyway, it's nothing to do with me.' He spoke quickly, echoing her thoughts.

'Thank you, Guy. It's lovely for me, being able to chat to my mum before we go to sleep and then seeing her when I wake up. It's been a long time since I've done that.'

She was obviously excited and Guy felt happy that his friend was reconnecting with her mother. Not that it helped him warm to Lorna. He wasn't surprised one iota that Don, whoever he was, had chucked her out. Guy had only spent a few minutes in her company and that was enough to make him want to do the same. He decided not to tell Meg that Lorna had asked for catering packs of ground coffee beans – six of them! – and had then snapped at him when he'd enquired what they were for. Instead, he held Meg's shoulders and kissed her on both cheeks. 'Happy Christmas, Meg. If I don't see you before I go, you have my number, so call if you need me.'

Meg nodded. 'Happy Christmas, Guy, and don't worry, I'm sure things will run like clockwork. With the holiday in the middle, we are only open a day or so without you.' She patted the counter as though it were a good dog.

Guy nodded and turned his attention to the order book. Meg swallowed the sudden desire to cry, hating even this slightest whiff of discord between them.

Lorna was outside, leaning on the display window. 'There you are! Did you sort him out?'

Meg shook her head. 'There was nothing to sort. Guy is my friend.'

'Yeah, you said that. I don't rate him much. Anyway,' she sniffed, 'I'm not going to let anything or anyone ruin our Christmas!'

'Where's our tree?' Meg looked behind her mum to check it wasn't propped inside the doorway.

'They're delivering it tomorrow. You didn't expect me to lug it home on my back, did you?'

'No, I suppose not, but I thought we might decorate it this afternoon.'

'We've got all the time in the world, love.' Lorna stepped forward and hugged her daughter.

Meg closed her eyes and inhaled the scent of her mum, remembering how this one small act could make everything feel better.

'Did you see the cake behind you?' Meg pulled away and turned her mum to face the display window where Dimitri and Anna elegantly swooped and swirled.

'What do you think?' She asked, eagerly.

'How much would a cake like that cost?'

'Oh, if it was for sale, hundreds and hundreds of pounds.'

Lorna tutted. 'What a waste of bloody money.' She shook her head and made her way to the front door.

Seventeen

Meg blinked, opened her eyes and reluctantly unfolded her limbs from the warmth of her duvet. She had overslept for the first time in as long as she could remember. It felt wonderfully decadent. She thought about the previous day's catch-up with Barbados. She had not only made out to Milly and Pru that she was still in New York, but she'd also failed to mention that she had a lodger for the Christmas period. It wasn't that she was keeping it secret exactly, more that she felt it would be easier to explain face to face, knowing that, like Guy, they too might judge Lorna a little harshly.

Meg smiled as she stretched and put on a pair of thick socks, excited about the day ahead. After cleaning her teeth, she crept along the corridor. It had been a second night of too much wine and while her hangover wasn't quite as bad as yesterday's, a headache certainly lingered. She didn't know how her mum did it – perhaps it simply required practice. Meg decided there and then that she and Lorna would only drink tea tonight; they would sit and admire the tree that was arriving today. With her fingers splayed, she clapped her hands in little taps, suddenly animated and as energised as a puppy.

She tiptoed into the kitchen and then the sitting room, not wanting to disturb Lorna. The tang of cigarette smoke clung to the curtains and cushions. Opening the French doors, she let the cold December air fill the room. Pulling the long sleeves of her pyjama top over her hands, she looked down at Curzon Street, where people scurried to and fro on the pavements. It was December the twenty-first, the stage in the month when Christmas shopping was either last minute and random or targeted and brisk.

The breeze from the French doors caused the door of the spare bedroom to slam shut. Meg winced and laughed, knowing that was no way to be woken after a night on the plonk.

Making her way down the hall, she stopped outside Lorna's bedroom and listened at the door. It was very quiet. Meg was sure the door slam would have jolted her mum into action. Slowly turning the handle, she eased the door open an inch and peered inside. The bed was crumpled and empty, the curtains drawn, allowing the mid-morning light to flood the room. Popping her head inside, she looked towards the bathroom door, which was open.

'Mum?'

There was no reply.

Venturing into the room, Meg looked at the drawers that had been pulled open and the pillows, haphazardly flung in a pile on the mattress. It was only as she was leaving the room that she noticed that Lorna's belongings were also missing. There were no bags on the floor, no pyjamas on the door hook and no toiletries strewn across the top of the chest of drawers.

'Mum?' she called again. 'How strange,' she muttered aloud. She rubbed her chin before pulling her hair into a loose bun.

Opening the front door, she trod cautiously down the stairs and peered through the door into the bakery. There was no sign of Lorna there, nor in the café. Still in her pyjamas, Meg was wary of being seen by customers, or by the Plum Patisserie team.

'Where the bloody hell has she got to?' Her question floated into the ether as she plodded back up the stairs. Meg's thoughts ran wild; maybe her mum had moved into a hotel and would reappear soon, ready to decorate the tree that would arrive any minute. Or maybe she had gone shopping and had stored her bags and belongings somewhere. As she ran through these scenarios in her mind, she knew that they were at best unlikely and at worst pure fantasy.

Meg's heart rate increased. She placed her hand on her chest. *Surely not?* But as she opened the front door of her flat she noticed the space on the console table where the silver-framed picture of Lucas usually sat. Walking over to it, she ran her palm over the flat wooden surface and scanned the area, as if she might make the frame reappear just by concentrating really hard. Crouching down, she felt along the wainscoting with outstretched fingers to see if it had fallen down the back and was nestling on the floor. It wasn't.

Meg sat back on her haunches; she knew at that point what had happened. Her mother had run away, creeping from the flat in the dead of night, treading softly to avoid a goodbye. Lorna had disappeared and by the look of things, she hadn't left empty-handed. Meg realised with a jolt that her mum had her credit card and pin number. Phoning her automated banking service, she punched in her security codes and passwords and listened eagerly for her balance. It was just as she feared: over a thousand pounds had been withdrawn in cash over two days and hundreds of pounds had been spent on purchases.

Meg stumbled back down the stairs, desperate to tell someone, only to remember that Milly and Pru were away and Guy had left that morning for France. Sweet Guy, who Lorna had been rude to. *Oh God.* As the strength left her legs, she sank down onto the cold, hard marble floor. She didn't care that the chill seeped through her pyjama bottoms, numbing her bottom in an instant. She didn't care about much. With her elbows on her knees and her head in her palms, she closed her eyes and thought about the day she had arrived there, four years ago. She could recall exactly how she'd felt: scared, sick, lost and vulnerable, and above all, fearful of what the future held. It was easy to remember because it was precisely how she felt right then. She might have the keys to a swanky flat, but when it came down to it, she was still scared little Meg, limping from day to day and hoping for the best.

The doorbell rang, making her jump. Meg leapt up.

Mum?

Her face fell as she looked into the face of a deliveryman in a tracksuit who in his outstretched arm was holding what looked like the rejected top of a raggedy Christmas tree.

'Meg Hope?' he asked gruffly.

She nodded.

'Happy Christmas!' He gave a lopsided grin and pushed the tiny tree with its bare branches and withered trunk towards her.

'What *is* it?'

'It's your Christmas tree.'

'But ... but it's tiny and dead!' She felt her throat constrict with disappointment.

'What did you expect for a fiver at the last minute? A lovely Norway spruce?' He smirked. 'And I only delivered it out of the goodness of my heart.' He winked.

Meg considered the image she had carried in her head for the last day or so: a full, green tree, artfully hung with baubles and strings of lights, the glow from which would grace their evenings as they drank tea and sat on the sofa, mother and daughter, together for Christmas.

'I don't know what I expected, but not this.'

The man shrugged his indifference. 'Either way, it's yours. Where do you want it?'

Meg reached out and took the spiky brown offering into the hall before shutting the front door. She set the brown plastic pot on the floor and laughed at the absurdity of the thing that barely reached her knee.

Her phone rang in her hand. It was Guy. Finally the tears fell.

'I thought you'd gone to France,' she

managed through her distress.

'I'm at the airport, but I had a sneaky suspicion that my girl might need me.'

'I do need you,' she whispered.

'What's happened?' His voice was gentle, as if he was addressing a child.

Meg stared straight ahead, not sure where to begin. Embarrassed. 'Lorna's gone.'

'Merde.' He sighed. 'Did you row?'

Meg shook her head. 'No. I didn't know she was going. She's just done a runner, disappeared.'

'Oh, Meg! I'm sorry. Truly sorry.' Guy's tone was warm.

'I don't know why I'm upset or surprised. Not really. I just wanted to believe that things were going to be different this time.' She found it easy to confess this down a phone line.

'That's because you are sweet and hope for the best, always. That's one of the reasons we love you.'

Meg considered this. 'I don't know about sweet – I think I must be bloody stupid. First Edd and now her!' She sighed. 'I wish I didn't always believe what people tell me, but I do. It's because I want it to be true; I wanted Christmas with my mum.' *And I wanted a life with Edd, a family life full of love and laughter.*

'So you must come to France with me. Go pack a bag, jump in a cab and meet me at the airport. Come on, chop, chop!'

Meg smiled. Usually when he said this he clapped his hands above his head, flamenco-style.

She thought for a second or two. 'I'd rather not, Guy. Thank you for asking me, but I don't want to go anywhere and I don't want to see anyone. I really appreciate you calling me – more than you know.'

Meg returned to her spot on the floor, sinking like a little rag doll, broken and lifeless. She held the phone in the crook of her neck and placed her face in her hands as she cried.

Guy uttered, 'Ssssshhh, don't cry, chérie,' between her sobs.

Meg sniffed and tried to collect herself. 'Every night that I was in care I used to convince myself that tomorrow would be the day she'd come and take me home, just like she promised. But she never did. I used to come up with reasons why – she'd had to go to the doctor's, or she'd missed the bus. I never gave up on her.' Meg dabbed at her tears with her sleeve. 'And it doesn't matter that I'm grown up now. I was so thrilled to see her here the other day, in Plum's. It meant she'd made the effort to find me after all this time. It meant she did love me after all.'

'I'm sorry, Meg.' Guy was genuine. No matter how much he had disliked Lorna, he still didn't want to see his friend hurting.

'No need for you to be sorry. It's not your fault, is it? It's hers. She lied to me. It was all about her on the make, seeing what she could get. It always was and it always will be. I fell for it because I wanted to believe her.' Meg sniffed again and paused before giving him the next piece of information. 'I gave her my credit card and pin so she could buy the Christmas tree. It's just arrived and it's pathetic, a cheap afterthought. It's shit.'

Guy sighed. 'Oh, Meg...' He clicked his tongue against his teeth and twisted his mouth. 'Does she still have your card and pin number?'

'Yep.' Meg nodded. 'I'll cancel it in a minute.' She didn't confess to purposefully having delayed calling the bank, but she knew what Guy was thinking. Illogical though it was, she didn't want her mum to get into trouble, didn't want Lorna to think badly of her for having involved the police. She also wanted her mum to have everything she needed for whatever twists and turns her sorry life took next. And, even more illogically, she still hoped beyond hope that it had all been a bit of a mix-up and that Lorna would bluster through the door at any second, with a bag full of Christmas decorations and a reasonable explanation about her absence. Even she had to admit that, with every minute that passed, that was becoming ever more unlikely.

'You need to do that, Meg. You don't know what she might do and it will only make things worse in the long run.' She knew he was right. 'I have to go, Meg. Call me whenever you want, day or night. I mean it.'

Standing, Meg ran her palm over the backs of her thighs and sniffed as she wiped away her tears. As she walked towards the staircase, she held the mouthpiece close to her lips, trying to get closer to her friend. 'Guy?'

'Oui?'

'She took the silver-framed photo of Lucas from the hallway. I keep hoping that it's because she wanted a photo of him to keep. Do you think that might be why she took it, so she can look at him, remember him?'

She heard his sigh.

'I think so, yes,' he lied.

Eighteen

It was Christmas Day. Meg was woken from a dream about Edd by the buzzing of her phone, heralding the arrival of a text message. With bleary eyes and the creases of the pillow still visible on her cheek, she lifted her head, raised one arm from the duvet and scrolled through the screen until the message opened. The breath caught in her throat as she read the lines: *I can't stop thinking about you. Miss you beyond words. Happy Christmas.*

Her heart leapt at the words she had wanted to read more than anything. Edd's texts and attempted calls had stopped after a couple of days of her not replying. It saddened her how easily and quickly he had given up. More proof of the insincerity of his words and actions, if any were needed. This single text, however, made her heart sing. It was Christmas and he was thinking of her! It wouldn't make a difference in the long run – a liar was a liar – but his words were a salve to her broken heart on this special day.

Sitting up, she rubbed her temples and pushed her hair behind her ears. As her eyes focused, her heart sank. The words were exactly as she had read them, but the text wasn't from Edd; it had been sent by Piers. Meg sank back into the pillows and fought the wave of melancholy that washed over her. It couldn't have been further from the Christmas morning she had envisaged.

Rising from the bed twenty minutes later, she fetched a glass of water and slumped onto the sofa. With neither the need nor the inclination to shower and dress, Meg simply stared out of the window. The day was grey and overcast. She watched the lights of passing vehicles flicker and rebound around the walls, like eyes in the gloom searching for prey. Though it was a tad chilly, she lacked the strength to jump up and turn up the heating or fetch a blanket, rather liking the way her shivers matched her mood.

Her mind was preoccupied not with Lorna and her betrayal, but with memories of Edd and the way he had made her feel. Standing on the ice at the Rockefeller Center with his arms around her waist as the snow settled on their noses and eyelashes, he had looked at her as though there was only her, as if he loved her just as she was. Meg blinked, dry-eyed as she wrapped her arms around her trunk. That was how she wanted to be looked at, how she wanted to be loved. Not as Bill had loved her, second best; or how Lorna loved her, when it suited her; or even Piers, who loved only the idea of her. But a real deep love with someone who knew how to make her feel safe like no one else ever could. That was what she wanted more than anything in the world. But like her list of toys copied from a ragged-cornered out-of-date catalogue, she knew the chances of it being hers were extremely unlikely, if not impossible.

It was midday in London when the Skype call came in, rousing her from the stupor in which she had spent the morning.

Lucas's head bobbed up and down in

front of the camera; his sun-kissed face beamed. 'Happy Christmas! It's Christmas here today, Mum, but I know it's not Christmas in England until I get back.'

That's right, Lucas. It could never be Christmas without you. 'Happy Christmas, my beautiful boy. I miss you so much!'

'I got a diving Action Man.' He held up a plastic figure that was dressed in a wetsuit and orange plastic flippers and had tiny scuba tanks on its back and a rather nasty-looking spear gun clutched in its right hand. 'I'm going to take him in the swimming pool and I got a iTunes voucher and I can get games for my iPad, Christopher is going to help me do it. And I got sweets and new pyjamas with pirates on!'

'Wow! You are such a lucky boy. I hope you said lots of thank-yous.'

'I did! And we are going to go to the beach and we are going out for our lunch and I want fish fingers and Pru said I can have whatever I want because it's Barbarbados Christmas and so I'm going to have two puddings which are both chocolate cake.'

Without warning and as per his usual modus operandi, he leapt off the stool he had been perched on. Meg found herself staring at the white tiled wall of the kitchen.

'Hello, anybody there?' she called at the screen.

It was a good thirty seconds before she got

a response. 'There you are!'

Milly came into view. 'I thought you were chatting to the boy!'

'I was, but he's hopped off somewhere.' Meg smiled and raised her hands.

'Happy Barbarbados Christmas, my love.' Milly's tone was warm.

'And to you! Are you all still having a lovely time?'

'Oh, the best! We've been up since the crack of dawn, quite literally! We're having a ball, but we do miss you.' She was sincere.

'I miss you too.' Meg couldn't disguise the catch in her throat.

'Everything all right, Meg?' Milly frowned and squinted to better see the screen.

Meg tucked her lips over her teeth and nodded, not trusting what might slip from her mouth and give her away.

'Just missing Lucas?' Milly hazarded.

Meg nodded again.

'Oh well, here he is, back again!' Milly shunted sideways and lifted Lucas on to the stool.

'Look, Mum!' He beamed as he thrust a rather limp-looking starfish towards the camera. 'He's called Steve and he's been my pet for two days! Say hello to my mum, Steve!'

Milly grimaced over his shoulder. 'Let's put Steve back in his bucket, mate. Remember what we talked about, keeping him nice and wet?'

Lucas once again clambered out of view.

'Aren't you going to say goodbye to Mummy?' Milly enquired.

'Bye, Mum! I love you!'

Meg smiled at the voice that drifted back towards the microphone. 'I love you too, so much.'

Milly took up the space on the stool. 'Poor Steve! We found him on the beach, already half dead. Lucas revived him somewhat but I think his TLC is making Steve wish he'd ended his days there and then. He was part of a moon-landing re-enactment yesterday involving a colander and a sand dune. I think Steve is miserable. He certainly looks it.' She shook her head. Meg laughed.

'We'll see you real soon, Meg. Can't wait to get back to you.'

Meg nodded. For her, the time couldn't pass fast enough.

'Give *everyone* my love.' Milly winked.

Meg knew she was referring to Edd and smiled weakly in response. 'Will do.'

As the computer screen went blank, Meg was aware once again of the silence in the flat. It looked uncharacteristically depressing without the lamps on to ward off the dull winter greyness. The smell of cigarette smoke, whether real or imaginary, filled her nostrils. She shuddered at the foul lingering reminder of Lorna's presence. Cracking open the window, she shivered once more as the icy blast of this Christmas Day whipped around the room. A quick glance at the clock reminded her that she hadn't eaten since she had picked at cheese and biscuits the previous evening. As she opened the fridge and then the food cupboards, she realised that there was nothing in either that might constitute a meal, let alone a Christmas lunch.

Stepping into her fur-lined Ugg boots and pulling her padded walking coat over her pyjamas, Meg made her way to the Tesco Express store further down the street, the only one open on this day and at this time. She collected the wire shopping basket from a stack by the door and traipsed up and down the neon-lit aisles as 'Ding Dong Merrily on High' reverberated from the speakers. The contents of her basket sat limply against the wire: two oranges, a tin of tomato soup and a packet of oatcakes, which she would devour with the remaining Brie and some sweet onion chutney. She pictured Brenda, Edd's mother, and the seven relatives she had invited for Christmas. She imagined bowls of roasted spuds, buttery parsnips, chestnut stuffing and moist, white turkey, all slathered in thick pale gravy and with a booze-soaked, flaming Christmas pud to follow. Even the idea made her mouth water.

'Don't suppose you've got any turkey?'

Meg shouted to the perky man who sported a tinsel bow tie and a Santa hat. He looked like he was having the best day.

'Ah, in the freezer, I think,' he shouted back. 'Or there are fresh turkey portions in the fridge.' He pointed. 'Leaving it a bit late, aren't you?' He smiled, lifting his eyes from the tray of sandwiches that he was stickering as 'Reduced' and placing back in the chiller cabinet.

Meg shrugged, not willing to explain how or why she had ended up in this situation on Christmas Day.

'Help!' a woman shouted in a jovial tone as she trotted in black patent heels into the store, her beautifully coiffed chestnut locks cascading over her shoulders. She smelt of expensive scent but was rather incongruously wearing an apron with the words 'Santa's Little Helper!' emblazoned across the front. Like Meg, she had clearly given little thought to the fact that she might encounter other last-minute shoppers.

'Okay there, Mrs Miller?' The store assistant seemed very pleased to see her.

'Yes! Merry Christmas! Having a bit of a crisis – I've forgotten the cranberry sauce. Please tell me you have some?' She wrung her hands as though this were the biggest disaster that could possibly befall her.

The man abandoned his task and loped off up one of the aisles, returning with not one but two jars of Tesco Finest cranberry sauce.

'You are an absolute darling and a total life-saver!' the woman gushed as she handed over a bank note and the man popped the jars into a bag. He was beaming, clearly enjoying being a total life-saver and an absolute darling.

Meg looked at the woman. Her face was flushed, probably at the sheer joy of Christmas Day, perhaps helped by a generous slosh of champers in her celebratory morning Buck's Fizz. She wished her own woes could be wiped away by the purchase of two jars of condiment.

She scanned the freezer cabinets, letting her eyes rove over blocks of mint-choc Viennetta ice cream, ham and pineapple pizzas and packets of frozen peas until there it was staring back at her: a frozen Christmas dinner for one. She pulled back the sliding door of the freezer, plunged her hand into the chill and lifted out the plastic package. Clearing a window through the dusting of snow-like grains on the lid, Meg could make out a ball of brown stuffing the size of a ping-pong ball, four strips of frozen carrot and three thin slices of meat – 'prime turkey breast!', according to the large green sticker on the front. She doubted there was anything 'prime' about any of it. Prime was what Brenda would be serving to her seven relatives, and what Milly, Pru and Chris would enjoy a few hours from now at their ocean-view restaurant; it might even be what Edd and Flavia would be picking at on trays in front of the television. At least theirs would be organic.

She stared at the square packet in her hands. This was it. This forlorn-looking processed meal represented her shitty Christmas and her shitty luck. Why had she fallen for Edward Kelly, with this fabulous body and floppy fringe? Why had she been so stupid? And then she'd gone and let herself be duped by her mum – again. Imagine, her mum finding her just in time for Christmas! 'What a bloody mess.' Meg closed her eyes and thought of Lucas, who was so very far away. It was Christmas Day and she missed him. She missed him so very much.

When she opened her eyes there was a man in the aisle and he was staring at her with a fixed smile. She had never seen him before, but he grinned at her as though they were old friends. 'Forgive me for asking...' He paused, licked his lips and eyed the 'Dinner for One' box in her hand. 'But I bet you're single!'

Meg smiled at the memory of that first abrasive encounter with Edd in the Greenwich Avenue Deli. How quickly they'd made amends. Edd had made her so happy, even if it was only for a short time.

He had lifted the lid on her indifference and given her a peek at what it might be like to love and be loved. She had liked that. She had liked it a lot. What was it he had said? *'I'm right, aren't I? You aren't married or even involved. It's just a guess, but mainly I've come to that conclusion because you are really, really ugly.'*

The man in front of her coughed. 'Am I right?'

Meg felt her tears pool and shook her head; she didn't have the energy to reply. She placed the sorry box of food back into its chilly home, leaving it as a treat for someone else to enjoy, and set the basket on the floor. Then she calmly walked out empty-handed, back to the flat where nothing awaited her except the odour of stale cigarette smoke and a cold breeze that blew in from the open balcony door.

Kicking off her Uggs and shrugging her arms from the sleeves of her coat, Meg peeled back the duvet and wriggled down to the middle of the mattress. She wanted today to be over and decided to spend it sleeping, waking up only when it was all over. Rolling over, she buried her face in the pillow and closed her eyes. 'Happy Christmas,' she whispered into the cold, still silence.

Nineteen

'Wow, look who's up early as a lark!' Guy said as he walked past Meg. 'All set?' he added.

She was vigorously polishing the brass fixtures on the front door. It was December the twenty-eighth and her baby boy was coming home.

'Yep. They won't recognise the place, it's shining like a new pin! I've gone cleaning mad, Guy. I've done nothing but scrub and iron and hoover for the last few days. I've even washed and re-hung all the curtains. This is proof that I have absolutely no life!' She laughed. 'I've put up a little tree that I got from the market and covered it in lights. Hope Lucas loves it – I'm sure he will, there's presents under it, which has to be his main concern, right?'

'Right.' Guy smiled, happy to see his friend full of the liveliness she had been lacking over the last few days. 'Why don't you pop down and pick up some cakes and brioche? Lucas will have missed Plum baking I'm sure and he might be hungry. You can have a nice lunch or afternoon tea, non?' He wanted to make doubly sure that there were no hard feelings after the whole Lorna incident. His friendship with Meg was far stronger than any demand for packs of coffee beans made by a woman on the make.

'Actually...' Meg snapped the duster in the air and leant back to avoid the fall-out. '... I am planning on making a cake for everyone. I was thinking of an apple and walnut loaf or a really good banana bread, in homage to Barbarbados!'

Guy placed his hand on his chest. 'Oh, poor things. As if having to travel home from paradise, exhausted, isn't enough of a challenge, you are going to inflict one of your cakes on them as well?' He sighed.

Meg twisted the duster into a fat orange rope and flicked it at Guy's legs as he hopped out of the way, squealing. He grabbed the duster and held it fast. The two laughed as they tussled and skipped around on the pavement like a couple of excited children.

Meg stood on tiptoes on the half landing in the hallway, spraying the air with her new cinnamon and spice room scent. She wanted the smell of Christmas to greet her family the moment they walked in. The doorbell rang. Meg checked her face in the mirror before leaping down the stairs taking two at time, beaming at the prospect of holding Lucas's little body against hers. God, she had missed him! She opened the door and took a step back. It was the last person she expected to see. Her expression was one of genuine surprise.

'Hello, Meg, is this a bad time?' Piers shuffled nervously from foot to foot.

'Oh, Piers! It's lovely to see you!' And it was. She felt a genuine rush of affection for this man, in the way she might feel towards an old friend or neighbour in whom she had zero romantic interest. He may not have been the one for her, but his snobbish views and less than accepting attitude towards her childhood were far less hurtful than Edd's lying and cheating. The temptation to fall into his arms and be hugged was strong, but she couldn't risk leaving him with the wrong impression. Nonetheless, she felt warmed by the familiarity of him, his ancient Barbour with the elbows and front worn shiny from use, his green paisley scarf and favourite camel-coloured cashmere sweater. She knew that Piers had been wearing similar clothes since he was thirteen and would be wearing them still at eighty-three. She smiled at him.

'You look tired.' He reached out and tucked a stray tendril of hair behind her ear. He was, as ever, sweet and concerned about her wellbeing.

Meg inclined her cheek towards his hand. 'I am. I've been waitressing and cleaning for the last few days and it's a darn sight harder than swanning around with my briefcase.' She saw a flicker of disapproval cross his brow, knowing he preferred her in a managerial role. 'As Guy says, I've gone a bit soft. Are you coming in? I'll pop the kettle on, I was just going up.'

She stood to the side and gestured with her arm. Playing host to Piers was the last thing she felt like doing right now; she wanted time alone with her family to hear every detail of their Caribbean adventure. But she hoped he hadn't sensed that.

'No, but thanks.' He looked down at the pavement. His expression told her he couldn't cope with being mates and had no intention of making small talk over a cup of tea, not when his heart still lurched at the sight of her.

Meg prayed he wasn't going to mention the Christmas Day text. Poor Piers, he was and always would be unable to fathom her lack of interest.

'I'm not staying. I just wanted to drop this off for Lucas.' He reached down and picked up a square box, beautifully wrapped.

'Oh, Piers, you sweetheart!' Meg placed her arms around his neck and rested her cheek against his chest. To her mind, anyone that thought of Lucas was worthy of a hug on a cold winter's day. She pulled away, but kept one hand on his chest. 'That is so kind of you; you shouldn't have done that!' She was genuinely touched and felt an even stronger longing to have her little boy home.

'Well, I got it a few weeks ago, before ... you know. And, err ... I didn't want to ... you know.'

'Right.' Meg felt herself blushing, embarrassed that he was hurting and she was indifferent. She had once read that the most powerful person is the one who doesn't love you back. It was a concept she hadn't really understood until now. She thought firstly of Edd and then of the lovely Piers standing in front of her with his kind gift for her son.

'It's one of those robot bugs.' He rattled the box. 'There's a remote control. I know he likes that kind of thing and the robot element looks like fun. It says aged five and up, so watch him with it.' He nodded; fatherly, kind.

'I will.' Meg took the box from his hands. 'I know he'll love it. Thank you.' She was sincere. 'Look, Piers, it's freezing. If you are not coming up, then at least step inside for a moment.' Meg reached out and pulled his sleeve until he was safely inside the warm hallway.

She didn't notice the tall red-haired Yank in the taxi outside, just out of earshot, who was watching the whole exchange and apologising to the cabbie for what appeared to have been a wasted journey as he gave a change of destination.

'Has Lucas had a great time?' Piers shoved his hands into his deep front pockets. Far better to hide them and quash the urge to reach for her.

'Yes, although he's been away. He went to Barbados with Milly, Pru and Chris.'

'Oh really?' His eyebrows knitted quizzically. 'Didn't know that was on the cards.'

'It wasn't, but then I've been working and travelling a bit and it just seemed...' Meg hesitated, staring at the back of the door, trying to find the words to cover exactly what she had been through in the last couple of weeks.

Piers took in her expression. He didn't know what was afoot, but a sixth sense made him realise that there was zero hope of a reconciliation. She was lost to him and that was that. Meg watched his smile fade.

'I have to go.' He was abrupt, suddenly awkward.

'Oh, right.' She shared his embarrassment. 'It's been lovely to see you, Piers.' She smiled. 'And please give my love to your parents.' She raised the box in her hand. 'And thank you once again so much for Lucas's pressie. He's a lucky boy.'

Piers' face crumpled as he swallowed his emotion. His words were gentlemanly. 'Sorry about the text on Christmas morning.' He addressed the floor. 'I was still one over the eight and you know how things can seem like a good idea at the time. Then you sober up and wish you could turn back the clock and apply a bit of reason.'

'I liked getting it, Piers. It made me feel happy.' This was the truth.

He smiled. 'When you do find someone you want to be with, Meg, never forget how very fortunate they are to have you.'

And when I do, Piers, they will love me for me, exactly as I am.

He shifted on the spot. Turning his head as he made to leave, he asked, as though it were an afterthought, 'Did you ever love me, Meg?'

She thought of Edd, his honesty crushing and yet, strangely, with hindsight, appreciated. It had helped her move on. No moping over maybes.

'As much as I could.' She held his gaze.

Piers nodded and tightened his scarf around his neck. With his head down, he strode out of the door and walked briskly along Curzon Street before disappearing from view.

Meg stood in the kitchen and tapped her fingers on the counter top. She was agitated, killing time until her boy came home and she couldn't wait!

Her phone rang, flashing up 'Private number'.

'Hello?'

There was a second of hesitation before a voice she recognised came down the line, making her stomach knot. 'Meg?'

'Speaking.' She was unsure what tone to adopt or how this call might develop.

'It's Flavia here. We met before Christmas...'

Meg closed her eyes. 'Yes. Yes, I remember.' She cringed. How much did Flavia know? She felt her muscles tense in anticipation of a tirade from this woman she had wronged.

'I got your number from Edd's phone and I wasn't sure whether to call or not, but I wanted to talk to you.'

Meg was silent, waiting for more.

'This is hard.' Flavia took a deep breath. 'He told me everything after you turned up and I just wanted to say that I wish you well and that I understand. Edd and I have been more like friends than a couple for a long, long time, but things have been tough for me and I guess I didn't want to face it, y'know?'

Meg nodded. 'Yep.' Her voice was small.

'We are done now, totally. I can see that we have no future and I should have let him go earlier. I guess I just didn't want to be on my own. It's been a really bad year for me. I lost my mom...'

'I'm sorry.' And she was. *I found mine and then lost her too. Or, rather, she lost me.*

'Thanks.' Flavia sighed. 'He's a good man, Meg.'

Meg felt flustered. 'I appreciate your call, Flavia, I really do. But I think we are done too. It was just one of those whirlwind things, the kind that's good for your soul but has no future. I'm just sorry that you got hurt.'

'Honey, I was already hurt. The thing is, he deserves a second chance – everyone does, don't they?'

Meg considered this. 'I don't know. A liar is a liar and if you don't have trust then I don't think you've got anything...' She let this hang.

'Well, look – I've said what I needed to. Give him my best regards and tell him that for what it's worth you have my blessing.'

'That's sweet, Flavia, and I appreciate it more than you know, but it's irrelevant. I am never going to see him again.' Meg winced at this.

'But he's with you in London, now!' Flavia sounded confused.

'What?'

'Yes! He left for London yesterday and I told him to text me to let me know he'd arrived safely. I got a message from him a little while ago saying he was at the Premier Inn County Hall, wherever that is!'

Meg ended the call and stood there in shock, wondering if and when he was going to pitch up at the flat; the thought both thrilled and horrified her. She decided she couldn't risk a nasty showdown in front of Lucas. With her finger trembling, she wrote and sent the text that she should have sent days ago. *I don't want to see you. Please do not contact me again. My feelings haven't changed, what I said to you in New York still stands. I have moved on. Meg.* It was curt and resolute, just as she had intended.

His reply came through within a matter of seconds: *So I see.*

It puzzled and angered her. *What on earth...?*

After showering and slipping into her jeans and her favourite baggy white cotton jersey, Meg again checked the clock. It was nearly 11 a.m.; they would be here any moment! She scanned the sitting room with its neatly plumped cushions, clean, fresh scent and dust-free surfaces, smiling as she made her way into the immaculate kitchen to fill the kettle and turn her banana bread on to a wire tray for cooling.

She heard the kerfuffle on the landing before they had a chance to knock or find a key. Sliding in her socks, she ran to the front door, threw it open wide and in they spilled! Christopher, carrying bags and wheeling a suitcase, came in at the same time as Lucas and they were almost wedged in the door-frame.

'Mummy!' Lucas wriggled past Christopher's legs and leapt at her.

Bending, Meg caught him and held him tight with his head tucked into the crook of her neck. The relief at having her little boy safely back in her arms was sweet and instant.

He pulled free of her grip and held her face between his little palms. 'I was going to bring Steve my starfish home, but he *died!*' He pushed out his bottom lip, indicating that he was sad – something he'd done since he was a baby.

'Oh darling, never mind. Plenty more fish in the sea.'

Christopher bellowed his laughter, still in holiday mood. 'Very good, Meg! Plenty more fish in the sea!' He chuckled as he rested the suitcase against the wall.

Milly and Pru filled the hallway with their handbags, exuberance and chatter. Pru stepped forward and patted Lucas's back as he sat in his mum's arms. 'He has really missed you.'

'No I didn't! Not even a bit!' Lucas piped up, shaking his head, unaware of the etiquette when it came to returning to the family home.

Meg laughed as Milly reached up and kissed her over Lucas's shoulder. 'I'll stick the kettle on.' She wandered into the kitchen before shouting back, 'Blimey, what happened? The place looks fantastic, have you got a cleaner?'

'Ha ha!' Meg beamed. 'No, I just wanted it to be nice for you all. I've done your flat too.'

'Well I think we should go away more often in that case.' Milly chortled.

'You all look wonderful!' Meg looked at the tanned and smiling faces of those who loved her. 'Have you had a wonderful time?'

'The best,' Christopher confirmed.

Lucas jumped from his mother's arms. 'I need to go and see Thomas! Has he been good?'

'Oh, an absolute angel. I've hardly heard a peep out of him,' Meg said.

'You look tired, love. Wonder why that is!' Pru's eyes twinkled. 'I want to hear all about it. When did you get back?'

Meg felt her chest heave and her tears pool.

'What's the matter, did I say the wrong thing?' Pru stepped forward. Her words alerted Milly, who came out of the kitchen to stand next to her cousin. Both stood there staring at her, concerned.

Meg looked at the floor. 'I'm so glad you are all home. I've had a really, really horrible Christmas.'

'Oh, love!' Pru placed her hand on her back and steered her into the sitting room.

Meg sat on the sofa with Pru and Milly on

either side. Christopher busied himself with the making of tea in the kitchen, happy to be occupied rather than have to listen to girl talk. It took Meg a full half-hour to recount the basic story of her New York trip, along with the brief epilogue of Lorna's visit.

'I'm sorry I kept it from you. I didn't want it to spoil your holiday and I knew you'd just rush back.'

'You should have told us, Meg. I can't bear to think of you here all by yourself over Christmas. I'd have insisted on you coming over.' Milly sighed.

'I know. But to be honest, Mills, I just wanted to stay here and wallow for a bit. And I have.'

'I'd like to get my hands on him.' Pru ground her teeth. 'What kind of piece of work is he, stringing you along like that?'

Meg nodded. *Indeed.*

'I thought he sounded too good to be true, a bit too smooth. I knew it was a mistake. I could sock him one, I really could!' Milly balled her fingers into a fist and shook her head.

Meg gave a small laugh, remembering Milly's words just days ago. *'He sounds very special, Meg, and as we all know, special don't come along that often. You've got to grab it, my girl, and run with it.'*

'And as for your mother...' Milly shook her head, unable or unwilling to say any more.

Lucas and Christopher came into the room. The latter holding a pirate flag.

Christopher made his way across to Meg and whispered to her, 'Do you know, Meg, this is one of those very rare occasions when I desperately hoped that my instinct was wrong. I'm sorry it didn't work out for you. I know you had high hopes.'

'I really did. I saw a future for us, Chris.' She was touched, as ever, by Christopher's fatherly concern. 'And the worst thing is, I've just heard from his ex that he is here in London, staying at the Premier Inn County Hall. It's all a bit weird. God knows why he'd come all this way and not make contact. How strange is that?'

'Very.' Christopher straightened up.

'Is it Christmas here today, Mum?' Lucas's eyes were wide.

'Oh...' Meg wasn't sure how to respond. She had assumed that 'Christmas' would take place in a couple of days, once everyone had got settled. 'I'm not sure.' She looked at the other adults in the room.

'I think it might be!' Milly urged.

Pru glanced at her watch, as though this was where the answer lay. 'Do you know, Lucas, I think you might be right. I think it could be Christmas here today!'

The cousins exchanged a knowing glance; a Christmas celebration might be just what Meg needed.

Lucas jumped up and down on the spot. 'It's Christmaaaaas! And I get to open my preseeeeeeents!' He was beside himself at the prospect as he spun around and ran from the room.

Meg jumped up and turned to face Milly and Pru on the sofa. 'Right. That's it, decision made. It *is* Christmas today! Milly, you get peeling the spuds. Pru, can you shove the turkey in the oven? And, Chris, you can make something fab for pudding!'

'I think, if it's okay with everyone, I shall go and buy a pudding. There is no way I'm going to put one of my efforts on the table in front of three competent bakers.'

'Competent? Talk about damning with faint praise!' Pru tutted.

Christopher winked at her.

Meg was in full flow. 'I'll go and get the other odds and ends we need – crackers, tinsel and any other bits of glittery shite I can lay my hands on! We shall feast like kings and Lucas will have a day that he will never forget! Okay?' She was practically shouting.

Pru looked at Christopher, who stared at Milly, who nodded. It wasn't like Meg to give out orders.

'Okay!' Pru replied on behalf of the trio, who all looked a little shell-shocked.

'Great!' Meg clapped. 'This is me taking control of my life and making it happen! See you in a bit, Lucas. I shall be back in a little while!' With that she grabbed her keys and raced out of the flat, wondering where she could find everything she needed to make the day absolutely perfect.

Twenty

Meg placed her key in the lock and bundled through the door with her numerous bags and boxes. The smell of her roasting turkey crown dressed with bacon and bay leaves hit her nostrils. She breathed in; it was intoxicating. *Oh, Mum, I wish you were here!* She had managed to acquire Christmas crackers at less than half price; three strings of tinsel had cost mere pence and the ready-prepared roast parsnips, minted peas, red cabbage, and cranberry and walnut stuffing had all been marked down.

'I'm back!' she called from the door, digging deep to find the happiest voice she could.

The hallway looked lovely. Someone had turned on the lamps and Simon and Garfunkel wafted from the CD player. It was sedate and calm. Meg took a deep breath, feeling a burst of happiness. This was going to be a fantastic day! *This* was the Christmas she had dreamt of; she would smile and make it great! Her family was home and this would have to be enough. There would be plenty of time in the coming months to lament the loss from her life of Lorna, Edd and the future that had seemed to be within her grasp.

Waltzing into the kitchen, she smiled at the sight of the sherry trifle heaped with fresh cream and the chocolate-smothered profiteroles that Christopher had snaffled from downstairs. Lovely desserts – no boxed slices of cake or crumbs for her today. Looking around, she was struck by how busy the three adults were. Pru washed cups and handed them to Christopher who passed them to Milly who placed them on the appropriate shelf in the cupboard. All three worked in an unnatural silence, with almost pained expressions on their faces. The whole set-up was a little odd, to put it mildly.

'Oh look! A little washing-up production line! Why don't you just shove them in the dishwasher?' she wondered out loud.

Milly shrugged and Christopher averted his gaze. Pru hummed. This was the second clue that all was not as it seemed inside her home. It was as if they were afraid to speak.

Meg smiled. 'Okay, you weirdos, I'll make a start on the table. Can someone deal with the veg and stuffing?' She passed the food bags to Milly and gave a little clap as she made her way into the sitting room.

Milly nodded, silently, avoiding her eye.

Meg walked into the sitting room. 'Oh, Lucas!' She sighed, half exasperated. She loved watching him play creatively but hadn't banked on such an extravagant display, not today.

'Do we *have* to have a pirate ship in the middle of the sitting room?' Her plans for a fancy Christmas lunch were somewhat thwarted by the presence of his vast sheet-covered galleon. She had to admit that he had done a fine job, not the usual upturned chairs and strewn towels. His trip to the Caribbean had obviously inspired him.

With her hands on her hips, she waited for the sheet to lift and for Redbeard to amble from below decks. When the sheet eventually fluttered and was pulled back, Meg felt her knees wobble as her breath caught in her throat. For a fraction of a second she smiled as she came face to face with the man she had fallen for. He smiled back, briefly. Then she remembered his lies and her smile disappeared, to be replaced by a scowl. Her heart continued to hammer inside her ribcage nonetheless. She placed her hand over it. *Sssshhh...*

'What ... what are you doing, Edd?'

'Oh, it's quite simple really, basic design principles.' He ran his fingers through his hair. 'I've left the two chairs the right way up – that's been their first mistake.' He turned to face the galleon. 'We've used the broom to gain more height in the middle and thus create useable space at either end.' He nodded, admiring his work.

'It's true, Mum, I can stand up in here now, it's brilliant!' Lucas poked his head out into the choppy waters.

Meg grunted. 'I don't mean what are you doing with the bloody pirate ship, I mean what you are *doing?* Why are you here?'

'For you. I came for you,' he said quite matter-of-factly.

'Well you have had a wasted trip, as I mentioned in my text. You can leave now.' She pointed towards the door.

'I'm not going to do that.' He shook his head.

'Can Edd come back inside my ship now?' Lucas was standing by her side.

'Why don't you come and help *us,* little chap?' Christopher's voice boomed from the doorway.

'But I want to play with Edd!' Lucas shouted, easily impressed by the stranger who had been willing to take on the role of captain and had built the best pirate ship ever.

'I need some help with chocolate tasting,' Christopher continued, 'and I thought you might be the man for the role.'

Lucas ran towards the kitchen. For that kind of job he was always available.

Meg sat at the dining table and let her eyes wander over the unexpected guest. He looked wonderful. His rolled sleeves revealed his strong arms and his hair as ever fell over his forehead, just so. Her stomach knotted.

She spoke quietly. 'You lied to me, Edd, and I can't get over that.'

'Well you need to get over that. And I didn't lie to you, I just didn't tell you everything, which I admit was a mistake. I was just trying to figure it out as I went along, trying to hurt people as little as possible. And in the process I hurt the one that mattered the most.' He sat down in the chair opposite her.

'I spoke to Flavia. She told me you were here.' Meg folded her arms across her chest and jutted out her chin like she could care less.

'Yes, I know. She's a great girl. And I wish her well, I really do. She's not a bad person, just not for me.'

Meg thought of Piers. A lovely man, despite his flaws, just not for her. Her thoughts then went to Flavia and her kind offer of coffee that awful day; from one needy, messed-up girl to another. 'She sounded like she was bring brave on the phone. Is she okay?' None of this was her fault, after all.

'Not really, no. But I have every faith she will be. I think things will work out for the best.'

'How did you know I'd spoken to her?'
'Christopher told me.'
'Christopher?' Meg squeaked.
'Yep. He came to see me at the hotel. He told me to leave you alone and to get the hell out of town. I was quite shocked. He is so proper and British, he sounded like a James Bond baddie.'
Meg smiled at the thought of Christopher squaring up to drive this Yank home.
'But I told him the full story and said I'd seen you with Piers, earlier–'
'You did?' Meg blushed.
'Yep – and you were right about the Barbour.' Edd waved his hand and continued. 'Anyway, Christopher told me you never loved Piers and that you never properly loved Bill because he wasn't the one meant for you.'
'Christopher said that?' *Dear Chris, Bill's uncle...*
'Uh-huh.' He nodded. 'And I told him that I thought I was the one for you and that I wasn't going anywhere because I love you and I just wanted a chance to talk to you and if that didn't work I would come back day after day until you believed me.'
'Well you've had a wasted trip because I don't believe you.'
'Maybe not, but you will. I won't give up until I've made things turn out right.' He smiled at her from beneath his fringe.

'How can you believe that things will turn out right when they are such a mess?'

'Sometimes I do and sometimes I don't.' He held her eye.

'What about right now? Do you think things will turn out right for us?' She thought of Lucas on the other side of the wall and of the future, a future with this man.

'Yes I do, I really do. And deep down, Meg, you know it too. I'm telling you the truth. This is the start of our adventure, remember? It was never going to be easy, coming at it from opposite sides of the Atlantic, but you knew that, right?'

'I don't know anything!' Meg ran her fingers through her hair. 'I can't believe you are here. Half of me is over the moon to see you, wants to jump into your arms and never leave and the other half is telling me to keep my guard up and chuck you out.'

'Jump, Meg. Please.' He placed his hand over hers and the warmth shot up her arm and spread around her body, weakening her resolve.

'But you said you were single,' she whispered.

'No, I didn't – you did!' He was firm.

'But it was implied by the way you asked me if *I* was single!'

'Really?' Edd looked confused. 'So if someone asks whether you're vegetarian, you can assume that they don't eat meat either?'

'What? No! What's that got to do with anything? Christ, Edd. You're being a knob. You lied through omission!'

Edd sighed. 'I know and I'm sorry. I'm really sorry and, believe me, if I had known what that one omission would do to us, what we would have to go through over Christmas, I would have come clean in a heartbeat. I'm still learning, Meg, and I now know I need to be upfront about how I'm feeling and I promise you I will. You need to give me a chance and we can learn this stuff together, grow together until we are perfect.'

Meg thought about Piers and recognised her own inability to face that situation, knowing it would have been fairer to walk away far sooner.

Edd continued, 'I did wrong, but for all the right reasons.' He smiled at her.

'Don't smile at me like that. There is nothing funny about this situation. This is my life and it's Lucas's life and I have to be so very sure.'

'You can be sure.' He raised her hand and kissed her knuckles.

'I wish I could be.' This was the truth.

'I think I'm ready now,' he said as he stood and reached into his jeans pocket.

'Ready for what?'

'To tell you.'

'Tell me what?' She tutted, perplexed and irritated.

'What my most treasured possession is.'

Meg sucked in her cheeks, remembering their conversation from just a couple of weeks ago.

'It's this, Meg.' He used the tips of his fingers to pull a small slip of white paper from his pocket. He unfurled it and handed it to her.

She placed it on the table and ran her fingers over it. It was a till receipt. The date and time were printed across the top – '12.08.14, 17.43' – and there in list form with the amount in dollars by the side was a food order. She read the words aloud. '"Swiss cheese on brown, two extras, one pickle."' Meg wrinkled her nose. 'It's for my sandwich!'

'Yes, it's for your sandwich.' He smiled. 'There aren't many couples that can pinpoint the exact day, the exact moment that they met the love of their life. My dad once explained it to me – that single instant when you see a face and you know; you know that you want to spend the rest of your life looking at it. But I can, down to the very minute. It was December eighth at seventeen minutes to six.'

Meg's eyes were full of tears. She felt like she'd been waiting her whole life to hear this. It was time to stop thinking of herself as poor, unworthy Megan and start believing that someone might love her for who she really was.

'I'm not going to let you go, Mary Poppins. I will love you and keep you safe, like no one else ever could. I'm not going to let you go. Not now, not ever. And that is just the way it is.'

Meg stood and threw herself into his arms. Edd held her tightly and the two enjoyed the sweet relief of reunion. She felt herself melt against him.

They were aware of the sound of clapping and laughter coming from the other side of the sitting room door. Meg walked over and opened it to find Milly and Pru in tears, clasping each other tightly, and Christopher bouncing Lucas high in the air.

Meg looked at the man who had warned her off Edward Kelly. 'What about your instinct, Chris?'

'I like the cut of his jib, Meg. And he knows I've got my eye on him.' He winked at Edd.

'I won't let you down, sir.' Edd looked serious.

She turned her attention to Milly. 'And I thought you wanted to sock him one!'

'I did, but he's straight as a die, Meg. And whilst I can't bear the idea of you not living here with me, it's time you grabbed a life. I want you to be happy and I've never seen you as happy as you were when you came home from New York and told me how he made you feel. "He's magic," you said; "he's everything," and you looked like you'd been lit from within.' Milly squeezed Meg's hands inside her own.

'And *you,* Pru! You said he was a piece of work!' Meg said, smiling.

'I did. But, Meg, he knows the exact day–'

'The exact *moment!'* Milly corrected.

Pru nodded. 'The exact moment he fell in love with you. He's a keeper, Meg.'

'And he builds a mean pirate ship,' Milly added, as though this might be the clincher.

Meg turned to look at her handsome New Yorker. 'There is just one small problem.' She twitched her mouth. 'You did once tell me that due to our lack of enthusiasm for baseball, London was nowhere you could ever live.'

Edd looked at her and frowned as if considering this for the very first time.

Twenty-One

ONE YEAR LATER

Brenda pottered in the unfamiliar kitchen, searching through the cupboards and peering into jars for a decent tea bag to put into the plain white china mug. She still marvelled at the fact that a property that cost so much money could have so little space and storage. What had Edward said? 'It's all about living in the right district.'

'I think if it was me, I'd move to the wrong district and have a bathroom a bit bigger than a biscuit tin,' she muttered under her breath.

'Morning, Mom!' He was as chirpy as ever. 'Sleep okay?'

'I always do. A clear conscience makes a soft pillow.' She nodded sagely.

'So that's why I'm an insomniac! It's all down to my misspent youth.' He laughed as he looked out of the window towards the city skyline in the distance and the bend of blue nestling between the buildings. 'Another beautiful Greenwich morning.' Edd sighed. 'I love this time of year: the frost on the ground, a nip in the air, getting ready for Santa!'

Brenda turned round, smiling at her boy, who sounded like a child. 'A big day for you, son.'

'Yes.' He grinned.

'I wish your dad was here.' She reached for the tissue lurking up her sleeve. 'He wouldn't believe it, you being made partner in a fancy firm of architects. He'd be so proud of you. As I am.' She sniffed.

'I know.' Edd nodded and adjusted the cufflinks that sparkled in his cuffs, sticking out below his jacket sleeves. He ran his finger over the two little seahorses that would always remind him of Meg. Ah, beautiful, beautiful Meg...

Meg shouted up the hallway, 'Come on, Lucas, you don't want be late on your very first day at big school!'

Lucas appeared at the other end of the hall wearing a black velvet cape over his school uniform.

Meg tutted. 'You can't wear your Harry Potter cape to school. Take it off. You're going to be late!'

'But Milly said I should take my spell kit. In case I need to make myself invisible or turn my teacher into a frog.'

Meg shook her head despairingly. 'You are not going to need to turn your teacher into a frog, I have met her and she is lovely. Ignore Milly.'

Milly slunk back into the sitting room. A coffee could wait.

'Is he nervous?' Isabel peered from beneath her specs, the *Daily Telegraph* laid flat on the dining table.

'He seems fine. I think we're more nervous than he is.' She sat on the floor.

'I remember William's first day at school. He looked so sweet in his little cap and shorts. He marched in mid afternoon and said he'd had a nice time but didn't think he'd bother going back again!' Isabel shook her head. 'That was him all over, really; thought he knew it all already. I loved his spark, his confidence.' She swallowed.

'He was confident,' Milly agreed. 'And funny.'

Isabel nodded, not wanting to give in to tears, not today.

'Lucas is very much like him,' Milly offered.

Isabel beamed. 'He certainly is. He's the image of him actually. Oh, did I mention I bumped into Piers? He was at a point-to-point up the road from Mountfield.'

'Ah, how was he?' Milly thought about sweet, dull Piers.

'Very well, gloriously happy and getting married!' Isabel mouthed the last two words as though it was a secret.

'Oh well, that's a good thing. Who to? Anyone we know?' Milly meant the 'we' sarcastically – she and Isabel knew hardly any of the same people.

Isabel leant across the table and whispered, 'A rather homely-looking girl.' She tightened her jaw and let her mouth droop. 'I honestly thought it was his sister. They were dressed in identical clothes and she had that chin thing going on, the same as him.'

'What chin thing?' Milly tried to picture Piers' face in more detail.

Isabel flapped her hand. 'Oh, you know

what I mean. That look that suggests all betrothals have happened within the cousin-once-removed category.' She nodded conspiratorially.

Milly snorted her laughter; Isabel was good fun when she was this cutting. 'Blimey, sounds like Meg had a lucky escape!'

Lucas stamped his foot on the hallway floor. 'Dad said I could wear this! He said I needed it to learn about witchcraft and wizardry.' Lucas pushed out his bottom lip and folded his arms across his chest.

'Ignore Dad. I have already told you, this is not wizard school, it's James Wolfe Primary, a normal school, for non-wizard children.' Meg ran her palm across her brow. Who knew it would be this hard to get him out of the door?

'Dad said you'd say that.'

'What did Dad say? Are you getting me into trouble, pal?' Edd bent low and picked Lucas up, sitting him on his arm.

'I just want to wear my cloak and Mum said I had to leave it here,' Lucas whined.

'Sure you can wear it!'

'Edd! No he can't.' Meg put her hands on her hips, exasperated.

Edd placed Lucas on the floor. 'You are going to have a great day, pal. And remember, no matter what the day throws at you, the real world is what is behind our front door; everything on the other side ain't important. And you will be back here before you know it.'

He walked over to his wife. Pulling her towards him, he kissed her face and whispered, 'When we arrive at school and he's settled, I'll take it off him. Trust me.'

'Trust you? I tried that once before and look where it got me!' She batted him away. 'You look rather dashing, if you don't mind me saying, Mr Partner.' She smiled.

'I'm wearing my lucky cufflinks!' He showed her his wrists and raised his eyebrows.

'Very smart.' She winked.

The sound of a mewling cry came from the small bedroom.

'Gabriel is awake!' Lucas yelled and ran to where his new baby brother lay.

'I'll get him!' Brenda shouted as she dashed from the kitchen at lightning speed. Her cup of tea could wait. 'What *are* you wearing?' She paused to stare at the face on Meg's T-shirt as she tore up the stairs. 'Is he not a baseball player?'

'No!' Lucas shouted as he ran back down the hallway. 'He *is* baseball!'

Edd high-fived his son. His training was going well; he'd make a Yankees fan of him if it was the last thing he did.

Brenda appeared minutes later with Gabriel wrapped in a white blanket and lying in her arms. 'It's okay, darling, your grandma has got you.' She kissed his little face and took him into the sitting room.

'You might want to loosen that blanket, Brenda. He doesn't like to be too swaddled,' Milly commented from the floor.

'William always liked to be tightly bundled, I think it helped calm him.' Isabel abandoned the newspaper and offered advice from the dining table.

None of the three grandmas had wanted to miss Lucas's big day, or the first week of having Gabriel home, or the dinner to celebrate Edd's new position. A big day indeed.

'I had fourteen stitches when I had Edward,' Brenda recalled. 'I was in agony. Haven't been right since in that department.'

'Stitches? I couldn't sit down for a fortnight! The doctor said my haemorrhoids were the worst he had seen in forty years of practice,' Isabel countered. 'I had a Filipina mother's help at the time and she only ever saw me sitting on a rubber ring, thought I was part mermaid.' She shuddered at the memory.

Brenda glared. 'I endured nine hours of labour with nothing but gas and air.'

'Gosh, gas and air would have been a luxury! I had William at home and had to survive on nothing but a big dose of grin-and-bear-it.' Isabel smiled.

Milly looked from one to the other. 'I

think I'm very lucky.'

Brenda and Isabel both looked over at Milly, who was building a Lego pirate ship, ready to play with when Lucas came home from school.

'I've had no stitches, no haemorrhoids, no stretch marks and no bloody pain, yet I get to be a nana to both of your grandchildren, kind of like I took a shortcut! Bosh!' She chortled, chopping at the air.

They both ignored her.

Edd strode into the sitting room. 'How do I look?'

'Very handsome!' Isabel remarked.

'You look lovely, mate. Like a very important partner at one of London's finest architect's.' Milly winked.

'That he does,' Isabel added.

Brenda wanted to speak but tears and pride stopped the words in her throat.

Meg walked in behind him. Edd grabbed his wife around the waist and kissed her gently. 'See you later. I love you, Mrs Kelly.'

'Sames.' She smiled.

Having waved Edd and Lucas off, Meg wandered through Greenwich with Gabriel asleep in his pram. She felt unexpectedly tearful. She smiled, figuring it was down to pregnancy hormones and a big dollop of not wanting her little boy to be starting school and growing up quite so fast. She stopped and looked through the gates into the grounds of the old Naval College where an ice rink had been set up for the season.

She thought of Dimitri and Anna, packed away in a box and currently living in their loft space; she would get them down and make them part of her Christmas decorations. Guy would appreciate the gesture. It was to be their first Christmas in their new home and their first as a proper family. It had been quite a year.

Meg twisted the gold band on her finger and felt her stomach flip as it always did when she pictured her handsome New Yorker, who at that very moment was taking up residence in his new office in the City. She couldn't wait to hear all about it later over dinner at the Oxo Tower on the South Bank, and to meet up with Pru, Christopher and Guy, who would be joining them there.

Reaching down into the pram, Meg pulled the edge of the blanket from Gabriel's face. He was so beautiful. She felt the usual pang of regret that Lorna wouldn't meet him; funny how, despite all that had happened, not having her mum in her life didn't get any easier.

Meg had been concerned about having a second child, worrying that it would be impossible to love another in the way she loved Lucas. When the midwife handed him to her, like a gift, her reward for all that huffing and puffing, she had peered at the little bundle, wrapped loosely in a pale blue cotton blanket, and she had known her worries were unfounded. He was perfect and he was theirs. Meg loved him the way she loved all the boys in her life – fiercely.

'Do you have a name for him?' the midwife had asked.

'Gabriel,' she had answered with certainty as Edd openly sobbed in the corner. 'He's an angel sent at Christmas, what else are we gonna call him?' She had smiled.

Gabriel reached up from his pram and batted the air with his mittened hand.

'Hello, little mate, are you awake? I'm just standing here having a good old think. I wonder what your story will be? I think about my own sometimes; it's been a bit of a bumpy old ride at times, but I think the life I have now is my reward for the times when I was so unhappy. You will always be loved, baby. You will always have a family that puts you first and you will always, always have a wonderful Christmas. And if ever you want me or Dad to take you to the seaside, no matter what the time of year, you just shout and we'll bundle you into the car and take you. Lucas will be there to hold your hand.'

She smiled at her youngest son. 'I expect we'd better be getting back. God knows what the competitive grannies are getting up to while we're away.' She laughed.

A young couple caught her eye, laughing as

they swirled on the ice. They were good skaters. The boy caught the girl around the waist and pulled her towards him. The two twirled and spun, holding each other fast. They reminded her of seahorses bonding snout to snout as they spiralled up towards the surface. Together, as one, ready to take on the world.

ACKNOWLEDGEMENTS

Thank you to Jo Ward, to whom I dedicated this book. She has always been there for me, a brilliant mum to Luke and Alice, a great sister, fabulous aunt and a lovely friend. She is celebrating a rather big birthday – I was going to write her a poem, but the only words I could think of that rhymed with her not-to-be-mentioned age were Twixty, Flixty and Blixty, which I don't think are actual words!

We love you Jo – Happy Birthday!